River of Gold

Theresa Rose

[signature: Theresa Rose]

BLACK ROSE writing™

© 2015 by Theresa Rose

All rights reserved. No part of this book may be reproduced, stored in a retrieval system or transmitted in any form or by any means without the prior written permission of the publishers, except by a reviewer who may quote brief passages in a review to be printed in a newspaper, magazine or journal.

The final approval for this literary material is granted by the author.

First printing

This is a work of fiction. Names, characters, businesses, places, events and incidents are either the products of the author's imagination or used in a fictitious manner. Any resemblance to actual persons, living or dead, or actual events is purely coincidental.

ISBN: 978-1-61296-579-6
PUBLISHED BY BLACK ROSE WRITING
www.blackrosewriting.com

Printed in the United States of America
Suggested retail price $16.95

River of Gold is printed in Calibri

Special Thanks

I would like to thank a number of my friends and colleagues, without whom this novel never would have happened.

To my Red Feather Writer's group whose patience, enthusiasm and encouragement steered me into the realm of genuine novel writing instead of the pile of slop I started out with, thanks so much for your support.

To Scott Driscoll, my writing professor friend. Thanks so much for your invaluable expertise and attention as you taught me how a true novelist writes.

To Lou Philippe, another writing buddy who put aside his macho hunting and fishing persona to read my decidedly feminine novel and actually enjoy it.

To my husband, Dan Slack, who supported my efforts from the very beginning and was never anything but honest with his comments.

Many thanks and much love to all who were so important to me as I launch my new career.

Sincerely,
Theresa Rose

River of Gold

Chapter 1 - Flight

It was the largest firestorm in Larimer County history and it was only June, but I was already on my way out of town for good. All night long the foothills had glowed with patches of sparkling red, occasionally exploding into bright yellow flames. Fort Collins was choked with smoke, burning eyes and throats and impossible to escape, even in my air-conditioned Toyota with the windows closed. I was headed north on 287, passing bewildered evacuees lining the sides of the highway, their vehicles piled high with hastily salvaged belongings, coolers, pet crates, sleeping bags, suitcases and office equipment with tangles of cords dangling like entrails. Adults were milling around anxiously, hoping to get some kind of information from the firefighters. Children, some bored and others frightened, peered out of car windows. Dogs panted in the smoke and the heat.

Two weeks earlier it had become clear that my life in Fort Collins was over. I'd been at work building ads for the *Northern Sun*, a small but smart local newspaper where I was proud to be employed. But that morning I was getting one of "those feelings" – a combination of anxiety in my head and lead in my gut that always signaled bad news. I hoped that it was a minor problem with one of my ads or a reprimand from a printer about my files but I already knew better. I didn't know just what. I was waiting for the bomb to drop when, sure enough, one of our ad salesmen charged in with a newspaper in his hand and strode over to my desk.

"What's up, Rick?" I asked. He was frowning at me as if I'd done something terribly wrong. Strange, because Rick and I usually got along pretty well.

"Jasmine," he said. "He's at it again!"

He handed me the paper. It was called, *Zeitgeist,* one of those righteous little independent papers, always produced by some college kid with more money than brains. I never would have given the silly thing a second glance but Rick seemed to think it was important. I unrolled the tabloid to expose the front cover, took one look, and gasped.

A most unwelcome image took up the whole cover. Greg Ross, my wicked ex, lounged in a recliner, the ever-present cigarette in his fingers. He looked smug and evil and sure of himself. The headline read "An Astonishing Bias – Preferential Treatment of Women in Cases of Domestic Violence."

"You'd better look at that story," Rick said.

I knew I had to, but I didn't want to.

I'd finally escaped from Greg Ross over two and a half years earlier, restraining order in hand, after several nightmare years of being an unwilling prisoner and slave to a guy who was incapable of taking care of himself. Now I lived on the edge of town where I hoped he wouldn't find me. I'd finished a long-neglected degree in graphic design and found a new job. Maybe I had changed my life, but apparently Greg had nothing better to do than to continue to seek his revenge on me for escaping from him. The hopelessly mislead editor of the stupid rag had obviously not bothered to check his source or his facts and printed everything Greg had said verbatim.

The story began: "A person with serious mental health issues is not to blame for her actions but my ex, Jasmine Anders, was a violent, out-of-control woman who was physically abusive..." My God! They published my full name! Greg went on to describe unpredictable rages, inexplicable betrayals of friends, compulsive lying and any number of sins that I was supposed to have committed. The truth was that I wouldn't have been capable of any such behavior, having maintained a listless docility through a constant cloud of marijuana in order to tolerate the situation. I could never believe that anyone could take Greg seriously, yet here it was again.

"He's talking about himself!" I cried. "Not me!"

"I know." Rick replied. He shoved his black-rimmed glasses back up his nose. "We know you're not like that. But this guy is relentless! Doesn't he have anything to do other than make trouble for you?"

Anita, the female half of the *Northern Sun* ownership spun around in her office chair.

"Let me have a look."

She shook back her ice-blond hair, grabbed the tabloid and skimmed it.

"This dumb kid has violated every journalistic code of ethics that ever was!" she exclaimed. Anita was a serious journalist, a demon for detail and an over-the-top professional. "You could actually sue him but I think you have a bigger problem here. This guy is never going to stop trying to ruin your life!"

"Not only that," she continued. "He's disruptive to the business. I know it isn't your fault but I'm tired of the way he attacks our paper in order to harass you. That letter to the editor in the *Larimer County Courier* was an embarrassment even if they did have to print a retraction. Then there were all those phone calls!"

I sighed miserably. One of Greg's favorite tactics was to call, repeatedly, whatever place I was employed, trying to get me fired and back on the streets with him. Anita had called the police and he'd spent time in jail for violating his No Contact order but apparently, he wasn't through. What did I have to do?

Did a single naïve mistake on my part involving a predatory con artist mean I could never live like a normal person, whatever that meant?

"Hey, Jasmine, how 'bout a cup of coffee?"

Tonio, the swarthy male half of the *Northern Sun* ownership, looked up from his desk. Expertly brewed gourmet coffee was his solution to every problem in life, so without waiting for an answer, he got up to fetch me a cup. After handing me a fragrant steaming brew, he gestured to Anita.

"Could we talk for a minute?"

Anita nodded and they both went out the front door and down the stairs. I sipped my coffee. It was black, hot and exceptionally delicious but it brought me no comfort. Ad designers with my level of skill were spit out of the university every semester. I could be replaced as easily as a light bulb.

Tonio and Anita came back up the stairs and I steeled myself for the inevitable bad news. Just when I thought I was a human being with a real job and a real life, Greg was going to smash it apart again. I already felt so far behind my peers, 33 years old with a brand-new degree, struggling to pay for a cheap apartment and a used car. Dating was out of the question and I had very little social life at all, as I was always trying to hide from Greg.

"Jasmine, we need to talk to you." Tonio began.

Rick looked up from his desk and over the rim of his glasses, clearly concerned for me. I waited with a lump in my throat and a gravestone-sized rock in my belly. My job at stake, my fate on the line, I thought, "This couldn't be happening." But it was.

"We didn't want to say anything but now I think we'd better." Tonio began. "We don't want to lose a hard worker like you but if you're willing to relocate, I think we might have a job for you."

"It's in Moab, Utah," Anita beamed. "Working for a Rodeo magazine. Would you like to go there?

"Moab? Isn't that where Arches National Park is?" I asked. *Yes*, I would move there in a heartbeat if anyone wanted to know.

"Well," Tonio chimed in. "If you're willing to move, we got a call from a friend who owns a rodeo magazine and she really needs some help. She's kinda crazy and she'll work you to death but she's a good gal otherwise."

"We'll put in a good word for you, Jasmine." Anita offered. "We'll be sorry to let you go but this might be a good opportunity. Plus, you'll finally get away from that guy. Would you think about it?"

"I think I'm already there!" I replied. The desert! Mountain biking! Petroglyphs! Canoeing on the Colorado! And no Greg Ross! Had something finally gone right?

Of course I had to wait a few anxious days while Anita and Tonio tried to contact the owner of the magazine. It was as though someone handed me angel wings when Anita finally got the call. The rodeo gal, whose name was Kate, didn't hesitate. "Send her on over," I heard her holler over the phone. "You give her some severance and I'll give her an advance. I need her NOW!"

Now I was racing a wild fire. The entrance to Poudre canyon was closed, which didn't surprise me. Smoke poured down the hills, occasionally exploding into flames. Favorite hiking trails, lovely campgrounds and picnic spots along the river were being destroyed. What did surprise me was that I-80 was also closed due to a fire near Laramie. The side of the highway was lined with semi-trucks, the drivers standing stoically with arms folded, discussing whatever there was to talk about, trying to kill the time. It was Friday and I needed to be in Moab on Monday for my first day of work. I was going to have to take a chance.

The Forks hotel off of Hwy 287 was once a busy stop on the Overland trail. Many failed incarnations had nearly left the place in ruins but then the right guy had bought it and given the beloved old building a facelift and another chance. Now, with a coffee shop, convenience store, and bar, the place was doing a lively business. In the parking lot, next to the usual motorcycles, pickup trucks and horse trailers were a couple of police cars. I parked and ran up the rickety steps to find the answer to the crucial question – could I get over the pass to the western slope? But the minute I entered the coffee shop, my pesky clairvoyance took over and I knew the rumors about the place being haunted were true. This wasn't just one ghost; the place was full of the imprints of two hundred years of activity, with layers of the same stuff going on. Coffee drinking, cooking, and other wildfires were being re-lived. At times it was difficult to separate the living from the dead as they stood in front of the windows, anxiously watching the smoke rise. I sensed a couple of spirits floating past – of the kind that were unable to cross over, confused and not understanding that they were no longer a part of this world. A dried-up apparition in an old-fashioned black dress noticed me and frowned, expecting some kind of response, but I didn't have anything to say to her and couldn't afford to be distracted by the abundance of spirit energy.

Two deputies in modern uniforms sat at a table sipping coffee and I needed badly to talk to them. Was Boy Scout Road closed? What were my chances of getting over the pass? I had to take a breath and focus, clearing the mist from the world of the dreamtime to re-enter the one made of flesh and blood.

The atmosphere of the place was eerily normal considering the catastrophic event happening just over the hill. The cashier nodded at me and waved a greeting. The line cooks swayed to reggae music as they made sandwiches and served ice cream. I was attempting to quiet my nerves when a familiar voice behind me startled me out of myself and landed me firmly on the physical plane.

"Hey! That isn't country music you're playin' and this is a

historic landmark! That's a violation of Larimer County ordinances!"

Laughter rippled through the coffee shop as the tall, sixtyish, uniformed officer sauntered in the door. It was Vern, our local sheriff, and my personal knight in shining armor. I turned around.

"Vern! Hi!" I said. "How are you doing?"

"Hi," he replied brightly. "I remember you. What was your name again? Magnolia? Wisteria?"

"It's Jasmine." I smiled. "I'm trying to get over the pass. Do any of you guys know if Boy Scout Road is open?"

"Oh yeah, it's still open but they're all on pre-evac so you're gonna have to hurry. That fire is moving real fast with this kind of wind. How 'bout you? Is that weirdo still chasing you around?"

I shook my head. "I have to leave town. That guy just won't quit. But I have a job lined up in Moab and I'm supposed to be there by Monday. I gotta get over that pass."

One of the servers, a diminutive girl with nose studs and eyebrow rings, sneered in my direction and mouthed the word, "Bitch!" Boy! Greg did have his groupies and I'd just met another one. At least I wasn't the only easily conned female on the planet. But, oh no! Did she hear me say, Moab?

"Well, good luck, then." Vern said. "Moab's a beautiful place." The other officers toasted me with their coffee cups and nodded in agreement. "Don' worry. You just get a move on. You'll make it." Vern gave me a friendly wink even as the nasty little girl server rolled her eyes. He sat down with his fellows.

"Oh, I hope so." I said.

Back at my car I stopped a moment to watch the smoke rising over the foothills. Helicopters passed back and forth, looking like tiny flying insects in front of the billowing clouds. The smell of smoke was still pervasive but not as choking as at the entrance to the canyon.

Just as I was getting into the car, the righteous little female marched up to me, snarling like a Pekinese puppy.

"Just because you're so good looking you think you can get away with anything! That was real mean, what you did to Greg all those years. You really..."

I slammed the car door in her face and backed out of the parking lot, having heard it all before. Yes, I had been mean to Greg Ross. I'd growled, barked and yanked at my chains like any other trapped creature. But now was not the time to dwell on the past. I had to get to Moab.

Driving up the mountain as fast as I dared, I saw a long line of trailers coming down the other side of the road, hauling horses, cows, llamas and sheep. On either side, the vast ranches and mountain suburbs seemed deceptively peaceful and the air became clearer as I gained altitude. As I turned onto Boy Scout Road, more trailers hauled livestock up the other side. At the entrance to the scout camp, scouts and scouts leaders were loading camping equipment into buses and cars. Hippie folk with tattoos and dreadlocks were evacuating the Buddhist Center, piled into the backs of pickups and squished into vans.

My anxiety was peaked when I finally got to the canyon and was confronted by two National Guardsman.

"Hey!" yelled one of the guards as I rolled down my window. "Where do you think you're going?"

He was a big, fierce-looking black guy. I'd already heard that the National Guard could be very firm with people trying to get to their properties in the fire zone, probably risking their lives in the process.

"I want to go *up* the canyon, not down!" I cried.

"Oh," he said. "You're going that way?" He backed off and pointed up the canyon.

"Are you sure that's where you're going! You're not pulling any wool over *my* eyes, you know!"

"Yes!" I shouted back.

"Well, get moving then." he ordered. "That fire is coming this way and it's coming fast!"

"Yeah, I know! I'm going!" I called. My whole *life* was burning down behind me. Wasn't I already stressed out enough?

Safe on the other side of the pass, I stopped at the dilapidated little town at the base of the mountain and bought a quart of beer. It was illegal, of course, but I knew these high-mountain ranchers often drove around the back roads with beers in their hands. While the mild buzz dampened my anxiety, it did nothing to relieve my distress as I drove through the famous pine forests of the Colorado mountains, so ravaged by beetle kill that there were almost no green trees left. There were clear cut areas everywhere, leaving huge piles of slash and a few spindly pines bent over as though in shame. Mountainsides that used to be blue-green were now almost entirely a sinister red. My proud Colorado mountains, the mighty Rockies, subject of a century's worth of scenic calendars, revered by painters, photographers, songwriters and poets, weren't so proud anymore.

But when I stopped for gas in Kremmling, the forests had receded, making way for scrub and sagebrush. Many of the mountains at this altitude seemed to have almost no vegetation at all. I bought a sandwich at the Subway and munched in the car as I continued along the Colorado River, flipping on the radio for company. Only one station had any reception at this altitude and country music wasn't my favorite, but it made such a wonderful soundtrack for my flight through the mountains I felt like I was getting away with something slightly rebellious. Not so long ago, I would never have been allowed to listen to country music. Even to have that kind of a choice available to me was a luxury that I hadn't had for years. I was gloriously alone, not owned by anybody, not under anyone's control. All my choices were my own.

The DJ played an old song I'd never heard of called "River of Gold" just as the sunset was turning the muddy Colorado into a bright golden ribbon. A gentle, rambling piece of cowboy poetry sung in a dark-chocolate drawl and underscored by a velvety guitar, it caught my ear in a way that music rarely does the first time through. I'd never been to Texas but the guy was singing about loneliness and lost love. I felt like he was singing just for me. A warm feeling of excitement bloomed in my solar plexus. An omen perhaps? Or did I just like that song?

"If I'd only been different, but if I had been, would I really have been me?"

I wasn't one bit lonely and had lost not love, but ten years of my own life. I had plenty of sadness of my own to sing about. The DJ announced that we had just been listening to the only known recording of that particular song, performed in Austin in 1982 by the late, great artist, Tom DeVries. He also announced that the station would be doing a three-hour Tom DeVries special the very next day. "Terrific," I thought. I liked that musician. There was also lot more driving to do to get to Moab.

I took it as a sign and parked my car in a sandy lot on the banks of the golden river, now turning a shimmering red. I wasn't sure it was legal to camp there, but I felt so relaxed and free and lucky, I decided not to worry. I grilled my lamb chop on my garage-sale hibachi and drank most of the bottle of wine I'd brought while I watched the sun drop behind the mountain. The lovely song had firmly planted itself in my psyche, rambling sweetly through my brain as I snuggled into my folding chair, wrapped in a cuddly sweatshirt, and watched the stars come out. I don't think I had ever felt such peace in my solitude.

The hatchback of my car made a chilly bedroom due to a cheap sleeping bag but I managed to sleep anyway. Leaving at about 5:30 a.m., I drove through misty mountains on steep, gravel roads and got to Wolcott and I-70 at about seven. The Wolcott Yacht Club, named because of all the rafting and kayaking on the Colorado, greeted me with the comforting scent of fresh coffee and pancakes. It was all warm and mountainy, log construction, with an upper deck inside, glass cases full of pastries and racks of postcards and souvenirs. I was their first guest of the morning. The round-faced waitress took my order for a plain omelet and filled my coffee cup with a weak brew.

"So where are you going so early in ze morning?" She had an accent that came from some other country but I couldn't quite place it.

"I'm on my way to Moab." I answered. "I'm starting a new job working for a rodeo magazine."

"Rodeo? How exciting! So wild west!" She gestured to the cook, a dark young man with a round belly and a beard, his hair tied with a red bandanna. The bacon he tended on the grill produced a heavenly aroma. "Hey Steve! Did you hear? This lady is going to Moab to work for a rodeo magazine! Cool, no?"

"Moab, huh?" Steve called out. "You'd better be into mountain biking."

"I'm not. Not yet." I replied, realizing that my lifestyle was about to change along with my location.

"You know, there's a law in Moab that you have to mountain bike. And go rock climbing! Hey, you sure you don't want some bacon? You're not supposed to have eggs without bacon."

Other patrons arrived, stepped down out of RVs, climbed out of cars with heavily loaded racks on top, and pulled up on motorcycles. Though I'd lived in Colorado all my life, I had never been on the western slope and it seemed like a whole different country. How I longed to relax and take my time, stroll through a picturesque mountain village, visit a hot springs or take a scenic hike. But there was too much at stake.

Back on the road, I realized for the first time that I-70 through Glenwood Canyon was an engineering marvel. The double-decker highway snaked alongside the Colorado River with the rugged rock faces of the beautiful canyon rising up on either side, pine trees growing out of the cracks. There were rafts and kayakers already on the river. An oddly appealing sulfurous stink rose through the pines from the hot springs, the vapor caves and a big, steaming pool alongside the highway. I was just a little sorry but I couldn't stop here either, except for gas. A new life called as I happily flew past towns named Rifle, Silt, and Parachute. The Colorado rocked and rolled along beside me. Battlement Mesa rose in front of me, bronzed, sandy and massive like a scene out of an old western movie. My wild road trip hardy seemed real, too beautiful, too romantic, too far from the seediest parts of Fort Collins, where I'd been confined for so long.

I passed the orchards and vineyards of Palisade and imagined a wine tasting afternoon. Pumping gas in Grand Junction, and gazing longingly at towering rock formations on the edge of Colorado National Monument, I promised myself I would come back and explore. Crossing the border into Utah, I remembered to turn on the radio. The previous day's DJ returned to reverentially eulogize Tom DeVries as one who in his short lifetime had never attained the fame and fortune he deserved. Only now was the singer being recognized as one of the finest of all country songwriters, ever. With modesty rare among his kind, the DJ admitted to being more interested in listening to Tom DeVries than in hearing himself talk so the next three hours would be uninterrupted music. As I settled into what I promised to be the perfect soundtrack for my drive through the desert, I again felt the fire in my core, growing, expanding and full of promise.

"Today I smelled smoke outside of Medicine Bow," he sang. "And it was really burning...

"I tried to say no... I tried to say... not now," he went on. "But it wasn't my decision anyhow."

Wasn't mine either! And boy, did I know how *that* felt! Who was this guy and how come he knew me so well? He didn't, of course. He'd been dead for 15 years but was more alive to me now than almost anyone else I knew. So, my escort to Moab was this fine gentleman cowboy. What did he look like, I wondered? What else could he do? I bet he found notes on the guitar no one had ever heard before. And his voice! I was in the throes of a crush on a radio cowboy.

"I loved her and I hated her
And I never figured out why
She shut down my heart
But she opened my eyes.
Some things are just those things
That stay with you 'till you die
I'm never gonna be the same guy."

Better than drugs, a psychoactive substance in human radio form, Tom DeVries was closing the gates of my old life, the one full of shame and misery, and escorting me to a future.

I was drawing near the town of Moab just as the last note of the exquisite "River of Gold" faded from the airwaves and the radio program came to a close.

"River of gold
River of lonely
River of only
Time to start again..."

Strange silhouettes appeared on either side of the highway, rising out of the flat desert floor, golden red on the west and indigo shadows on the east as cast by the sharply angled sunlight. The entrance to the touristy little town came into view, framed by glowing canyon walls and cris-crossed overhead by cables holding bobbing gondolas. Friendly signs lined the main street, welcoming me to Moab. Had I been Dorothy just landing in Oz, I couldn't have been more bedazzled. The LSD flashback feeling got a little less psychedelic when I realized I hadn't consumed anything but Tom DeVries since my early breakfast. I pulled off at a grubby little grocery store just off the main drag.

The CitiMart cashier whose nametag said Marge and whose hair appeared to have been set with sponge rollers, chatted as she rang up my roast chicken and a bunch of grapes.

"You on vacation?" she asked. "By yourself? Or are you visiting someone?"

"I'm moving here from Fort Collins." I said. "I'm starting a job at the rodeo magazine."

"Oh dear!" Marge grimaced, but not unkindly. "With Kate Bernanke? She's a really great gal but you'll be working your butt off. Tends to fry her employees pretty fast. Anyway…"

She handed me a business card for the Wagon Wheel motel.

"My sister and brother-in-law own this place." she assured me. "It's not expensive and they keep it nice and clean. It's also perfectly safe for a single woman"

She pulled out her cell phone.

"I'll let them know you're coming. Welcome to Moab!"

The Wagon Wheel motel was single story stucco lined with pots of petunias, marigolds and spiky grasses. A cactus garden graced the front entrance where a smiling woman with the same sponge-roller hairstyle and bright red lipstick as Marge instructed me on where to park. She introduced herself as Maybelle and, like her sister, chatted merrily as she checked me in.

"So you already brought your supper?" she observed. "Those chickens are good but they're greasy. I'll see you get a TV tray and some napkins. So you'll be working for Kate, huh? Everyone loves her but oh my goodness…"

Back in Fort Collins there were places I couldn't go, acquaintances I had to avoid and people I didn't even know would have nothing to do with me. Here, the nice woman called me "ma'am" as she accepted my credit card as if I was a real person, and brought clean, fresh sheets and towels to my little motel room. She and her husband fussed over me, made sure I knew where the ice machine was located and that I had shampoo and soap in the bath. Other guests nodded politely in greeting.

That evening, I cozied into my rented bed with a beer in my hand and flipped on the evening news. It seemed like every western state in the country was on fire somewhere. The Larimer County fire was one of the biggest, costliest and most resource-consuming, with firefighters coming from as far away as Montana and Washington State. A reporter was trying to interview one of the county fire chiefs but without much success. Big, burly and bearded, the guy was doing his best to answer the questions but he couldn't get the words out. He was in tears.

Meanwhile, I listened to the friendly conversations of the other motel guests and locals as they sat on the front stoop. Neon lights blinked through old-fashioned curtains with a wagon wheel motif. The air was dry but the evening was pleasantly cool and the flowers outside perfumed the air. The sip of beer on my tongue was sweet and refreshing. Was this truly the beginning of a whole new life?

Chapter 2 – Kate

I arrived right on time the next morning but the address I had turned out to be an old feed store and not the office I expected. Signs for products and various feed companies were nailed all over the outside of the clapboard exterior, some recalling the 1950's. A bright new neon sign advertising organic horse feed shone through the front window, but there was nothing about the *Rodeo Review*.

I shrugged my shoulders and entered the building through a tattered screen door. A symphony of peeps from what seemed like a thousand baby chicks assaulted my ears and the sour smell of bird poop mixed with sweet horse feed shot up my nose. The noise wasn't deafening but it was certainly distracting, and I almost didn't hear the gruff male voice call out to me.

"Can I help ya, ma'am?"

"Yeah, maybe," I called back as I wound around stacks and stacks of dusty feed bags, salt blocks, tubs of supplements and cages full of fluffy yellow birdlings. Baby bunnies cuddled in straw at the bottom of a deep watering trough but they weren't making any noise. The walls were hung with bridles, ropes, gloves, ancient rodeo posters and signed photos of cowboys and cowgirls, some framed and some not. A palpable spirit presence floated through my psyche, quiet, subtle and a little sad. I felt nostalgia, broken dreams, a wistful resignation and a longing for simpler times.

"This is sweet," I thought to myself. "An adventure!" I finally bumped into the counter where the proprietor stood, smiling through an old-fashioned handlebar mustache. He gently packed up baby chicks in cardboard boxes while an earthy looking woman in Wellington boots cooed and clucked like a mother hen.

"If you'll take these, I'll bring out the feed," the old guy was saying. Then he looked over at me.

"I'll be with you in a minute. Let me finish up with this lady."

They walked out front together, chatting amiably, he with a big bag on each shoulder.

"So," he began when he came back. "What can I do for a pretty lady like you? You sure don't look like one of my clients. No shit on your shoes or anything. You in the right place?"

"Oh, I'm not." I said. "I'm looking for the *Rodeo Review*. I have a job there if I can find out where it is."

"You must be Jasmine, then. Kate's not here but I'll letcha in." He reached for a set of keys behind the counter. "She's in Rock Springs waitin' for Lucy to bail her out of jail but that'll probably happen today." He extended a thick, rough hand. "Bud McClintock," he said.

I pretended not to notice the hand was missing a couple of fingers.

"Yes, I'm Jasmine." I said. "What's Kate doing in jail?"

"Aw, don't worry. She and a bottle of tequila were entertaining a client. Almost hit a deer on an overpass right in front of a state patrol car. But it'll be OK. Anyway, you just follow me."

I followed the old guy through the back of the store, every bit as musty and dusty as the front. The splintery floorboards creaked under my feet and the cloudy windows hardly let in any light. I had to watch my every step. Bud led me out of the dark and into the painfully bright sunshine where stood a tiny clapboard shack that looked to be the same age as the feed store, but sporting a fresh coat of white paint. The little front porch was bordered by turned-wooden railing and a beat-up wicker rocking chair sat next to the door.

"Welcome to the *Rodeo Review!*" Bud announced as he put the key in the door, worked it one way and then the other and shook it. His plaid-shirted belly spilled over an oval belt buckle that must have been six inches wide. He made steady conversation, intending to put me at ease.

"Kate and I go back a long way." He was saying. "'Fact I used to do some team ropin' with her daddy but that was a long time ago. Kate did quite a bit of barrel racing in her day… anyway, door's open. You can go on in."

He held the door open for me as I entered.

"Don't let the mess fool ya. Kate has got this thing down to a science and she knows where everthin' is. And don't even think about trying to straighten up cuz you'll foul up her organizational system."

"Thanks for warning me, Bud." I said gratefully. I could have made a huge mistake just trying to be neat and orderly.

I looked around at the tiny office. Three desks were untidily stacked with papers, photographs and order sheets. A single printer sat precariously on a stack of magazines. The walls were festooned with rodeo posters, newer than the ones in the feed store, and also framed photos, old and new. One in particular was a real standout.

In color and a couple of feet tall, it featured an astonishingly if artificially beautiful girl with wide blue eyes framed by the longest of lashes. Blond curls cascaded out from under her white cowboy hat. I would soon learn that this was the requisite hairstyle for a rodeo queen and sure enough, a banner behind the girl read: Lucy Bernanke. Grand County Rodeo Queen 2011.

It was pretty strange... cowgirl android. I didn't know there was such a thing.

"Gorgeous, isn't she?" Bud proudly admired the photo. "Kate's daughter, of course. You'll meet her too since she works with her mother."

He turned to go. "I gotta get back to the store cuz those chicks are selling real fast. You'll have to find your way around the place by yourself but don't worry, Kate'll call soon." He touched his old felt hat and gave me a wink. "Good luck, Jasmine. You can ask me if you have any questions, but I might not have any answers."

"Thanks, Bud," I said, wishing that I was working in the feed store instead of lost and lonely on another planet. The place was such an obvious firetrap it was a good thing there were no ashtrays in sight. A former bouquet of dried up, wilted flowers drooped out of an old cowboy boot. As I tossed them over the porch railing, my cell phone rang.

"Uh, *Rodeo Review*." I answered.

"Jasmine? It's Kate." "Sorry I can't be there but you'll catch on. The desk in front of the window is yours and there's a whole stack of ads to get started on. Your username and password is on the top. And if you have any questions you can call me on my cell, in my cell!" She laughed out loud at her own joke.

"Well, Kate, are you okay?" I had to ask. I was pretty sure this jail was no nicer than the one I landed in when I finally lost it and slapped Greg.

"Oh yeah, I'm fine." Kate answered cheerfully. "The food's terrible but I gotta tell ya. Jesus must have been lookin' out for me cuz I met a guy who used to be the Evel Knievel of bull ridin' back in the sixties. He's just an old drunk now but he can still talk about the old days. I'm in here gettin' a story for the Buckin' History column. Can you believe that? Might be hard to track down the photos, though. See if you can find somethin' on the internet. His name's Drake Wilson."

"When do you think you'll get out?" I asked.

"Lucy's gonna bail me out this afternoon." She said. "Anyway, you're gonna be getting' all kinds o' phone calls with all kinds o' crazy questions so just take messages and I'll deal with 'em when I get back. Oh! Here' comes Drake again. I gotta go."

The phone started ringing as soon as Kate hung up. I punched on the speakerphone.

Ring! "*Rodeo Review.*" At least I'd gotten *that* part down.

"I got the results of last week's Junior Rodeo in Eaton, Colorado," said a husky female voice. "Can I talk to Kate?"

"I'm sorry, Kate isn't here today and I'm a brand new employee. Can I take a message?" "No need," she answered. "I'll just e-mail 'em. When's Kate gonna be back? D'ya know?"

"Late tomorrow, I think," I replied, but I sure didn't *know*.

"I'll talk to her on her cell, then. So Kate's got a new slave! I knew that geeky wuss she hired wasn't gonna last What's your name and when did you start?"

"Just today. My name's Jasmine. So I'm a slave, huh?"

"Aw. Don't let me scare you, Jasmine. Kate's quite the character, but everybody knows that. I'm Suzy Braeburn and me and my husband own the Braeburn Rodeo Arena in Provo. You'll be hearin' from me now and then. You have fun. Bye!" Her phone clicked off and there was another ring immediately after. The avalanche had begun and I was already in over my head.

Ring! "*Rodeo Review.*"

"I need to know, when's the team roping championship in Huntington."

"I'm sorry, Kate isn't here today. Could you call back the day after tomorrow?"

"Can't you tell me?"

"I'm sorry. This is my first day here and I wouldn't know where to find that information."

"I *bet* you're sorry!" the male voice snapped sharply but then he backed off. "Naw, I understand. I'll call back."

"I can take a message."

"Jus' let her know that Tuff called. She'll know what it's about."

I wrote down a message that said "Tuff called: 9:15 a.m." Yeah, I bet he *was* tough.

Ring! "Rodeo Review."

"I want a full page ad for my team roping jackpot series. Where's Kate anyway?"

"I'm sorry. She's in Rock Springs, Wyoming."

"Still? That rodeo was over two days ago! Why is she still there?"

"She's working on a story about a bull rider named Drake Wilson but she says she'll be back the day after tomorrow."

"Oh yeah? Why would she bother with him? He was great in his day but he's been all washed up for years. Oh well. I'll just e-mail the info. Who are you, by the way? Did Kate find herself another victim so soon?"

"Victim?" I thought. "Slave? Uh oh."

"My name's Jasmine and I just started this morning."

"Well, I guess we'll just have to wait and see if you're still there tomorrow. My name's Julie and my husband's name is James and we own the Double J Ranch outside of Green River. You from Moab, Jasmine?"

"No. Fort Collins, Colorado."

"Figures. I kinda thought she'd been through everybody in Moab. So how did you get this job?"

The *Northern Sun* had been all business, with phone calls restricted to only the most pertinent issues. These folks all wanted to chat and their friendliness was taking up precious time. By noon I hadn't built a single ad, and hadn't even opened up the ad file. I didn't know what the deadline was, hadn't checked my username or password, and I was getting hungry.

Just after one-thirty, Bud McClintock poked his head in the door and asked if I'd brought any lunch.

"No!" I said. "I'm way too busy to go out for any. This place is crazy! I haven't been able to work on my ads at all."

"That doesn't surprise me," Bud chuckled. "You tell me what you like on your pizza and it'll be my treat. Kate asked me to look after you and you're gonna need it. We both knew you'd be doing three or four jobs at once."

Wow! Bud to my rescue! He returned with the pizza and sodas and insisted that I take a lunch break, which I didn't think I had time for. We went around to the side of the feed store where there was an old-fashioned metal patio set reposed under an umbrella made out of old Volkswagen hoods.

"Like the umbrella?" he asked. "I welded it together myself after seeing a couple of these in a junkyard in Colorado."

"I love it!" I said. "Uh, Bud. Tell me something. I've been talking to people on the phone who've been using words like 'victim' and 'slave' in reference to my job. What do they mean by that?"

"Oh," he smiled through tobacco-stained teeth. 'Well, you see..." He sat back in his chair and folded his hands over his belly. "That's why I brought you out here, 'cause I knew you were going to work through your lunch if I didn't. I love Kate for a lot of good reasons. But," he went on, pointing at me with his pinky, which happened to be one of his few whole fingers. "She's a workaholic and doesn't even know it. It's really hard for her to wind down and she thinks everybody else is just the same as she is.

You're gonna have to stand up for yourself or the workload might kill you. You'll be doin' the job of office manager and ad designer at the same time, workin' twelve hours a day every day if you don't say somethin' to Kate. Make sure you get your days off during the summer even though it's rodeo season, and see if you can talk her into hiring an intern or somethin'. I jus' thought I oughtta warn you."

"Thanks, Bud. I feel like I have a lot to prove, but I don't need to kill myself doing it."

"No you don't. But Kate's a terrific gal otherwise. You'll see that too."

I didn't get to my ads until after 5 when I turned off the phone. I called Kate to let her know to call me on my cell.

"Good idea!" she chirped. "I'm glad you don't mind stayin' late. We startin' into cowboy Christmas and there's gonna be a lot of days just like this one."

"What's cowboy Christmas?"

"That's the summer time. That's when everybody makes their money. It slows down around the middle of August. I hope you like that office cuz you're gonna be there a lot."

"So I'm told," I replied. "Bud bought pizza and made me take a lunch break."

"Isn't that umbrella he made just the cutest thing? Hey, did you find any photos of Drake Wilson on the internet?"

"I'll start looking right now. There wasn't any time earlier." That was true, but I'd completely forgotten to look for the photos.

"I believe it. Okay, I'm out of jail but I don't think we'll be back until late tomorrow night. You're stuck with another day by yourself."

I got about half of the ads done and went back to the motel at about eight, thirsty for beers and needing some downtime to reflect on what I'd gotten myself into. I was prepared for a major change but this was a whole different world and appeared to require a different species than all too humanoid me to do this job. But when I thought about Greg Ross, so far away and unable to ruin my life any more, working myself to death didn't seem so bad. I tossed back another beer, watched the local news and went to sleep.

The following morning started just like the day before,

except the printer on top of the magazines had begun to slide off to the left. Tragedy was imminent but I barely had the time to straighten it out before the phone calls began.

Ring! *"Rodeo Review."*

"Jasmine! How *are* you? You find any photos of Drake Wilson yet?"

"Let me look." I opened up Firefox. "Sorry, Kate. I had so many phone calls I forgot about it. Is there a headset in the office? Maybe I can do double duty if I don't have to keep picking up the phone."

"Good idea. I'll pick one up when I get back to Moab. What about Drake?"

I opened a site and found mostly old, grainy news photos. One showed him flying through the air in a back flip off of a huge Brahma bull. I sent the image to Kate's IPhone and she let out a genuine cowgirl whoop. Maybe this was going to be more fun than I'd thought.

"You're a good girl, Jasmine. I'll see you tomorrow and get you off the phone."

The next day was just like the day before, with the telephone blaring every few minutes, so when my cell phone rang I flipped it open and said *"Rodeo Review"*, already on automatic pilot.

"Jasmine? Oh good! I found you! Listen, I've been thinking that we might have a chance to salvage our relationship..."

Okay, I see. Little nose ring girl had lost no time.

I flipped my phone shut and turned it off but it was too late. Greg knew where I worked! Oh no! I was going to have to tell my new boss that this guy would likely tie up her phone line trying to get to me. I turned my phone back on, dialed *69, and learned that he was calling from the Open Door Mission. Didn't

30   River of Gold

those places usually kick everyone out in the morning after breakfast and not let them back in until evening? Greg must have found someone gullible enough to con into letting him stay and use the phone, long distance at that! I'd been that dumb at one time so I could see how it could happen. But Kate wasn't going to want to change her phone number and screw up her client list.

I went back to doing my job, grateful for the distraction but sick to my stomach with worry and dread. At five Greg hadn't called yet but I knew he would as soon as he harangued someone long enough and hard enough to let him use their phone. Embarrassed and worried, I slunk over to the feed store and told Bud, who frowned even as he was reassured me.

"You tell Kate right away," he advised. "She's a woman of the world and she's picked the wrong guy more than once. She won't let you down."

Nice words, but they didn't make me feel any better. I called Kate to tell her I'd turned off my cell and why.

"Oh yuck!" she spat into the phone. "Jasmine, you'd better be worth the trouble! But never mind, Anita and Tonio already told me a little about why you had to leave town. We'll deal with it somehow. I'll see ya tomorrow."

I reminded myself that this gal had just landed herself in jail with a DUI. Maybe she would be more understanding than I thought. But back at the motel, I drank more beers than I should have as I tried to calm my nerves. When Greg was on to something he could be as persistent as hell.

When I showed up for work at nine, a lanky, fortyish-looking cowgirl with wavy blond hair and a blinding sunshine grin was pulling the weeds out of the tiny garden in front of the porch. She wore jeans, of course, cowboy boots and a man's sleeveless muscle shirt over her sports bra. Her arms were long, lean and tanned, with freckles on the shoulders. A tiny gold cross glinted at the base of her throat.

"Hey girl, you gotta get here at eight if you're gonna do this job," Kate shouted almost before I even got out of the car. "I know the office hours say nine but that's for the clients. Got your cell number changed yet?"

Yes, but that wasn't going to help with the office phone. My hopes rose a little when I realized that every time Kate answered the phone, there would ensue a discussion about new babies, grandparents, kids in college and sick horses. Ad prices and sizes were almost an afterthought as Kate kept the phone line so busy that it seemed possible Greg wouldn't have a chance to get through. It was business as usual until about 11 a.m. when Kate answered the phone and hung up right away.

"He asked for you, Jasmine. Does anyone else know you're here?"

"No," I replied. "Just the folks at the *Northern Sun*. I had to leave Fort Collins and everyone in it behind me. Practically drove right through the fire. Kate, I'm sorry!"

"Oh hell, we'll figure it out," she barked impatiently. But then she flashed me a sly grin and a nod. "You just get to work on those ads. I may have a plan."

She took a few more chatty business calls and then another that she hung up on. There was a third right after that. Another business call and then another Greg call. I was horrified, had a hard time focusing on my job due to frayed nerves and shame, but I had a two-inch stack of paperwork for a distraction. Kate had done good business in Rock Springs. She even joked merrily that her client with the tequila had purchased a double-page color spread to apologize for the jail time.

"Whole new way to sell ad space!" she joked merrily. "But I don't think I'll do it quite that way again. Shit, now I have to pay a fine and take alcohol classes…oops! There goes the phone!"

I gritted my teeth but Kate saw the number in the phone display and growled at it. She punched on the speaker with a calculated wink.

"I have to talk to Jasmine!" I could hear Greg shout. "This is important to both of us and I…"

"I had to fire her, you goddamn asshole!" she yelled. "This is a business, not some couples' counseling service…

"Oh! She's fired?"

Greg sounded hopeful. Typical of the tactics he used to drag me down and keep me bound to him. He kept talking.

"Is she going back to Fort Collins, then? Do you have…?"

"*What?* No I don't know if she's going back to Fort Collins. Now fuck off! I don't have time for this shit! I have to find somebody to replace her, you lousy jerk!"

She slammed the phone down in its cradle with a satisfied expression on her face. So that was Kate dealing with the impossible Greg Ross. He might continue to call her and harass her like he always did but he didn't have a chance this time. Kate could push back as hard as he could push.

"Sorry, Jasmine. I usually don't like that kind of language but some situations just call for it… Oh, hi Gerald."

A stocky, tow-headed young man had just come in the door and, for now, the whole Greg Ross interlude was over. Kate was already on to the next thing.

"Hi Kate," said Gerald. "Lucy here?"

"Naw, I gave her the day off. She had to do all the driving from Rock Springs so she needs her rest. She'll be here tomorrow but don't forget, she has a job to do and you can't be hangin' around all day!"

"'Kay," he grumbled as he skulked out.

"Who was that?" I asked after he'd left.

"Oh, we get a lot of those. Guys looking for Lucy. I think

Gerald has been a hopeful since the second grade but Lucy doesn't date just anybody."

I met Lucy the next morning when she showed up at about 10:30, wearing jeans, a T-shirt that should have been put in the wash days earlier, and fuzzy slippers. Without makeup, her complexion was sallow and her eyes baggy. Hair spilled out of a clip and her attitude stunk like a restaurant dumpster. She took one look at me, then saw the empty cowboy boot.

"Where are my flowers?!" she screamed before snarling back at me. "Did you throw 'em out? Those were from Dwayne Shade, you know!

"That was more than a year ago, buckle bunny." Kate snarled. " He's been ridin' a lot more than bulls since then, you can bet on it. And you're late, by the way!"

"What right does she have to throw my flowers out anyway? And what about that creepy ex-boyfriend of hers that kept calling yesterday? You were pretty mad about it last night!"

"I was mad at him, not her." Kate snapped back. "And who are we to talk about creepy ex-boyfriends?" Kate waved a hand at me. "Jasmine, why don't you take a little walk down by the river while I knock some sense into my ditzy daughter? Come on back by noon."

"Okay, Kate," I replied casually. "I'll be back."

Whew! I shut the front door on an explosion of female fury hot enough to burn the place down. Glad it wasn't my problem. Did this happen every day?

Two vehicles sat in the parking lot next to mine. One was a sturdy, late-model Subaru hatchback with *Rodeo Review* logos plastered all over it and loaded with magazines. The other was a gigantic purple 4x4 Ford truck with a license plate that read Lucy, a star on either side of her name. Okay, so the rodeo queen business had gone to her head. I felt sorry for her mom.

This was my first chance to walk by the river since I'd arrived in Moab so I was grateful to the gals for kicking me out of the office. I turned on the car radio to get myself in the mood. The DJ advertised a used car sale at a local venue and then made an announcement

"Now here's another rare beauty by the late Tom DeVries. Oh, what I wouldn't give for just one more note by this guy. This is the rarely heard classic "Come On Home With Me". Listen good 'cause I don't play this one very often."

I waited, holding my breath as my magical DJ put on a delicate, folksy, fingerpicking number I wouldn't have expected from a Texas cowboy:

"Little darlin' take my hand and come on home with me.

That life you left behind is gone forever.

Follow me and you will see

That nothin's like it used to be.

As long as you and I agree

To be together."

Wow! The pretty tune effervesced around me like the bubbles in a cold glass of beer. I parked next to the gently rolling Colorado and stepped out of the car with my head in the clouds and my feet not quite finding the ground. Did everybody feel light-headed and wing-footed after hearing that song, or was it just me?

I took off my shoes and strolled through the warm sand. The Colorado had cut a deep canyon, and the massive, craggy, sun and shadow colored walls rose up with the river on one side and the highway on the other. Boaters on vacation floated lazily on the muddy waters in canoes and rafts, and some waved to me as they passed.

Another strange, unexpected feeling seemed to blossom from my interior, one of love, or longing, or desire for something that seemed so close and yet not really there. Love I didn't believe in, and romance was a con job. I'd been through all this and I knew better. Yet here I was being lured out of my jaded and disillusioned self into some otherworldly realm where love songs were true and fairy tales weren't stupid, and I knew I couldn't go back to work like this.

To bring myself back to earth, I bought some coffee and a bratwurst at a roadside stand and ate my lunch. Back at the office, Lucy was alone at her desk and Kate was nowhere to be seen as I poked my head in the door and looked around.

"All clear?" I asked.

"Oh yeah," Lucy looked up but she didn't quite meet my eyes. "My mom went out for sandwiches. She told me to call her if you hadn't had your lunch and she'll get one for you."

Then she screwed her mouth into a twist. "I'm sorry, Jasmine. That was mean of me and I know it but I was still mad at my mom for what happened in Rock Springs. I shouldna said what I said."

"That's all right," I said as I extended my hand. "I'm Jasmine Anders and I'm happy to be here."

"And we're just as glad to have you," Lucy smiled. She was much prettier in real life without all the fakery of the rodeo queen photo, even with untidy hair, dark circles under her eyes and a grumpy attitude. Trying to make friends, I told her so.

"Oh yeah," she agreed. "Don't they just goop it on? I swear I got home from that shoot and my own dog didn't know me."

"So, when do I get to go to a rodeo?" I asked her, mostly to make sure the conversation stayed friendly.

"Oh, you won't be going to any rodeos," Lucy replied. "I'm sorry about that cuz they're so much fun but we need somebody to be in the office and you're already doin' great. My mom says so."

A bit disappointing but I was in, for now anyway.

Kate gave me another advance, and Friday off so that I could find an apartment over the weekend. I took the first one I could afford, on a corner so I wouldn't have neighbors on both sides, my first impression being that most of them made their livings in ways they didn't want to talk about. I reminded myself that the stained carpet, peeling paint, ugly sofa and questionable mattress were only temporary and I insisted on signing a month-to-month lease. To cheer myself up, I traded in my long, limp dishwater blond hairstyle for a jaunty bob in a deep auburn and felt awake, refreshed and better than I had in years. No Greg Ross, a crazy but loveable job, an enchanting hometown and something else that I couldn't quite grasp. A feeling that I was meant to be here, an invitation or a calling. I could only wait and see.

Chapter 3 - My Cowboy Angel

I was used to working my summers away but this was worse than it had ever been as I did double duty in rodeo land. Kate and Lucy were almost always somewhere else. Managerial duties were so many that I never got to my ads until late in the afternoon. Also, that rickety excuse for an office was probably the only building in Moab that wasn't air-conditioned and I had to make do with a couple of fans that blew the paperwork all over the place. Kate didn't trust me and made a pest of herself by calling some twenty times a day about every detail of the business, making it impossible for me to do anything else she wanted me to do.

"Kate!!!" I finally exploded at her. "I can't work with you calling every minute! Give me a chance to do my goddamned job!"

"Oooh, sorry." Kate apologized. "I'm so busy I don't know what I'm doing."

We agreed to limit her calls to once in the morning and once in the afternoon but it still didn't help all that much. Kate was faxing me all kind of scribbly ad designs and pages of copy that hardly looked like articles. I was working from eight A.M. to almost midnight every day. I still wasn't all alone, either. There were visitors, friendly locals who stopped in to chat, rodeo folk passing through Moab asking about a good place to eat or where to find a liquor store, and any number of hopeful yokels looking for Lucy.

Some were a real pain in the butt. One was a washed-up 40-ish cowboy with a permanently injured hand that he'd gotten from bull riding.

"Jason," I would plead when he showed up. "I've got work to do. This isn't a good time."

"Oh, I just want to visit for a little. I gotta to tell somebody about what they did to me at Social Services this morning… "

"Jason, I'm sorry but I just don't have time for a visit. Please now, let me do my job!"

"Oh but ya gotta hear this one. Old bitch said they were gonna have to cut my benefits. Well I'll tell you what I told her. I said…"

Jason lived on disability and had nothing to do but drink. Kate told me to chase him away but I didn't know how, maybe because he reminded me a little of Greg. I finally started locking the door when I saw him coming.

Bud McClintock checked in frequently.

"Let's get you out of here!" he'd say. "We'll get some lunch and go for a drive. I know where there's some really good petroglyphs."

I couldn't resist his lunch invitations even though I'd have to work even later than usual, but I'd remind myself that he was an older guy who may not have had much more time left on earth. He had lost his wife after being married for fifty-four years and was obviously lonely. His politics were on the order of John Wayne's, which I ignored, but his conversation was always lively. He also watched out for me a little, even chasing me away from the office on a Sunday when I'd crawled in to try to catch up.

"Jasmine!" he scolded. "I told you to take some time off and get some rest an' now you're gonna have to do it."

I tried to protest but he wasn't having it. "No, you don't

work on Sundays!" He stood firm in front of the office door. "It's Kate's problem that you have too much work, not yours."

That day, I chose to believe him and went back to my crummy apartment with its bare walls, cheap TV and nobody that I wanted to spend any time with so I just slept all afternoon. No wonder I preferred work.

Many others dropped in and out of the office all summer long - the lady who sold homemade burritos; the guy who owned the building and who usually came by when Kate forgot to pay the rent; the gal with the western wear store who never liked her ads; the guy who sold horse trailers who always had last minute changes. They were not made particularly welcome even though I tried to be polite. I always apologized for being so rude but I just didn't have any time.

By the end of August, the season was finally over. I had never been so tired. The frenetic pace of the magazine had so swallowed me up that even my usual clairvoyance had shorted out. I was feeling none of the sensitivity I'd been used to. After six issues of the magazine, I never wanted to see another ad for anything rodeo ever again or anything else for that matter. So that morning, I sat grumpily in front of my computer, having arrived at 8 am sharp, waiting for Kate to show up with another giant pile of work and me wanting to die of exhaustion right then and there.

Kate breezed in shortly after me, her ultra-white grin blazing into my eyes. Someday, I was going to ask her what tooth whitener she used. She handed me an envelope.

"Here," she said. "Take this and don't come back until next Monday. We can do without you for a week."

I opened the envelope and could barely believe what I saw, not only my usual paycheck, but a big, fat bonus check and a gift certificate for the fancy western wear store with the bitchy owner. I stared at Kate with my mouth wide open.

"Well, don't just sit there!" Kate laughed. "Take the time off!

You deserve it." So I did.

My first stop was at the local garage for a new set of tires. I almost hated myself for that when I should have been doing something fun and celebratory, or at least, going home and back to bed. But I dropped off my car and walked to the bank and then back to the garage where I sat on one of the cold metal chairs in the waiting area and stared at the walls for what seemed like an interminably long wait. Old concert posters, photos of fancy cars and outdated girlie calendars stared back at me through the combined odors of new tires, motor oil and gas. But I noticed something in the corner; a sepia-toned poster headlined "Cowboy Angel" advertising a concert at a long gone venue and dated 1967. I dragged myself out of my chair and leaned over a case full of car parts to get a closer look.

"Ooh! What a doll!" I thought, admiring the star of the poster. I lifted up the corner of one of the girlie calendars to find the name of the lanky cowboy with the lopsided grin, black hat and jacket, string tie, hair a little too long and…oh wow!

The name said: Tom DeVries.

I ran back to the shop, poked my head around the door and asked if I could get an oil change along with the new tires. Then, sneaking back to the corner, I squeezed my butt around the case of car parts and broke two fingernails prying the rusty thumbtacks out of the wall. Carefully rolling up the brittle old poster as tightly as I dared, I hid my purloined prize in my tote bag and sat back in my chair, waiting patiently for the $600 and some dollars' worth of tires and service I'd ordered, reasonably sure that even if anyone noticed that the poster was missing, which was unlikely, they would hardly say anything to *me* about it.

Driving away, feeling newly secure with the tires and clean oil, and positively smug with my kidnapped poster, I began to get that "on vacation" feeling that I hadn't had before. So I went to a tourist shop and bought a sweatshirt, straw hat and beach mat. Then I went to the grocery store and bought a sandwich, chips, a small cooler and ice.

"So Kate finally let you out of jail," Marge said cheerfully through her ruby red lips as she rang me up. "Did you think you might never come up for air?"

I grinned back and nodded. "Time to spend the day by the river. And do I ever need it!"

"I bet," she answered.

"Anyway," she added as she handed me a plastic jug. "Take this and be sure to fill it up at Matrimony Spring. Best water on earth."

Before anything else, I stopped at the liquor store for a six-pack of good beer and then stalled between the whiskey and the tequila. Knowing that it was a terrible idea, I opted for a fifth of Maker's Mark. I was celebrating, right? I had a week off and had gotten a bonus check. I deserved a treat.

A series of signs led to Matrimony Spring, which is a spout of pure water that pours out of the side of a rock face and where everyone in the know fills up their bottles and jugs. It was also, apparently, where hopeful singles hung out, and had probably been so since the cave men dragged their women home by the hair.

"You new around here?" A lean young man on a mountain bike was filling his water bottles. He had on one of those skin-tight, gaudy outfits that all the bike riders wear.

"I don't think I've seen you before." He smiled. His perfectly straight teeth matched his helmet and goggles. This guy obviously had some bucks.

"Well, yeah. Uh, no." I said.

"Colorado? I see your plates," he said. "Fort Collins, maybe?"

For just an instant, I panicked. How did he know I was from Fort Collins? Did he know something about me?

"How did you know?" I asked. This was making me

nervous. Was I still on that same old walk of shame?

"Just a guess" His smile grew wider. Whew! He was just being friendly, hoping for a date.

Yeah, he seemed pretty nice but I didn't want a real boyfriend just yet. I wanted my Tom DeVries fantasy and now I had a little piece of him all to myself.

There were many secluded spots alongside the river and I found one where I could park and not be too far from my car. I left the radio on while I unpacked my picnic, cracked open a beer and unrolled my poster. Just for a little, I promised myself. I wanted my Tom framed and behind glass as soon as possible, for even though the paper was sturdy, the edges were crumbling and frayed, with some water damage in one of the corners. But I stared at that face for as long as I dared, just as a DeVries sequence began on the radio. I heard "River of Gold" and then a couple of his tunes that were new to me and then, enchantingly, a song called "Cowboy Angels".

When I'm all alone and I can't sleep
My cowboy angels come flying to me.
They ride black or white horses wearing black or white hats
Across great gray landscapes on a flickering screen
That never really looked quite like that.

Just as with "River of Gold", I turned off the car radio and let it play as much as I could remember in my own head, staring at the poster with the words *Cowboy Angel* blazed across the top in an old western font. Carefully, I rolled up the poster and placed it back in my tote, in the car and out of the sun.

I ate my sandwich, a pickle and some chips, drank beer, watched the folks on the river, and napped all afternoon, saving the whiskey for later. I must have slept for a long time because when I woke up it was early evening and my sunny spot on the sand was already cloaked in the shadows of the canyon walls. I smelled charcoal and lighter fluid and heard the faint conversations of the other campers. Many had pulled their canoes and rafts onto the sand and were reliving the day's encounters with the rapids.

I pulled on my new sweatshirt, warm from the sun and sand, and contemplated my bottle of Maker's Mark. I smelled whiskey even before I opened the bottle and began to get the feeling that I wasn't alone, although there didn't seem to be another living person anywhere near my secluded little space. No, this was my kind of company, real and not real, a presence known only to me. The scent of whiskey became even stronger and mixed with tobacco smoke, the scent of freshly showered male and old-fashioned after-shave. Tom DeVries sang in my head as though he was right near me and I truly felt that he was. He might not have been real but he sure wasn't wrong as I sprinkled whiskey like holy water in a wide circle around my sandy little spot, dancing a little, turning, and weaving my own spell, waltzing to music heard only by me.

The whiskey went down warm like nectar from God and I felt the embrace of someone no one could see. We made wordless conversation, saying nothing, but nothing needed to be said. My body was on fire with whiskey and the sweet presence of my cowboy angel and I drank even more to tame it down. I lay in the warm sand with my arms out on either side and I knew how drunk I was already but I gave my tired self to the drink, and the stars and the neon white moon while my cowboy angel took me flying. I felt I'd launched myself clear out of my body and at last had wings but then the stars started spinning and I gave myself to gone.

The sun was rising and the scents of wood smoke and coffee began to float over the campground as I woke up with a pounding head, but I also had that luscious heady feeling left from a night of romance. I reached out for my Tom and called out his name but he wasn't there anymore. The hangover didn't seem nearly as painful. The knowlege I'd somehow I'd made love to Tom DeVries was the only thing that mattered.

By the next morning, I had recovered from my drunken binge but not from my romantic encounter with the ghost of my country star. I put on a dress, sandals and my new straw hat and took my poster to the frame shop, hoping that they wouldn't know that I'd helped myself without permission to my crumbling relic. This was a small town. Anyone could have been in that garage and seen that poster. But the clerk, young enough that she probably didn't even own a car, took my order with caring efficiency and recommended acid-free backing and mat board.

Next, I sought a rental at the bike shop where the too flirtatious, too-young-for-me clerks saw the way I was dressed and picked out a single speed with a flowered basket for me.

"Better take a Power-Ade, maybe even two," the one with the goatee insisted while the blond with the dreadlocks nodded in agreement. "Even if you're just riding around town, you can still get dehydrated."

"And buy yourself some chips or something else that's salty," the blond suggested. "Salt gets a bad rap but you really do need it in the desert."

So I bought the Power-Ade and promised to take their advice. This would be my first real look at the town of Moab.

Chapter 4 - The House

The house was irresistible, front door wide open with a real estate sign in front of it. I parked the bike at bottom of the stone staircase, three-tiered and steep, leading up to the little adobe. There was a sturdy one-car garage right off the street. Locking my rented bike to a two-hour parking sign, I indulged in a fantasy of home-ownership.

The house was tiny, flat roofed, and a pale brownish-pink. It was shaded by huge old cottonwoods that someone had lovingly pruned over the years and kept strong and leafy and relatively free of dead wood. The era was nineteen-twenties. The hardwood floors needed attention as they were scratched and scuffed and the varnish had long since worn off. An arched brick fireplace graced the living room. There was a single bedroom off to one side and another small room on the other that suggested no particular purpose but it really didn't matter since the room was framed on two sides with glass brick. A green room for plants? I was charmed. I just let the fantasy roll. Two older women were talking to the realtor, a Spanish-looking woman who politely answered all their questions, knowing all the while that these were not potential buyers but just a couple of ladies with nothing to do that afternoon. The kitchen had these nifty old nineteen-fifties appliances and enameled metal cabinets and the floor, of course, was Spanish tile, worn to a velvety smoothness by years of meticulous scouring. And the back patio, (oh, such enchantment!), had a stone floor and was surrounded by a stone wall with an archway leading to a tiny, neglected garden area. Unkempt roses climbed rickety trellises. Sitting on the stone wall, I allowed myself to dream the dream. Then I realized something that I had suspected when I first walked in the door. I knew the place was haunted.

Free of the dreadful workload, I had recovered my psychic sense. Although I knew the little adobe was haunted, I was not at all frightened. This spirit was not the scary kind but an emanation of comfort, and *familiarity*. The whole property seemed kind and welcoming. While I was sure that the same spirit could be very firm with that of which it didn't approve, I was not one of those things. Nor was I frightened of the slight whiff of whisky and cigarette smoke, or of the long-stemmed rosebud that dropped off of the trellis and fell on the stone wall next to me. And I was anything but frightened of the unmistakable scent of freshly showered masculinity that teased my senses for just a moment and then dispersed. I had met this spirit before. I may have been drunk but that didn't mean he hadn't been there. I'd been drawn to this place, deliberately, first seduced by the music and then pulled into this house. Tom? What do you want from me?

Feeling a little goofy, I got up, curtsied playfully and went to find the realtor lady. The poor gal was still being monopolized by the same two old women who were expounding enthusiastically about the other tours they had done and other houses they had seen. My polite inquiry into further information about the property was met with obvious relief. I explained, apologetically, that I hadn't plucked the rosebud but that it really had fallen. Doña Martinez smiled appreciatively, grateful that I had come to her rescue. The house had been vacant for years and had only gone on the market very recently. Did she know the place was haunted? Could I ask her? What if I told her I'd just met the ghost and that I'd liked him? I didn't, though. I just asked for the flyer and told her I'd be back in touch.

I went back to my stupid, cheap apartment with it's stupid "don't care" furniture, opened up my cheap refrigerator and looked at my reasonably healthy but stupidly dull food and spent the rest of the evening tossing back cheap beer and watching a rosebud bloom. I couldn't wait to go back to work. The job may have been hard work performed at an insane pace but it was inspiring, exciting and it kept my mind off my past. It had its roots firmly planted in the sheer love of the sport and the lifestyle that came with it. I hardly even belonged there! Well, that's not quite true. I not only got the job done, I did it with flair. I made really fun ads. I answered the phone with bright, friendly efficiency. I took down the right information and remembered the phone numbers. I made sure that Kate got all her messages. I did one hell out of a job. It was time to do something about my life!

Just for grins, I brought the flyer into the office with me and showed it to Kate.

"That's really cheap for around here. Why don't you buy it?" Typical Kate comment. There was no way I could get a loan.

"Kate, I couldn't..." I began.

"Sure you can. It's a good deal, especially for that neighborhood. Let's see if we can make an appointment for sometime today. I wanna do something different anyway. I'm sick of this place."

Kate, being herself. She was not just a good person, but a great person. A great person who drank too much, shot her mouth off and sometimes crashed her car into things. Everybody who knew her was better off for it and I happened to be one of them.

We made an appointment for right after lunch. Kate wanted an adventure and I wanted to, uh, "see?" the ghost guy again.

Doña met us at the foot of the three-tiered staircase.

"Look at all those stairs! You can't really want to do that every day!" This, from one of the most on-the-go gals I'd ever known in my life?

"Wait until you see the house. You'll see why." I wasn't really telling the truth and I didn't think I'd better. We ascended the stairs with a minimum of puffing.

Doña filled us in on the history of the property. Built in the late 1920s, the house had changed hands in the 1950s (Aha! The appliances!) and been sold again in the 1970s, not really lived in but used to bring in some vacation rental income. It had been empty since the early 1990s, but someone had done some conscientious maintenance, which explained the healthy condition of the large cottonwoods and the lack of crumbling adobe.

Yes, the price was exceptionally reasonable considering the location, and the owners were anxious to sell. Kate loudly explained that I didn't have any money but that she was willing to help me.

Was anyone else been interested? Well, not so far. It was very small, and wouldn't be suitable for a family of more than two.

Kate admired the fireplace, "But these floors...!" She almost shrieked with delight at the kitchen. I was anxious to get to the back porch and the garden and I explored with nostrils flaring. There was something that I'd gotten a whiff of that I wanted to whiff again.

The olfactory sense is the sexiest, the strongest and the most accurate of all the human senses. Combined with my own sixth sense, my olfactory cranked up as high as it could go, I sniffed around but was disappointed. In the meantime, Kate had decided the deal was on.

"Tell you what, I'll co-sign for you and even if you do something stupid, I'll still have the house!"

I was thrilled but still cautious. It was an old house and had been unoccupied for many years and I wanted to know why. I suggested that we consult a building inspector before making any commitments. Doña and Kate readily agreed.

I tracked down a county employee named Dishta and put the fee on my credit card. We made an appointment for the next morning and I waited at the foot of the stairs for some balding old guy with glasses, a bellyache and a bad attitude like the ones they had in Larimer County. But they didn't make them like that around here. Rob Dishta was one fine Native American with a shimmering black braid that hung all the way down to his shapely behind. He was thoroughly pleasant as he did his job, flipping switches, checking the breaker box, accessing the plumbing.

"These are probably lead pipes," he warned. "Get yourself a filter and be sure to run the water for a full minute before you drink it."

He hauled himself up on the roof in a single, fluid motion. I was poking around in the kitchen when I noticed a weird, narrow, floor to ceiling cabinet that suggested no use to me at all. Then I caught the faintest waft of whiskey and cigarette smoke and opened it right up.

It still seemed to serve no purpose, with strangely positioned shelving. Was it a spice cabinet, maybe? I looked from top to bottom but couldn't see all the way to the back. With the help of a step stool I found in the bathroom, I searched the back of the top shelf and found a metal case, a little bigger than a briefcase, with a lock on it and a key in the lock. The handsome Dishta descended from the roof and I shoved the case back in the cabinet. Immediately, I was enveloped in a cloud of that freshly showered male that I had previously found so delicious. It dispersed right away but it had its effect on me. I figured that if Dishta found me a little weak in the knees, he'd think it was all about him anyway.

He certainly was thorough! We checked every corner and

opened every door, miraculously not opening the mysterious cabinet. The cellar wasn't creepy at all since the walls were neatly lined with sturdy metal shelves that must have once held gleaming jars of fruits and vegetables. There was a little dry rot in the beams that held up the floor,

"That can be fixed." Dishta assured me. Those floors had to be refinished but he knew someone. He left a business card and said to give him a call.

The deal was signed with a minimum of fuss. Kate dumped $20,000 into my pathetic savings account to make it look to the mortgage company like I had enough money to do this thing. She took it all back after the papers were signed. Nobody said a word. I had good credit because I'd never missed a payment on my Toyota. The monthly mortgage payment was affordable, hardly more than my apartment rent. This couldn't be happening to me. I couldn't help but wonder if I was getting a bit of assistance from the other side of existence. I asked myself if I was crazy but I already knew better.

Chapter 5 – Tom DeVries

Without my even asking, Kate gave me a much-deserved raise. I immediately bought a laptop computer so I'd have something to do in my empty house. Since remodeling can be disturbing to spirits, I felt I had better make sure the refinished floors wouldn't ruffle any supernatural feathers. Keys in one hand, deed in the other with my signature: Jasmine Bethany Anders, at the bottom, I went back to the house that weekend. The first thing on my mind was the mysterious case! I took the stairs two at a time and was out of breath by the time I got to my (my own!!!) front door.

Sitting on the stone wall at the edge of the garden, I opened the case as the heavenly scent of whiskey and cigarette smoke drifted past my nostrils. Heavy bubble wrap surrounded something important and I had to use my keys to get the tape off. Apparently, it was music! Several reels and about twenty cassette tapes were carefully dated and labeled. A little packet of desiccant fell out of each package as I opened it and the name on each package was the name I so loved, Tom DeVries.

"Is that you, Tom?" I called out jokingly as a red rose fell off the trellis and rolled over my shoulder into the case.

That elegant, gentlemanly presence was so real and so right that I lost my sense of time and sat on the wall until it began to get dark. I really didn't want to leave. We were just hanging out.

It's not like we could have a conversation or anything. Then I remembered; would it be all right to re-finish the floors? I couldn't move in until I did. The hearty laugh that rolled through me immediately after didn't even feel like me, probably wasn't, but I think he said okay to refinishing the floors.

I put the case back, locked the cabinet, added the key to my key chain, and drove back to my hated apartment, my laptop and YouTube. I was in such a rush to get to know this guy better that I had forgotten about food and had to settle for a burger and fries from the stand on the corner where the line seemed interminably long. But I'm glad I waited. It turned out to be an all-beef, charcoal-grilled burger with nice, fat, oven fries that were all crisp and brown on the outside with just the right amount of salt. I already had beer, thank God. My evening with my burger, beer, headphones and laptop lasted long into the early morning as I listened to one song after another after another. Oh, could he write! And he sure knew his way around an acoustic guitar! The swaggering, western, total, "guy thing" going on was something that I could have eaten with a spoon, by the bucketful. Oh, when was the last time I'd lain in the arms of someone I truly desired? Way too long ago!

So I looked him up on Wikipedia. Apparently, he was a notorious gambler, an insatiable drinker and a true Texas ladies' man. He could swing dance, fox trot, two-step and waltz. He'd been married three times, said "I do" and then didn't. He'd been on stage with everyone from Glenn Campbell to Johnny Cash to Waylon Jennings and strutted around with Hollywood movie stars on his arm. Several albums were produced but he'd never had a hit record or single in his lifetime. Since his songs were in every contemporary country star's repertoire, that seemed a little strange.

I went through the image gallery. In one photo, Tom wore a beaming smile, having Julie Christie on one arm and Karen Black on the other, both women appearing fully prepared to fight a duel to the death over their choice of manflesh for the evening. How could this guy have flown under the radar all this time? I speculated that he may have chased too many of the wrong skirts and had scored a little too often. Tammy Wynette told a story about how he'd tried to steal her from Glenn Campbell and how much she regretted that he hadn't. Sadly enough, Tom died just a few weeks short of his fiftieth birthday. He'd been flying through the Arizona desert in his beloved T-Bird, rag top down and most likely with a whiskey bottle in his hand. The body was found many yards away from the burned-out car. He probably never knew what hit him.

Just before I crashed out at some weird hour in the morning, I went to Amazon.com and ordered all the Tom DeVries they had. It would be the last piece of mail I would receive at this address.

Rob Dishta showed up at my new house with a couple of geeky white guys who re-finished the hardwood floors in a day. Moving in was easy since I didn't have any furniture, cookware, dishes, or anything else that might have signified real civilization other than my laptop, which was fast becoming my most prized possession. I wasn't feeling sorry for myself. My evenings spent on a mattress on the floor with a beer in my hand and Tom DeVries in my ears were absolutely divine. My cowboy angel poster smiled down from the wall. I felt blessed. I didn't always sense the presence of ghostly romance in any direct way but I always knew there was someone around, warm, sweet and welcoming and I never felt lonely. It was almost like a honeymoon in our own little love nest. But only almost. And my past continued to haunt me.

One night I dreamed I was wandering aimlessly in the streets of Fort Collins. It was either very late at night or very early in the morning. It was raining and I was wet and shivering. Whatever it was I was supposed to do wasn't done and I couldn't go back home so I could only stand in the street, lost and afraid. I woke up with my heart pounding and a sob in my throat.

A terrible scene flooded my memory. Greg Ross was dragging me through the streets looking for free marijuana or anything else he could get. There wasn't any money because Greg had spent all of his SSI check on pot and meth. My cashier's job became history when Greg took it upon himself to call my manager and demand an advance on my paycheck, even threatening to call the Better Business Bureau to file a complaint. The manager responded by ordering me into the office and handing me my last check.

We were walking past an old building turned free clinic when Greg suddenly stopped.

"Let me show you something," he said.

We went to the back of the clinic where he pointed to a basement window.

"I bet you could get through that. My old girlfriend, Gigi, did it once and came out with all kinds of goodies, a big bottle of Hydrocodone, codeine cough syrup. I bet if you looked hard enough, you could even find some laudanum hidden way in the back!"

Greg was nodding excitedly, as if this was some wonderful idea. I was shocked.

"Come on! Give it a try! I'll hold your jacket!"

"No!" I screamed. "They probably have it all wired up to an alarm system! I'll just get caught!"

"Oh, come on. Just try it!"

"No!" I screamed again. "No way! I'm not going to do that!"

Greg hit me in the face and tears sprang to my eyes. He shoved me down on my knees in front of the window as though he was going to force me through the glass. Someone driving a car through the alley honked and shouted. Greg let me go.

"I'm going home." He growled through clenched teeth. "Don't even think about coming back empty handed."

Theresa Rose 55

Then he turned and strode away.

That evil memory was just one of many that occasionally burned through my brain and kept me awake at night. If this was symptomatic of post-traumatic stress disorder, I didn't have the time for it.

The warm, fragrant cloud that was my ghostly boyfriend surrounded me and I remembered where I was, embraced and protected in my own little home, paid for with a real job. These dreams and flashbacks were infrequent but scary and toxic and I always spent the next day feeling depressed, tarnished and as though my present life was not quite real. I feared that one day I'd be found out and everything I had, my home, my job, Moab and Tom DeVries would dissolve into a fantasy and I'd be slammed back down into homelessness, poverty and abuse. I thought about getting some counseling but I was just too busy.

Instead I furnished my home, paycheck by paycheck. I bought cool pieces of furniture that didn't go together. I bought antique plates and cups and glasses that were yellowed with age. I spent the winter happily curled up in a recliner in front of my little fireplace with no one for company other than my laptop and Tom. Spring rolled in and summer loomed ahead. Rodeo season revved up its engines and Kate apologetically explained that I wouldn't be going to any rodeos this season either. Not wanting to wind up in jail, I was fine with that. There were only two places I wanted to be at that moment. One of them was at work and the other was at home wrapped in the otherworldly presence of my own cowboy angel. The pathetic wreck of a human being who used to be me was gone. I had a job I was good at. I was an asset to society rather than a trashy street person. I owned a sweet little home. I was in love with a ghost.

Chapter 6 – A Request

I was hurrying down the stairs to work one morning when I met another friend, although it wouldn't have seemed so at the time. The startling rattle nearly made me jump out of my skin and I looked down to see the tail end of a rattlesnake slither into a space under the stairs. Now, I may have jumped but I am not one of those people who automatically hate snakes. I've always thought rattlesnakes were rather polite in giving you a warning before they struck so I decided the snake was my bodyguard and named it Fred. It could have been a female but I couldn't tell and wasn't about to look any closer. Stomping my feet as I approached alerted Fred in the same way a deer or an elk would do in the wild. Fred would answer with a rattle and slither under the stairs. I did make sure to warn visitors, and thanked heaven the mailbox was next to the garage.

My next important purchase was made at a local pawn shop and cost me all of thirty-five dollars. The cassettes and reels were old-fashioned technology and it was almost a miracle I found a working boom box. I wouldn't have known what to do with the reels anyway. By then I knew all my CDs frontwards and backwards and it was time to get a little more intimate with my out-of-this-world boyfriend. The cheap machine had surprisingly good sound for such a Stone Age relic and the first cassette rolled out those rich chocolaty vocals almost as if Tom were there in the room. The cassette was an informal recording with two other voices besides the unmistakable Tom. One of them was female. I got jealous. Anyway, I caught a reassuring scent of whisky and cigarettes and knew I was in the best of company. The recording was obviously a jam session, obviously whiskey-fueled. "Pour me another glass, my dear?"

It played snatches of song, notes and chords with lots of fussing around with equipment and finally, three actual songs, just the way I liked them, with Tom doing most of the singing and the other two harmonizing with practiced expertise. The songs were not on any of my CDs. I hoped that I would finally hear a recording of the exquisite "River of Gold" but I couldn't listen to all of the cassettes in one evening so I'd have to pace myself. Now I knew for sure why someone like Tom DeVries would have hung around this place in spirit form, probably scaring off unsuitable tenants until the right person showed up. If I'd had any doubts about my gentleman ghost being that person, they were dispelled at the end of the last song on the tape. I heard distinctly my Tom saying in that smoky Texas drawl of his, "Jasmine, I need your help."

I did an Alice in Wonderland for a moment and grew as tall as my cottonwood trees with a sense of my own importance. Then I crashed right back down to earth when I realized this was something I could do very, very wrong. This material could be incredibly valuable and I knew no one in the music industry. I also knew the industry could be corrupt, dangerous and exploitative. Tom! Dammit! Can I really do this?

There are all different types of spirits and hauntings. Some are merely impressions left by dramatic events. Some are phantom beings who don't realize they're dead, and some just don't want to leave. Tom was a personality with unfinished business, looming above the physical plane, searching for a way to bring completion to a life cut short. He had left something undone in his life and now was doomed to guarding that case of music until it could be safely released into the right situation. Searching on the web in old issues of *The Star* and *Nashville Enquirer* Magazine, I researched Tom's life on earth. I wasn't just being nosy, either. What if that case had been hidden deliberately from some unsavory characters? What do I do and who do I call? TOM!!!

I don't really care for those types of magazines but I do believe that they know how to do business. Every issue of *The Nashville Enquirer* had been carefully preserved for 50 years and you could pay to access specific subjects. I sighed as I realized that I've have to pass on that great red and white striped 50s style skirt that I saw in the store window but this was more important. I spent my money on Tom DeVries.

Tomcat DeVries!

Screamed a headline from June 1975. It was accompanied by a photo of Tom and Jerry Hall, the long, tall fashion model and fellow Texan, intimately conversing in a restaurant booth. Before or after she married Mick Jagger, I wondered? I scrolled down to read the brief article.

```
Mrs. Emmaline DeVries, second wife of country
star, Tom DeVries, has filed for divorce, citing
infidelity, gambling and his long and frequent
absences as the reason for her actions. She is
quoted as saying that she would always love him
and regrets the divorce but she can no longer
tolerate a chronically straying husband and the
constant financial difficulties. She went on to
say that she wishes Tom all the best in his life
and that she hopes they will remain on good terms.
The couple have no children.
    When asked to comment on the impending divorce,
DeVries would only say that he didn't blame her a
bit.
```

Another one of the boys, really. Just ask June Carter. There was a photo of Emmeline DeVries on the courthouse steps, next to her lawyer. She was slim and stylish in jeans, leather jacket and cowboy boots, with smooth, straight hair slithering down her back almost to her waist. Her classic features included a dimple on each cheek, a sweet feature implying a certain impish appeal, but the expression in her eyes almost made me cry. The lovely lady was in the worst stage of grief.

My Tom wasn't one of the worst of the wildmen and he wasn't in the magazine all that often. But the story about the copyright dispute gave me the creeps.

Tom DeVries in Court Battle!

```
The acclaimed country star, Tom DeVries has filed
a lawsuit against Jim Ed O'Reilly of the
Nashville's Finest recording company, claiming
that early in his career he was coerced into a
whiskey soaked poker game with O'Reilly, John
Hammond and Phil Lafayette and lured into a
contract that had him sign over the rights and
ownership of all of his music, past and future, to
Nashville's Finest. He was to be paid a percentage
of record sales and for his stage appearances but
Nashville's Finest would own everything he wrote.
O'Reilly claims to have given DeVries a sizable
advance on future recordings and states that
DeVries had walked out on a legitimate contract
and he had been been fully aware of what he was
doing when he signed it. O'Reilly intends to file
a counter suit over the breach of said contract.
    As of this writing, Nashville's Finest has been
unable to provide any evidence of an advance paid
to DeVries. DeVries, however, has produced a
blatantly exploitative contract and one would
indeed have had to be very young and very drunk to
sign.
    Maybe he did sign the contract but this
reporter wishes the superbly talented Tom DeVries
the best of luck in the courtroom.
```

He only produced two albums after that and spent much of the rest of his life either on the road or in open warfare with

Nashville's Finest, fought in one courthouse or another. Little wonder he hadn't been more popular during his short life. Even my Tom, my dashing hero, had been made a slave at one time. We had more in common than I'd thought.

Rumors abounded about a series of secret sessions that took place in an unknown location in order to hide the work from Nashville's Finest. Ownership of the legendary music was disputed by a number of people, including Mrs. Candice DeVries (3rd wife) and Mrs. Emmaline Hughes DeVries. The first wife wasn't mentioned. I got back into Wikipedia and scrolled down a little further. That now familiar warm scent of my favorite ghost, whiskey and cigarette smoke floated around behind me. I almost felt his arms around me, resting his chin on the top of my head as we read the entries together.

"Which one of your ex-wives is still speaking to you, Tom?" I said out loud, "You're going to have to let me know who to contact." It seemed simple enough to continue to listen to the cassettes as they might contain more cryptic messages just for me. I listened to two more cassettes before I got too sleepy and had to go to bed. I heard more dinking around, discussions about major fifths and minor sevenths and time signatures. I'm pretty sure I heard something being snorted. I heard a couple of sassy, swaggering, irreverent numbers, funny as hell. I heard one long, mournful, beautifully poetic song about a young girl who falls in love with a gambler and dies of a broken heart. I wondered who the other two performers were but Tom wasn't letting on. I listened but there was nothing else. No specific messages for me.

Well, not that kind of message, but there was another kind. Between the music, the scent, and that warm, welcoming presence, I was being seduced into something that I couldn't define. I always had that voice in my head, crooning, caressing my senses, and telling me stories. Night after night I'd dance to my Tom, sometimes waltzing or slowly turning to the most romantic singing I had ever heard in my life. I undressed while my poster watched from the wall, longing to lie in his arms and I went to bed naked to try to get some kind of sense of what it might have been like to make love with my Tom. He was there all right. I felt his presence. It was so real, so tender, he held me in his way but he couldn't touch me. My desire for him only grew as the needs of my own healthy body bloomed forth in longing. I put my hand between my legs to try and get some relief but my own very efficient fingers couldn't give me what I wanted. I wanted Tom and I wanted all of him. I wanted his mouth on mine and his tongue down my throat. I wanted his hands on my body and his firm belly against mine. I wanted his knees forcing my legs apart. I knew that his thrusts would never be sharp but deep and smooth and rhythmic, as rich and intoxicating as his music. I wanted to hear moans, gasps and cries of ecstasy. My fantasies, as delicious as they were, they were also a form of torture. There's only so much fulfillment in being a fan in love with a poster on the wall.

Then it got worse. It was one of those nights when it was so hot that I had to take a shower just to cool off. I was standing in a towel, preening, when I saw his reflection right behind me, our eyes meeting in the mirror. My own Tom, dark hair, smoldering eyes, black jacket, string tie. He wrapped his arms around my shoulders and pressed his mouth to my neck and I felt those lips all the way down to my toes. I let my towel slide off, inhaling deeply into my lungs the warm fragrance of a real guy who never needed cologne or perfumy deodorant. I tried to lean back against him but he had already gone. Evaporated. Disappeared.

I must have sat for an hour on my bed wrapped in a navy and white silk kimono I'd ordered online for twenty dollars. I think it was a man's. Didn't matter. It did matter that if this had been a more normal circumstance, I would have been undoing the guy's pants with my teeth by now. I was yet another of the many women who had been frustrated by Tom DeVries, and if I knew anything about departed spirits not yet crossed over, they were the same personalities in spirit form as they had been in real life. Here he was, romancing yet another woman in his dashing, irresistible way. How does somebody just *forget* they no longer have a body?

Chapter 7 - Rescue

July in Moab was getting hotter and it wasn't just about the weather. I stomped out a *Good Morning* to Fred, who didn't rattle back that day. He was lazily digesting some big, bumpy lump I didn't want to know any more about.

"That had better be a rat and not a kitten," I scolded my creepy tenant. Just at that moment, Rob Dishta sailed by on his bicycle, all broad shoulders and ripped abs in a white tee shirt with his long hair loose and flowing behind him like black smoke. He waved to me and I waved back. Here I was *craving* human flesh and letting it get away.

Back in rodeo land I was doing double duty, *again*, working at my two jobs managing the office and working on ads. Even my Tom got shorted. Listening to his music in the office was too much of a distraction and by the time I was home, I usually just crashed out until the alarm woke me up. I think he understood. But oh, did I miss him.

By the end of July, I was fried to a crispy critter but not from sunburn. Kate and Lucy called from some noisy bar in Colorado to tell me they were on their way back from Cheyenne Frontier Days. Soon I'd get a day off. Maybe.

One night, anxiety nagged me as I locked up the office. What was I forgetting? I was getting out early, around 10:00 p.m., having tied up all the loose ends I could remember. I kept looking back at my desk; trying to think of the one important thing I might have blown off. But my inbox was empty. I checked my e-mails one more time. I listened to my voice mail. It was all taken care of. I thought that maybe I was just being over-conscientious since I was leaving early. Maybe my anxiety could have been due to extreme fatigue but this felt too real. Something wasn't right. A sensation of fear was trying to warn me of some kind of danger. I knew better than to ignore my instincts but what was I to do? You can't call the police about a *feeling*. Anyway, I was fifteen minutes from my own bed. Maybe DeVries would tuck me in.

Even at night, Moab was stiflingly hot at that time of year and I was sweating and thirsty. I noticed the beat-up old 80s Subaru parked on the curb by my house but didn't think much about it, figuring that someone was visiting the neighbors. I parked my Toyota in the little garage and began the weary climb up the three tiers of stairs, looking forward to a few cold beers and some trash TV before I crashed and burned.

But then I heard something I'd been sure I'd never hear again.

"Jasmine! There you are! I finally found you! Oh, you wouldn't believe what I've been through!"

I turned around. "Greg Ross. Oh, *shit!*"

In Larimer County, I'd had a restraining order. I never thought he'd be able to get to me in Moab. How did he even get a car?

"Now, Jasmine. I know you don't really feel that way." He held out his arms to me, seriously expecting me to come running. "Come on. Say hello to an old friend!"

Greg Ross was NOT my friend. I wasn't about to go near him. Under the streetlights I could see that he had deteriorated from an old hippie in worn jeans and tie-dye into a seedy, drunken bum. He was unshaven, his shirt was buttoned up wrong and his pants were big, baggy and held up with a piece of rope. His tennis shoes stank and I could smell his boozy breath from where I stood, several yards away.

"Greg, I'm not coming near you!" I screamed, but nothing I had to say would make a difference to this guy.

"Oh Jasmine, I know you don't mean that. Look, I've decided to forgive you and I want to give you a second chance. I came all the way here so that we could start again."

This was Greg all over. Always twisting the facts. Always blaming the other guy, or girl, as in my case. Always painting himself as the misunderstood counter-culture hero instead of the worthless, insane asshole that he really was. He forgave me? *He* forgave *me*? For what? I'd been a prisoner and a slave to that guy, terrorized into stealing, begging or whatever I had to do to meet his impossible demands. The hideous memory of my life with Greg Ross came right back and I felt the white-hot flash of frustration and rage shudder through my body, rendering me weak and out-of-control. He knew just how to push my buttons and he was coming even closer.

"Greg, you don't come near me. I don't want you! I HATE you! You fucking asshole! Get out! Get off these steps!" My words were worthless, completely impotent in front of that brick wall of fake identity that he'd built around himself. No amount of profanity would have any effect on him.

"Jasmine, I thought you would have had time to think about this but you're still the same, selfish, irresponsible brat you always were! You and your stupid bitch of a boss lied to me and now you're gonna pay for that! Grow the fuck up and let me in!" He gritted his teeth in that old, familiar snarl and started toward me. I knew what was coming. Same old shit.

I tried to reach for my cell phone. I always wore my handbag with the strap crossed over my chest so that I wouldn't drop or lose it. Greg grabbed the strap and he had me. I was too exhausted to fight back, feeling helpless, hopeless and *bored*. This guy was a disease with no cure.

He started to drag me up the rest of the steps. I resisted as much as I could, trying to sit down only to be yanked up again.

"Jasmine. You bitch!" he was yelling now. "You're going to let me in, we're going to work this out and you're never going to run away from me again! I can't even believe that I've decided to give you another chance, you selfish, lying slut! It's always all about you! Jasmine first, every single time! I thought you might have changed..."

Greg's rap always went on and on, losing all meaning as he spewed more and more phrases that had nothing to do with real life. Greg's way was always to build up this wall of words, thinking that if he just said it loud enough and enough times that his twisted vision would finally be true. There was never any reasoning with Greg, ever. I kept trying to fight him, to resist, but I just didn't have the strength.

A nasty cloud of tobacco smoke surrounded us and suddenly the air was freezing cold! My Tom, in a rage! Greg didn't notice. He was too busy shooting his mouth off.

"Tom!" I screamed out loud. "Help me!"

"Tom, huh! Who's this fucking Tom? We'll just see about..."

Then Greg's car blew up.

There was a loud BOOM and a ball of flame rose into the air. Greg lost his grip for a moment as he turned around just long enough for me to kick myself free and shove him off the steps. I started to run and Fred rattled. Greg shrieked. I kept going.

"Jasmine! Stop! It's a rattlesnake! I've been bitten by a snake! Jasmine! What are you doing?"

But I didn't stop. The front door flew wide open for me and every light in the house came on. I stumbled in the door with Greg still after me, screaming my name. The door slammed in his face and I was safe.

I was safe. I collapsed on the sofa, panting and shaking, sweating and in tears. The lights in the house went off one by one until only the porch and the living room lights were left.

Greg kept screaming outside and pounding on the door but I didn't have to be afraid any more. That familiar ghostly, gentlemanly, freshly laundered embrace wrapped itself around me and I sobbed more in shock than any sorrow. My heartbeat gradually slowed down. My Tom was old-school Texas. He didn't take it kindly when some jerk tried to rough up one of his lady friends.

Of course, the police showed up within the next couple of minutes. I could hear Greg screaming something about having been bitten by a snake and his worthless bitch of a girlfriend wouldn't let him in. The blabbering got fainter as one of the officers pulled him away from the front door and called an ambulance. I don't think the police were impressed but I wasn't sure. Greg could be one hell of a con artist.

The pounding on the door that followed came with an introduction that I could almost live with but still made me nervous.

"This is Officer Gravdahll. I need to know what's going on here!"

I stood up, still shaking, brushed the tears from my face and opened the door a crack. I looked past the officer to see Greg at the bottom of the stairs with another officer. He appeared to be in handcuffs.

Officer Gravdahll was broad and square. Even his hair was square. He must have noticed that I was exhausted and trembling, and his serious manner softened up a bit.

"Is anyone else here?" he began.

"No," I answered almost truthfully, knowing he wouldn't want to hear a ghost story. "Would you like to sit down?"

"Yes, I would," he said sternly. "I need to ask you a few questions. You seem like an awful nice lady to be involved with someone like that."

"I know." I replied wearily. "Where should I start? I was trapped. I was conned."

I dropped down on the sofa and Gravdahll took my vintage, pink leather recliner. I told him I'd come here to escape from that guy, that I'd had a restraining order in Larimer County but I never thought he'd find me here. I told him about the cycle of abuse, manipulation, violence and drug abuse.

No, we'd never been married. Yes, he probably had been bitten by a snake.

"Look, now I have a job I love and I own this house and the only drug I'm abusing these days is beer. I don't want the rattlesnake exterminated. He saved my life." I stopped short of introducing my snake friend by name.

"So how do you account for the explosion? Are you sure there was no one else involved?" Gravdahll wasn't buying my innocent victim story and I couldn't blame him.

"I think one of the neighbors might have done that," I said. "Greg is so dangerous and mean no one would have wanted to get between us. But I don't know who it was."

"Well, you'll have to come down to the station and make a statement. You can ride with me."

Damn! I was so tired. "Okay, I don't think I have much to hide. I'll be telling the same story I just told you."

Maybe it was the last time I would *ever* have to tell that story.

The explosion had only blown up the gas tank. Greg had almost no gas in the tank so there was no fuel for any real fire. He had been insisting to the other officer that his driver's license was in the glove box but when they checked, there were only empty booze bottles.

He was charged with harassment and drunk driving in Grand County, Utah, for which only spent a couple of weeks in jail. Later he was transported back to Larimer County where he had to face charges for parole violation and theft of a motor vehicle. Greg insisted the guy who owned the car had given it to him, which may or may not have been true. The car was such an old heap, whoever it was may have been happy to get rid of it and reported it stolen to collect the insurance. Greg Ross, who once seemed so brilliant, really was that dumb.

The next day was Sunday and I was so glad. I slept most of the day, safe and cool in my little house and having sweet dreams about my Tom, who had proved himself once again.

Kate burst in that evening bringing beers, pizza and the Sunday paper. While not the biggest headline, Greg's burned-out car made the front page. The story was a generic report about the police being called to the scene of an explosion where a man was harassing his ex-girlfriend. The paper identified Greg Ross as a drifter with a criminal record in Larimer County, which included assault, armed robbery and possession of illegal drugs. The explosion of the car was still under investigation. Kate wanted to know all about it, of course. "What were you doing in the office until ten at night anyway?" she began. "That was the same guy, wasn't it? It'd better be."

"Yeah, same guy," I sighed. "I'm not dragging around anyone else like him. I swear. One of those is already too many."

"What are you going to do about the rattlesnake? I almost dropped everything I was carrying and this is real expensive beer."

"He's my hero." I replied. "His name is Fred and he's kind of a wuss. All he ever does is rattle and crawl back under the stairs."

I told her that I'd been working until midnight most nights and the magazine was doing great. Both issues we'd put out since she'd been gone were huge and our advertising revenue was almost double. She and Lucy spent the summer growing the magazine by leaps. With all the dust and excitement, beers and handsome cowboys in a summer's worth of rodeo, they hadn't thought about me.

"But I knew that if you were doing the same job, you would do the same thing and I'm not a wimp." I said proudly.

"I suppose the extra large paychecks and another bonus

might make up for all the work. We had a great summer, you know." She took a big bite of pizza, followed it with a sip of beer and chewed thoughtfully. "Hey, maybe you're finally done with the jerk! I can't imagine how it happened to a nice gal like you."

"It happened," was all I could say.

I remembered the first time I met Greg Ross. I was a college dropout, renting a room in one of the stately old houses so popular with students and other young people on their own for the first time. There was a shared kitchen and I was making fried rice.

"That smells GOOD!" A voice called from the hallway.

He was tall, dark, with sparkling brown eyes and a mustache. I recognized him as the guy who held court at one of the local coffee shops, always expounding on one esoteric topic or another, surrounded by fascinated young listeners. His smile had an outlaw charm to it, which I reflected back to him by shifting into automatic flirt mode. He was just about to make some dinner for himself so he asked if I would care to share some of my fried rice if he made us an omelet with the fresh farm eggs he had. We cooked together amiably and sat down to share our dinner when he asked me the weirdest question.

"So, when's your birthday?"

"What?" I replied. "You don't even know my name yet."

"I'm an astrologer," he explained. "Tell me your birthday, the place and the time of birth and I can tell you all kinds of things that I bet you didn't know about yourself."

"Sounds interesting." I said. "My name's Jasmine, and I don't know if I believe in that stuff." I actually did, but I didn't want him to think I was too easy, so I feigned a healthy skepticism. He was 32, didn't drink, collected a disability and was immersed in his metaphysical studies. He invited me up to his room to share a joint and look at my astrological chart.

We ascended a curving staircase to his hexagonal room, the room that used to be the original Victorian parlor. It had big, leaded glass windows and was cluttered with books, candles and tarot decks. He took a fat volume off the shelf, applied the information I gave him to the study of a few pages and immediately asked me if I had any psychic abilities.

"Uh, maybe." I said. "Sometimes I think I can communicate with spirits."

He nodded. "That would be very likely. You have your Sun, Venus and Neptune in the eighth house. And I see that your Mercury is in the twelfth."

"That doesn't mean anything to me."

"It means that you really are a natural psychic."

"But everybody else thinks I'm just crazy."

"Well, you're not crazy at all. Some people would say you were gifted."

"I had some counselors try to tell my folks that, and then I'd never see them again."

"It does scare some people. But there are lots of folks like you. Some of them make a lot of money, working for the police. They find bodies and stuff."

Greg's brown eyes sparkled at me.

Fueled by mountains of marijuana, my world became magical. Even the music on the radio seemed to be part of the spell. Greg brought me books from the library about other people with the same experiences. He showed me scientific studies proving my abilities were real. I had never been allowed to think in that way by anyone I'd known before. He introduced me to the Tarot, Astrology, Wicca and Native American spirituality. I immersed myself in these studies. I read and read and read. I attempted spells, black and white magic, just to see what would happen. My personal psyche drifted very far from earth for a time as I embraced this separate reality. Those early days with Greg opened my mind to a whole different universe and we would converse long into the night, Greg being the enigmatic teacher and I the eager student. I may have fallen out of touch with the real world for quite a while but I also learned some things. Those were such bright beginnings. I just didn't know.

Chapter 8 - Delivery

Now I really did owe Tom a favor. I went back to the cassettes, promising myself I'd listen as carefully as I could to receive his next request. How sad it seemed that a voice once so strong and beautiful was now limited to the frail world of acetate and electrons. Imagine my surprise when I plugged in a cassette and got the message right away, before any music, even. After a little bit of static, and a couple of thumps and bumps, I heard it, clear as a summer day in the desert, "Call my wife."

Yeah, Tom. The same question again. Which one? Well, it made the most sense to look up the most recent. I looked her up on Google but didn't get much more than her genealogy. Then I invested twenty-five dollars in a service called PeopleSearch.com and was relieved to find there was only one Candice DeVries. Boy, this was one heck of a nosy site! All of her previous addresses and phone numbers were listed, and all in Nashville, Tennessee. Phone numbers, yes, but not e-mail. I was nervous as I picked up my cell and typed in the number. Praise the Lord! A message machine!

"Hello, Candice DeVries?" I realized I hadn't organized my thoughts as well as I should have. "Uh, my name is Jasmine Anders and I bought a house in Moab, Utah and I think I have something that belongs to you. I found a case with about twenty

74 River of Gold

cassette tapes and eight reels of music, all by Tom. I'm a huge fan of his and I thought I had all of his music but I hadn't heard any of the songs on these cassettes. I can't listen to the reels." I caught my breath. Why was this so hard? "Um, this really isn't a joke or anything. I just need you to tell me what to do with these." I gave her my e-mail and phone number and closed the phone.

Since I'd paid for a month's worth of PeopleSearch.com, I started an investigation just for myself. I looked up an old college boyfriend and found him. Dangerous territory, that. I found a much-loved girlfriend that I hadn't heard from for years and took down her number. I had just decided to give her a call when I heard my ring tone. There was a lilting, Tennessee Waltz of a feminine voice on the other end of space.

"Would this be Jasmine?" I could smell the magnolias through the phone.

"Yeah, that's me. This must be Candice?"

"Yes it is, and I am real interested in what ya have there but you gotta be reeel careful."

"I agree." I said. "I read about Nashville's Finest and that nasty trick they pulled on Tom to take control of all his music. Stunk to high heaven."

"You bet it did!" she snorted as her sweet lazy lilt turned unmistakably bitter. "Oh, damn, Ah still can't stand it! And he weren't the only one they did that to either, but I think Tom fought the hardest. They's always figurin' new ways to take advantage in Nashville. Makes me kinda sick. Sorry, I'll never get over it. Let me take a deep breath."

I waited as she heaved a few sighs. So this was Tom's widow, still angry and still grieving. I would be too, if I was her.

"Okay, I'm back," she said. "You're who? So you're in Moab? Where's Moab, anyway? And you found a case?"

"I'm Jasmine Anders. Moab is a little tourist town in Utah where I work for a rodeo magazine. And yes! I bought this house and I found it in a weird little closet. Everything's been named and dated. There are two other musicians on them but I don't know who they are."

I heard a door open and slam on the other end of the line as another southern accent called out,

"Hi, Mama. I just came in for my guitar strings. Who ya talkin' to?"

"Oh hi darlin'. Listen to this! It's a gal named Jasmine who thinks she might have your daddy's music. She lives in a town in Utah called Moab and works for a rodeo magazine."

"Moab! Nice! I'd love to go there. So she thinks she has some music? Maybe all them rumors are really true then? Wow! That's big! Make sure you get 'er number! Gotta go! Love ya lots!" The door slammed again.

"Sorry about that" Candice said. "That was my daughter Melissa, Tom's girl. Anyway, there's always been these rumors. Those two other musicians might be Emmaline Hughes and Dirk Castellano. Those two used to tell a story about secret sessions, a bunch of them, recorded when they were raising hell out on the coast. Then Tom died. I always figured that if there were any new recordings it all would have burned up in the crash. Sometimes I get calls from folks who think they got the secret music but I usually don't take it too serious. Tell ya what. You send me just one a those cassettes, so that I'll know for sure."

"Emmaline Hughes?" I said. "Isn't she his first wife?"

"She was his second wife and they broke each other's hearts. I don't think it was anybody's fault but that God-awful Nashville's Finest. Emmaline and Tom couldn't perform together without those creeps tryin' to take over her career and they kept havin' to go on tour without each other... Sad story. Emmaline's a sweetheart and her husband, Will, is real good to her. He's her manager, you know."

"Is anyone left from Nashville's Finest who could make a

claim to the music? This could get pretty weird. Legally, I mean."

"Ohhhh yeah," she agreed. "We gotta be careful. There was a lawsuit filed against Nashville's Finest just before Tom died. He and some others, including Emmaline and Dirk, worked on it for years. Then that creepy Jim Ed O'Reilly got shot and those other two guys got out with nothin' but debts. I still think we better watch our asses. You don't tell nobody else, ya hear?"

"I haven't said a word."

"Well, you just keep it that way. Know what? When Jim Ed got shot in his home studio I was real glad that he got what he deserved. Bullet right through the forehead and brains explodin' all over the place. He was so mean to Tom! Practically took everthin' he had. That's really why he couldn't pay any alimony, ya know. Worked his butt off, too!"

I was pleased at the way Candice defended Tom so fiercely. I was starting to like Tom's third wife even if I was a little envious.

"Tell you what, Candice. I'm going to disguise that cassette. My makeup company always sends the stuff in nice padded envelopes with their logo all over them and I always save them. I knew they'd be good for something."

"You do that!" Candice sounded better, even hopeful. "And thanks a whole lot, Jasmine. Maybe between the two of us we can finally set some wrong things right!"

So we exchanged e-mails and I promised I'd get the first cassette in the mail right away. Tom swirled around the whole time I was on the phone. I could sense his excitement and also, his obvious feelings for Candice. I was doing the deed. I'd started the process. Pretty soon, he wouldn't need *me* any more.

And that hurt!

Boy, did it hurt. I felt like just another starry-eyed groupie hanging out on the fringes of someone else's life, romanced, seduced and used as a tool for somebody else's agenda. What was in it for me anyway? Gee, thanks Tom.

But then I thought again and climbed partially out of my funk. Maybe the dark shadows of that other crazy jerk poisoned my mind. Tom came to my rescue when I needed him the most and helped put that other situation behind me for good. He needed my help. He needed me and me alone to bring his family their rightful inheritance and to bring all of his unheard music back to the airwaves. He chose me and trusted me to do the job. Was that such a bad thing? I felt special again.

About a week later, I got an excited call from Candice. She was sobbing, poor gal.

"It's him, darlin'! It's Tom! And Emmaline and Dirk, just like they said. Oh, let me get a tissue!" The cassette must have brought back a confusion of love and grief, joy and screaming pain at the same time. Fifteen years since Tom's death and her heart was still as broken as ever. I felt a little grief of my own since he was no longer all mine and would be crossing over once this last task of his lifetime was done. Tom, the anxious soul with unfinished business was almost done with his.

"Sorry I'm so weepy," Candice apologized. "I just miss him so much! Sometimes I get so depressed I can't get out of bed for days and days."

"Hey girl, I didn't even know him and I still get all choked up that he's not here any more."

"Oh he was so special. This is hard goin' ya know. Anyway, this is also like finding a great big diamond. Don't tell nobody. Ooh, I better warn Melissa. She oughtta know better but she's only nineteen and she sometimes runs off at the mouth."

Candice didn't want to come to my house in Moab because it might bring me some unwanted attention, especially from greedy folks who might want to know if there was more. I agreed. I didn't want creepy people trying to break into my house. We agreed to meet in Grand Junction at the airport. She asked me to send her some references just as a precaution. I understood. Candice would be coming with her daughter. She would hire a plane right away.

I told Kate when I found out that I was going to have to take a Tuesday off to meet Candice in Grand Junction. I told her why. I also mentioned I'd been reluctant to tell her the whole story.

""Well, it's a good thing you didn't tell me before. I probably would have blabbed to the wrong person and screwed everything up. Take your Tuesday. You deserve a lot more time off than you get."

God, I love that woman. I really do.

"Oh, Jasmine!" Lucy sang out. "I almost forgot to give you this message. Some lady called, said she was one of your old college friends and wanted to get back in touch. I gave her your cell number."

What? Who could that be, and how did she know I was here and where I worked? Well, Greg Ross had found out where I lived, hadn't he? Fort Collins could be a very small town sometimes.

"Did you get her name?" I asked.

"No. She said you'd know who she was."

No, I didn't.

I kept thinking I should make copies of the cassettes or show up in Grand J with some kind of a contract including me in what could be a very lucrative deal but I didn't know how to write such a thing or where to find anyone who did. It was too late to track down the outdated blank cassettes and the equally outdated recording device in order to make my own copies. I sure couldn't trust anyone to make me a set of CDs. I thought about keeping back one of the reels as insurance, but it wouldn't please Tom and I didn't want to take the risk of making him mad. I was on the verge of losing him for good and it made me gloomy. Having to be stupidly honest for probably nothing made it worse.

The morning I took off for Grand Junction, I stopped at the

grocery for bottled water and road snacks. In the fruit aisle of the produce section I spotted Rob Dishta looking tall, dark and handsome as usual. He saw me and nodded a greeting and I smiled back. I was thinking of a conversation opener that wouldn't sound too silly when a petite, female creature grabbed his arm. He looked irritated. She looked dangerous.

Oh, she was pretty all right. Positively slutastic. Caramel skin, big hair, full lips, fuck-me pumps and short shorts. Was this really his type? I felt quite ladylike in my khaki safari dress and red flats.

She turned around and gave me a scorching look designed to make me feel like an ant under a magnifying glass. But instead of cowering, I picked up an apple and took the biggest, loudest, crunchiest bite I could manage, chewing slowly as startled patrons and employees all looked my way. No spitfire Latina was going to keep me from stealing her boyfriend.

Dishta stormed out followed by the dark-haired she-devil. I went to the checkout counter, complete with the offending apple. Marge wasn't there that day but the lady at the counter bit her lip trying not to laugh out loud. She carefully wrapped the apple in a small plastic bag and packed it up with the rest of my groceries. I calmly paid my bill and went out to the parking lot where Dishta and the she-beast were engaged in a furious argument that I pretended was none of my business. Rob had already mounted his bike and she didn't appear to have one, not that anyone could ride a bike in those shoes. I knew they hadn't come in together.

I had other things to think about. Driving to Grand J with what could amount to several million dollars worth of Tom DeVries on the passenger seat was a little more important than possible future boyfriends. Every nerve in my body stood at attention. I set the cruise control at exactly the speed limit instead of my usual five or ten miles over, taking no chances. I had Tom in the CD player to keep me company but this wasn't the same as my first trip over this highway, which had been so romantic and exciting and free. I was nervous about having to ask directions to the airport, nervous about having to stop for gas, nervous about having to use the ladies room. Nervous, as in actually shaking and sweating. *What* was going on?

My cell phone buzzed and I picked it up, thinking that it might be the mysterious college girlfriend and did I ever need a diversion! I sang out a cheerful "Hello!" but the voice on the other end was no lady.

"This Jasmine?" it growled.

"Yeah. What do you want?" I said. Too late to just say no.

"Well, we think you have something that doesn't belong to you. We want you to pull over and do it right now!"

Oh no! I looked in my rear view mirror and *damn* if there wasn't an old black Cadillac on my tail. I couldn't see into the windshield but I didn't need to. That thing had teeth! The front bumper grinned at the back of my little Toyota like it was ready to take a big bite out of the trunk and eat me alive. I snapped my phone shut and stepped on the gas. Where's a cop when you need one? Getting pulled over might be my best chance for survival!

The Cadillac accelerated and pulled up beside me, dangerously close. The fool was trying to force me off the road! Here it was, everything I'd dreaded, everything I'd been warned about. My hands turned ice cold on the steering wheel as all the blood in my body drained into my feet. A cigarette dangled out of a flabby face in the passenger window of the Cadillac. The face scowled and an arm waved vigorously, motioning me to pull over. Taking a risk that I didn't feel up to, I floored my gas pedal enough to get ahead of the Cadillac, but I knew my little car was no match for the giant engine in that seventies cruiser. It pulled up beside me again.

My cell rang but I wasn't about to pick it up. I was so far out of town that there wasn't a gas station, convenience store or residence in sight. Where were the police? That damn cell wouldn't stop ringing and the Cadillac came close enough to ram my rear bumper. Shit!

"Pick it up, Jasmine. I'll take it from here." It was Tom, not heard really, but felt somehow. I flipped open the phone.

"Young lady, this isn't a game…"

"Ain't you two ever gonna dry up and blow away?" The unmistakable drawl took over my phone and the cigarette fell out of the face in the window.

"What? Tom! But, but, you're supposed to be dead!" The voice on the other end lost all its menace and shrunk to a squeak. "Shit, I just burned my pants!"

"And *you're* gonna be dead if you don't leave this little lady alone. I've been real sick of you guys for too damn many years."

I screeched my tires around a rock face and heard another voice call out "Tom? No! That's impossible! They matched the dental records! It can't be him!"

"It sounds just like him. But there's nobody else in that car!"

"It's just a trick! Lady, you pull over and do what I tell you to!"

"John Hammond, you scumbag!" Tom sounded so menacing that he scared *me*! "You and Phil take a good look at your last minute on earth!"

The Cadillac suddenly veered to the left and I was ahead again, ice cold and trembling but unharmed as yet. Even the music in my CD player joined in.

"Trouble looked around, and it got doubled". Tom, of course, singing a sassy little tune about a bar brawl where the guy who starts the fight pulls everyone else into the fray to cover his escape.

Driving like a true maniac, I put more distance between my car and the Cadillac, grateful there was no one else on this stretch of highway. Just as I rounded another curve, sliding into the wrong lane at 95 MPH, I lost sight of the bad guys and thought I caught a glimpse of Tom striding by on my left. Long, tall, dressed in black, cowboy-hatted and lighting a cigarette. Then I heard the screech of tires and a loud crash behind me. I kept going.

Chapter 9 – The Women

The airport wasn't that hard to find and was small enough that I could see my car from the terminal. I stashed the case under the seat, locked the car and waited for the women with my hands, underarms and underpants damp from sweat. How was I *not* supposed to be mad as hell at these two gals for spilling the beans? But how was I supposed to explain that the ghost of Tom DeVries had come to my rescue?

I immediately knew the tall, dark-haired, lanky gal that accompanied the slightly tubby blonde with the big hairdo. Tom's looks didn't translate well into a female incarnation. She was horse-faced and horse-toothed. Not a pretty girl at all, but her father's daughter, most surely. Something about her shone with that intangible thing called star quality. She sashayed down the causeway in red spike heels and skinny jeans. Her chestnut brown hair hung in loose waves to the middle of her back and her deep brown eyes sparkled with the sheer joy of living. She even greeted me with a drawl that sounded much more like Texas than Tennessee.

"Hi, I'm Melissa and this is my mom, Candice. I think you two already know each other."

Melissa shook my hand and Candice gave me a peck on both cheeks.

"I just can't tell you how much we appreciate you're comin'

all the way here." Candice beamed. "We really should have lunch or something and get to know each other a little better."

I badly needed a beer (or two!) so we all got in my car to find a restaurant. It didn't matter where, really. We settled for one of the nicer hotels at the edge of the airport but couldn't decide whether to bring the case into the restaurant or leave it in the car. Candice and Melissa were playfully secretive and whispery, as if the three of us were involved in international espionage and about to get exposed at any moment. I couldn't possibly tell them the danger had crashed and burned many miles back.

"What about the X-Ray machine?" Candice frowned. "They'll see everything in the case!"

"Well, it's just some old cassettes and reels." Melissa said. "There's nothing' illegal about those. And I don't even think there's that many people who would even know the name, Tom DeVries."

"I think you're okay," I said, hoping my irritation with the whole situation wouldn't show. "Neither of you look like international spies to me."

"But none of us knows what a spy really looks like, ya know." Melissa raised and lowered her eyebrows a couple of times as though we were all co-conspirators. She was having way too much fun with this.

The restaurant was dark and air-conditioned to a frosty chill that made all three of us shiver. The hostess, clad in a sweater, took note of the situation and brought us to a booth with padded leather seats next to a sunny window. The place was almost empty and the waiter almost asleep as he took our orders. We ate something decent but unmemorable. I do remember that I downed two beers before the food came and drank one more with my lunch. Then told them about how I first became acquainted with Tom and how much I loved his music.

"It's so timeless," I said. "Everything else from that era

sounds dated but none of his music ever does." I was coming from the dreamy realms of ultimate fandom. "I wish they hadn't slopped all that orchestration over some of his songs. It's like they're trying to drown him out or something. I've read comments like that from lots of his fans on YouTube."

Of course, Candice and Melissa agreed whole-heartedly. "Oh, he was so ahead of his time," Melissa drawled. Her voice had her father's dark chocolate tone. "All that over-production bullshit was Jim Ed O'Reilly again, along with those two other creeps that he was partners with."

"John Hammond and Phil Lafayette."

Coming from Candice, those names sounded obscene. She frowned at her gin and tonic as if both of those guys had spit in it before she took a big swallow. Well, they were unlikely to bother anyone ever again whether they were alive or dead at this point. But as Candice went on, I could almost taste the bitterness and grief left over from losing her Tom. I stopped being mad at her.

"What a couple of idiots, jerks and everything else that's wrong with the world." Candice obviously had a long-standing grudge against the whole music industry and not only for what had happened to Tom. "'*We* know how to sell records!' My ass!"

She was really getting riled and for some reason her daughter kept kicking her under the table. I tried to change the subject and asked Melissa if she or her brother were played music.

"Well, I play guitar and sing a little. My brother Brandon sings reeel good, but he's into somethin' he calls indie rock and he had to move to Seattle. I kind of like his stuff but *I* like to sing my daddy's songs."

"Oh, she does such a beautiful job with those!" Now Candice shone with pride. She inhaled deeply, her creamy bosom swelling out of her lacy collar. "But I wish she would do more acoustic, like our Tom did, and not all that electric stuff."

Melissa gave me a wry grin.

"My momma doesn't like it when I 'lectrify my daddy. Eeeew! That doesn't even sound right! But now I guess I'm gonna have a whole bunch of new songs that I can ruin."

"Tom DeVries left some big shoes to fill." I commented.

"Ya know," She stretched out a long leg and studied her foot. "I almost could fill his shoes but I don't think I could sing or write or take over the stage like he did. But seriously, I can't wait to hear his voice again. I think it will help with my career, too. But my momma doesn't really want me to do that."

"Oh, shit, Melissa," Candice wrinkled up her nose. "I know how good you are. It's just that I don't want any kid o' mine in that advantage-takin', talent-abusin' cesspool.

Whoa, Candice! Her soft, pretty face began to glow bright pink as the aging belle evolved into a mini volcano of blonde rage. No more gin for you, I thought. Melissa gave her another kick.

"You name me one musician has any say over their own career!" she almost shouted in a righteous rant. Her Nashville twang bounced off of the walls of the empty restaurant, waking up our waiter, who was leaning against the bar.

"They roped my Tom into a bad deal that he never got out of and he wasn't stupid or weak or anything like that. His career never went where it shoulda gone and it was all because of that damn Nashville's Finest!" She bit her lower lip. Melissa patted her shoulder.

"Now, mama. You calm down. You know what you're like when you get like this and there's nothin' you can do about it now."

"Oh, I know. I know."

Candice heaved her lace-draped bustline a couple of times. I longed to help soothe her and tried to steer the subject to something more pertinent, like the legal issues.

"So did they win their lawsuit?" I asked.

"Yeah, back in the eighties. Not that anybody got any money but they all got outta their contracts. I think we can get it sorted out in our favor. I just so wish that Tom coulda been here and see all his hard work and talent finally pay off."

She narrowed her eyes, pressed her frosted pink lips together and leaned forward toward me. She had something else to share.

"Ya know, there's some that think Tom was murdered. Probably by that awful asshole, Jim Ed O'Reilly."

Or a jealous husband, I thought, but after all, she was his widow. I just said, "Really?"

"Well," she continued. "The lawsuit against those creeps was just about to get served. Tom was at the top of a long list of people they'd ripped off. And you know what's funny? After Jim Ed got shot, they found out that Nashville's Finest didn't have any assets 'cept for the publishing rights. The stupid company had so many debts, those other two morons ended up losing everthin'. There's some kind of justice out there, comin' from somewhere."

There sure is, I thought.

Melissa spoke up. "Didja know that my daddy met Jason Poole one time?"

"No, I didn't." I replied, thoroughly amused. I'd gone a little ga-ga over Jason Poole when I was a teenager.

"Yeah, they was staying in the same hotel. Radio Lightning had this huge stadium show they were doin' and my daddy was playing in the hotel bar. It was a real nice gig, but he sure wasn't making a million bucks a night like Jason was. Anyway, my daddy was standin' there and Jason was done up in this black silk outfit with dragons crawlin' up his legs. Jason looks up all surprised and says, 'Tom DeVries!' and my daddy, well he was all long, tall Texan and Jason wasn't very big so he looks down and says "Boy, they make 'em small over there, don't they?' I guess Jason just cracked up and my daddy put out his hand and invited him down to the bar after the show. And ya know, Jason showed up! The other guys in Radio Lightning were partying it up in some god-awful way upstairs but Jason met my daddy at the bar! They even jammed a few numbers!"

Candice beamed. "I always loved that story. Tom always kinda liked Radio Lightning."

Melissa got back to business. "We need to put a clause in the contract that gets Jasmine some kind of, oh, finder's fee? We wouldna had a chance if she hadn't called us first."

Candice's head whipped around to stare at her daughter, pencil-thin eyebrows coming together just over her nose.

"Hey, it's fair!" Melissa retorted. Maybe she was like her dad in a few other ways.

"Yes, it's fair," I agreed, wondering how much it was worth to almost get run off the road. "I think I deserve some compensation but we don't have a contract, and won't until the value of the music is nailed down." I sighed. "You really don't have anything other than my word that I found the music."

Candice stuck out her lower lip thoughtfully, changing her mind about her moment of possessiveness. He had been her husband, after all and it couldn't have been an easy job. Something was owed to her, surely. "Ah, sure. Of course." She said. "We'll keep in touch with you, girl. I don't know what I was thinkin'. Bad habit."

I suggested a drive around the Colorado National Monument as long as they were in Colorado. The ladies were thrilled and their hired plane could wait. I turned on my CD player so Tom could serenade us. Candice said she couldn't wait to hear all those new songs from her Tom. Her Tom? Hadn't he been *my* Tom for a while? I was jealous again. She got the whole nine inches and two kids out of the deal while I might as well have been watching the TV. *My* Tom was about to evaporate into the ether. Neither Candice nor Melissa seemed to sense my plummeting mood.

We made the obvious small talk, enjoying the drive but unable to do any hiking because of the shoes they were wearing. We did get out a couple of times to take in the spectacular views. I stuffed the hurt as deep down as I could stuff it. These gals couldn't know that I'd had a relationship with Tom, as a ghost. They'd only think I was wacko anyway. And besides, it was almost over.

With a sinking feeling I finally handed over the precious case at the airport. I'd done my good deed and now I felt lonesome, empty and sad.

Driving back across the desert, I already missed Tom. I looked for evidence of our last good time together and spotted a tow-truck driver loading a mashed-up black Cadillac onto a flatbed. Utah's cheesiest tabloid TV station's news wagon was just pulling away. Well, at least the evening news would be fun. But I still couldn't talk any sense into myself. That Tom wasn't even a real person and he drove me kind of crazy; it was time to come back to earth. There was a cool new guy on the horizon who was obviously interested, slutty girlfriend and everything. Nope. This was the downside of having fallen for Tom DeVries. Candice, Emmaline and any number of other women knew all about it.

I recalled the rosebud, the initial flirtation, and the first flush of romance, trying to feel my grief all the way down and not try to hide from or deny anything to myself as a way of healing my achy heart. I tried to remember every moment as I drove that lonesome highway until I finally had to pull over and have a good cry. It helped a lot.

Once I got home, I felt better. The little house didn't feel as empty as I had expected, but greeted me with sunshine streaming in through the windows. I got a beer from the fridge and went out to the back patio. I began to feel good about myself for what I had done. I'd been trusted with something important and hadn't done too badly.

My tabloid TV station really delivered. The reporter named Joe Bob, whose feature was called "Strange But True", appeared on Highway 191 in front of an ambulance, the smashed Cadillac, and several police cars. Joe Bob never seemed to believe that this was a real job (which was maybe why I watched him whenever I could).

"Strange But True just got stranger as the Grand County sheriff was called to a motor vehicle accident on Highway 191." Joe Bob put on his most serious face. "A terrible thing happened to a classic 1972 Cadillac with Tennessee plates. Looks to have spun out and rolled four or five times, disgorging two passengers who were two guys in their 60s with booze on their breath. Both of these guys were babbling some story about seeing the ghost of the late country star, Tom DeVries, in an advanced state of deterioration! And another thing, they both said his suit was clean and pressed and his shoes were shined. Now you have to have gotten one hell of a head injury to remember that particular detail!"

Joe Bob furrowed his brow. "Now how many zombies do *you* know who get all dressed up to go out? You have to wonder what those guys were drinking. All I have to say is, that was an awful mean thing to do to that Cadillac and a major crime right there. A many crime scenes as I've been on, this one really broke my heart. What else were these guys up to anyway? Did they think they were on a page out of Fear and Loathing in Las Vegas? You can count on Joe Bob to stay on the story, reporting for Strange But True."

I love Joe Bob.

So I went back out to the patio as the sun went down and the stars came out. Unexpectedly, I began to feel something like pride in myself. I felt honored Tom had chosen me and in the process of helping him and his family, I had outrun a Cadillac! We had worked together to right a great wrong in his life. I had not been in control, but I had earned a merit badge from somewhere in the cosmos.

I had a future somewhere and was no longer such an insignificant being. Instead, my actions would have real consequences and would ripple out from my center and be felt in far distant places. All traces of the sad, shame-filled waif escaped from Larimer County just a year ago evaporated off and became a distant memory of some other person. I was clearly not the same and would never be again.

Chapter 10 · Rob

Back at work, nobody noticed that I had changed. It was cooler but still summery as September rolled lazily by and the RVs just kept on coming, driven by retirees on permanent vacation.

Rodeo season had backed off a bit but smaller arenas all held a flood of events and they all bought ads. There were always roping events, roughstock rodeos, practice rodeos and a local venue featuring amateur bull riding every Friday night. I did ads and more ads. I took call after call. I stuffed far too much magazine into too few pages and got it all done anyway.

I missed my Tom, who was never mine after all, but it was somewhat liberating to end a romance that offered no future and most frustrating of all, no physical fulfillment. Thinking of which, the handsome Rob Dishta and I mildly flirted whenever we happened to see each other. I couldn't help but wonder about all the other girls and why this guy wasn't permanently hitched already. Did it have something to do with that scary little Latina gal?

One Friday afternoon, unannounced, Rob came striding into the office, straight to my desk.

"Jasmine, Uh, hi. I think that you and me should go out sometime."

"Well, I think so too." I tilted my head flirtatiously. No being coy or playing any games with this guy. I introduced Rob to

Kate and Lucy who were momentarily speechless at my good luck, especially since all the best looking guys usually came in to see Lucy. Kate shoved her tongue back in her mouth and told me to take the afternoon off. Rob promptly picked up his cell phone and cancelled his last appointment. He asked me to wait while he went out and cleaned up his truck since he wasn't expecting to get this lucky. Wait, that's not what he meant...

I was gathering my purse, my tea thermos and my jean jacket when Kate flashed me one of her blinding white smiles.

"That's a quality guy there, girlfriend. You go get yourself good and laid."

I laughed out loud. Yes, I was ready to move but not quite as fast as Kate suggested, even thoroughly sex-starved with DeVries only making it worse. I joined Rob in the cab of his magnificent, bright red 4x4. All that flesh and blood and muscle and sweat were giving me bright ideas. His braid ended in a silky filigree on the seat and I really wanted to stroke it. I didn't though. He offered to take me to see some petroglyphs so well hidden that very few people ever saw them. While I was actually interested, I did have a question to ask.

"Rob, don't you have a girlfriend or something?"

Rob let out a long sigh.

"Or something is right. I do NOT have a girlfriend! I have a wicked little witch of a stalker named LaToya following me around. We were an item in high school, the basketball star and the talent contest queen..."

"What kind of talent?" I asked. She did seem inclined to the dramatic.

"Oh, she thought she was Janet Jackson. And she sang and danced pretty well, too, but she didn't want to take any classes or anything. Thought she didn't need it."

"So what happened after high school?"

"Well, I went to college in Provo, thinking it was over between us, but she didn't. She still doesn't! She still won't leave me alone! I don't know what to do!"

"I had one of those too!" I said. "That's why left Fort Collins! And he still tracked me down here. He's gone for good now but what a nightmare! I thought he'd never go away."

We stopped at my house so that I could get better shoes and a backpack. I warned him about Fred as we started up the stairs.

"You have a rattlesnake? I can call somebody..."

"Oh no, don't! He just doesn't want to get stepped on." I approached Fred's favorite step and stomped out my usual greeting. Fred rattled back and slid under the step, just like he always did. Rob had a funny look on his face, more creeped out than impressed.

"Jasmine, nobody makes friends with a rattlesnake," he said.

"Oh, they don't mean to be so bad. Thumping on the ground is the way to communicate with them. Why doesn't an Indian know about these things, anyway?" I wasn't about to tell him I owed actually one to Fred.

"Hey, don't expect any of that Indian bullshit from me," he said. "Let's go put together a picnic and sit by the river."

At the grocery we bought chicken, fruit, chips and potato salad. I bought a tablecloth in a Madras print. We bought beer, of course.

I wasn't disappointed by the glyphs at Rob's secret site. I loved the mysterious memoirs left by ancient cultures. Looking at the strange symbols made me feel all tingly. I could sense the presence of the spirits and felt they had something to tell me. Some looked like composites of different animals. Others that showed human figures all lined up, hand in hand. Had I been alone, I would have hung out quietly and listened to the old ghosts but Rob honestly wasn't interested in petroglyphs that day. He needed to talk. We ended up next to the Colorado under big shady trees blowing tufts of fluffy white seeds all over us. A group of canoes floated languidly by as we spread the tablecloth on the sand. The biggest one, filled with camping gear, looked like one of the beautiful canoes out of *The Last of the Mohicans*. We waved. They all waved back.

Rob started to spill his guts. "I think she's really crazy. She used to come to my dorm on the weekends even when I told her not to. I'd have a date and she'd butt right in and tell the girl that we were engaged. She even bought a ring and showed it off. I told her and told her. But instead of going home, she just sat by my door and cried."

It sounded so familiar. With Greg Ross, I was just a bit player in his movie. LaToya sounded much the same.

"She still lives with her mom. Her dad ran out on them a few years ago. She's been working at the same souvenir shop since high school. She says she's not moving out because she's waiting for us to get married. Jasmine, we haven't even been intimate since a couple of times in college when I gave in like an idiot. Scenes like that in the grocery store, when you ate that apple, are so typical. It was really funny that you did that, by the way. But to get back to LaToya, my family can't stand her and neither can I."

Remembering how tenacious Greg Ross had been, I also remembered why. "Rob, you said that her dad ran out on her and her mom. Can those women support themselves?"

"LaToya's job is part-time and I don't think her mom does anything."

"That might be the reason that she's so persistent. The guy I had to run from couldn't take care of himself without some kind of slave to do it all for him."

"Do you know what happened to him?"

"Some," I played it down. The dirty, miserable part of the life I left behind didn't belong on a first date. "He's been in and out of jail ever since. He always seemed really intelligent but he wasn't. Kept doing the stupidest things."

"No way am I taking on LaToya and her mom."

He continued, words spilling out in a stream of frustration

and helplessness. This guy really did need to talk to someone who had been under the thumb of a delusional puppet master.

"...Christmas, she shows up at the house just in time for dinner, brings my mom a fake Christmas wreath she probably took off the neighbor's front door, my sister gags, I try to call the police..."

"And they always say that they can't really do anything until something happens."

"So, you know about that?"

Oh, yeah. I knew *all* about that. But I had been so ashamed and so intimidated that I didn't go to the police even when something did happen. Rob and I had more in common that I had thought. Someday, I would tell him about the scene on the stairs with Greg Ross.

But I didn't want to spend our whole first date talking about our horrible past relationships. I asked him about his family and his face lit up just for a moment.

"Well, my granddad was a code talker in World War 2...But, I'm sorry, Jasmine. I've been talking about myself this whole time. Let's do something else."

We packed up the picnic stuff and took a walk along the river. By now we were holding hands. Human biology was much on my mind but Rob changed the subject to geology.

"Have you ever been to Canyonlands? Fall is the best time to go and by some miracle I don't have a soccer game to coach tomorrow. Do *you* have any plans for the weekend?"

I didn't, and told him I would absolutely love to go.

"Great! I'll pick you up at seven if that's not too early for you."

Suddenly I was five years old and tomorrow was Christmas. The chemistry spiked between us as we tried to make our mundane plans.

"I don't have any camping gear," I said.

"Oh, no problem. I've got everything we need. It's supposed

to be dry tomorrow so we can just roll out the futon in the back of my truck."

"Under the stars!"

"If that's okay with you."

You bet it was.

We shared a very promising kiss on the front porch.

I didn't sleep much that night. Heavenly visions of all the wonderful things I could do with this guy kept me awake and made me wonder how I was going to make it through the next day of driving and hiking and picnicking and all the other things I usually loved but now seemed like mere formalities getting in the way of the important stuff. I reminded myself to savor every moment. The weekend would be over in no time and real life would raise its boring head. Every moment, Jasmine, every moment. Anticipating the sound of Rob's truck, even packing my back pack felt magical.

He showed up right on time and I ran down the stairs. It was really hard to act nonchalant, greeting Rob with a light-hearted kiss, pretending to be interested in exploring Canyonlands. Once in the truck, I looked through his CDs and found names like John Hyatt, Lyle Lovett, Emmy Lou Harris and Hoyt Axton. Cool, those were some of my friends. But I also noticed a number of CDs by the newest country pop sensation, Tracy Simon. She was a delicate blond with a big voice but with a sugar pop style more suited to the tastes of high school girls. I had to ask.

"Hey Rob, are *you* the Tracy Simon fan?" It seemed unlikely.

"Oh yeah! I love her! Especially her videos." His enthusiasm was genuine. "My girl's soccer team turned me onto her. I figured as long as I was stuck in the van with her on the CD player all the time, I might as well be a fan."

Weird, I thought. Tracy Simon was too girly for *me*. Oh well, *I* was in love with a long-dead Texan.

"Have you ever heard of Tom DeVries?" I asked cautiously.

"Who?"

"He's someone I discovered last year. He's in the same category as Lyle, Hoyt and Emmy Lou but he's kind of obscure. I just thought you might know him."

"Oh, those are my dad's CDs. Sometimes he borrows my truck."

We ate the breakfast burritos that he'd brought and shared a thermos of coffee. I began to get excited in spite of myself about Canyonlands, something that not long ago would have been an impossible dream. Arches was only the beginning, I knew. The entrance to Canyonlands was only a few miles from Moab so we began our tour at the Island in the Sky with the panoramic views it offered and proceeded to Mesa Arch, the much-photographed formation which Rob insisted everyone had to see. Then it got interesting. Rob knew the park really well and he also knew most of the rangers so we were able to go places most tourists didn't go and to be alone for most of the day. It really paid to be with a homeboy.

We hiked into a deep canyon.

"I wanted to make up for yesterday." Rob looked apologetic. "All I did was talk about me."

"Oh, I think we needed to get clear on some things."

"Yeah," he said. "LaToya, for one."

"And Greg Ross for another" I answered.

"Well, I hope that crazy exes aren't the only things we have in common." He gestured ahead.

"See that? It looks like a staircase?"

I followed his lead to what really was an ancient staircase; steep, eroded sandstone steps leading up and over the canyon wall. The steps were shallow and not easy to negotiate. We had to crawl like rock climbers, finding secure holds for hands and feet. Rob had me go ahead, promising to catch me if I slipped. I wasn't used to this and it made me nervous but I didn't dare let him know. Instead I made a bad joke about the ancient people who had made this being more like monkeys than we'd thought. Rob chuckled.

"Wait 'till you see where we're going. It's worth the trouble."

After the last pitch, we found ourselves at the entrance to a cave. It wasn't a dark cave. It wasn't damp or musty either, but made out of warm, dry, golden sandstone. A stream of sunlight angled in through an opening in the ceiling.

"Look there." Rob pointed at one of the walls.

It was covered with pictures, animals of all kinds, deer, buffalo, bears, birds, and turtles.

Groups of human figures, stick figures carrying shields, a large spiral with lines radiating outward, probably the sun. Strange figures could have been spirits or space aliens. I was flooded with a sense of activity, dancing, drums, campfires and shadows on the walls. Animal hides lining the floor. I didn't really "see" with my eyes as much as with my inner eye, just as I hadn't ever "seen" Tom DeVries, but I felt I was getting a very real impression of what had happened in this cave. I mention this to Rob.

"My mother felt the same thing when I brought her here."

"So you don't feel it? Aren't you the Indian in this party?" I thought I'd challenge him a little. Just to hear what he'd say.

"Aw, not really." He kind of scoffed. "I told you. All that stuff about Indians having some special connection to the land and being all in tune with some great spirit is crap, most of the time. I really like it in here, though. Always have."

He looked around and gestured toward a couple of smooth, flat rocks.

"Natural lounge chair. Let's sit over there."

We made pillows out of our backpacks and Rob unrolled a self-inflating pad onto the warm stone. We had a perfect view of the painted wall. Rob started to put his arm around me.

"Let's get a little closer. You don't mind, do you?"

Hell no, I didn't! "Not at all," I said. I rolled onto my side and put my head on his shoulder. This may have been manna from heaven to me but I doubted that Rob ever lacked for dates. My body prickled with anticipation, so much so that I was afraid of moving too fast and putting him off. The beautiful cave, the warm sandstone and that powerful young male body extended an irresistible invitation. There would be more to come.

Rob pulled me over on top of him and took my face in his hands for our first really deep melting kiss and I sank into that taut, muscular body as though I'd always belonged there. I was so starved I was shaking at his every touch, which didn't surprise me and probably excited Rob. It did surprise me that he gasped when I pulled his shirt up in order to taste his firm belly and rub my cheek against his chest. This felt so new to me. It had been years since I'd had any real desire for another. Greg had been far more interested in drugs than sex and I had only turned to him because I had no other choice.

Rob kissed me on the neck and began working his way down, expertly undoing the buttons of my shirt. In a way, I could hardly stand it, trembling, gasping, moaning, on fire with his touch. Rob seemed young, eager and a little tenuous, maybe shy about being too forward. I felt his hard-on surge and I undid his pants, moving my lips from his belly on down. Since I was the older of the two of us, it felt natural that I should take the lead. I cupped his testicles in my hand and kissed his penis, gently, trying not to get too aggressive. He still had to beg me to stop. When I finally straddled his hips we began to move together in lush, smooth waves. He gazed at my breasts, caressed my neck. I planted my mouth on his. This was pure heaven.

Lying naked, side by side on the warm velvety sandstone, I felt as though we had always belonged together.

Rob sighed contentedly. "I was so looking forward to this."

"And so was I," I replied. It seemed such a shame to leave this place but the afternoon was wearing on and the cave would soon cool down. Besides, Rob had a futon in the back of his truck.

It only got more delirious. We couldn't even have a conversation any more, but just laughed and giggled at each other with anticipation as we got back to the truck and he drove us to the camping spot. We pulled ourselves together just enough to light the hibachi for grilled steak and shrimp while we shared a bottle of wine.

The sunset slowly descended over layers and layers of red rock and sandstone, turning the tans and reds to that darkest of blues. I felt as though the old spirits rose out of the rocks and arched over us, singing their strange and perfect rhythms that only the most blessed could hear. Rob rolled out the futon as the stars came out and the moon shone full with the light of love. We spent one of those nights where we'd make love, doze off in each other's arms and then, barely even awake, make love again.

Waking up all tangled in long black hair, wrapped in those powerful arms, I could have stayed exactly like that for the rest of my life but it finally got too hot in the back of the truck. We reluctantly packed up and moved out of our realm of sacred passion but we hadn't broken the spell. We weren't talking much. It felt like we were in some kind of bubble, floating around with no real relationship to the rest of the world. We visited a few more sites and hiked around and every place felt holy. Other people floated around us and greeted us pleasantly and every one of them was beautiful and kind. We finally left the park as the sun went down and our magical weekend drew to a close. We agreed that we shouldn't spend another night together since we both had to work in the morning but we must have made out in the truck for a good half hour before we were finally able to extricate ourselves and become two separate beings again.

I floated up the stairs on gossamer wings, crazy in love and looking forward to putting myself to sleep by recalling every detail of the last couple of days. But that's not what happened.

Chapter 11 – Tom again!

As I opened the door I was hit with a blast of freezing cold air and the raunchy smell of skunk. Tom? Yeah, Tom, mad as hell! Hey! I didn't remember making any deal to be faithful to a guy that wasn't there. How dare he string me along like that and then come back to claim me!

"Tom!" I shouted out loud. "I thought you'd crossed over! I thought you were done with me. I did what you wanted! What the hell is this?"

He couldn't answer my question directly but he certainly let me know how he felt. Along with the icy wind and the skunk, I sensed something that I hadn't expected at all. I felt pain and disappointment. I'd really hurt him. I hadn't meant to but I had. But Tom DeVries was awfully careless about the women in his life, afflicted with a short attention span at the very least. I hadn't thought that he might actually care for me. I put on a sweatshirt against the cold but it didn't help much. What had he seen in me anyway, other than needing my help with something he couldn't do by himself? Tom DeVries, always the ladies' man, dating music and movie stars. What would he have seen in this ordinary female with her dark, impoverished and drugged-out past? Knowing Tom, he was probably drawn to my sheer unavailability, the challenge being more than he could resist.

I resented having my sexy, romantic weekend snatched

away from me like that. I resented being made to feel guilty about something that wasn't even wrong. I felt hurt knowing that Tom was so hurt. I grabbed my sage wand off the mantle and tried to light it but Tom blew it out. I tried again but the lighter flared up so high that I dropped it and left a burn on the hardwood floor. I gave up and flopped on the sofa.

"Tom, please." I wasn't shouting this time. "You know that I adore you. I really do. You're sweet and sexy and you protected me when I needed it. But I live on the physical plane! You don't. As wonderful as you've been, you've been driving me kind of crazy too. We don't have a future together. Maybe you can go on forever just the way you are but I can't! This is all the life I've got!"

Tom swirled around the room and I could feel his rage, disappointment and frustration. This could go on all night! Goddamn! I was not going to be a prisoner again! I wasn't about to be held against my will by another guy who had the power to keep me in fear! I tried to walk out but the door wouldn't open. This was the last straw!

"Damn you, Tom!" I screamed this time. "How many hearts did *you* stomp all over in your lifetime? You're used to having women falling all over you all the time, doing what ever you want. You know what you're *not* used to? You don't even have that famous nine-inch dick anymore! So what's the point?"

My hands flew to my mouth. That was really mean. The front door flew open, a blast of icy wind blew and the door slammed shut. There was a crash from the bedroom as my precious Cowboy Angel poster fell to the floor.

I felt a sob rise in my throat and tears stung my eyes. I spent the rest of the night confused and weepy, sweeping shattered glass off the floor of the bedroom and trying to make sense of the day's events. It wasn't supposed to have ended this way.

I slunk into work the next morning trying to remember that I'd just had the greatest weekend of my entire life and that there were more in my future but I was feeling so sad about Tom that it didn't look right. Kate and Lucy noticed right away.

"So, Jasmine, it looks to me like your hot date wasn't so hot after all." Kate was ready to hear the whole story but I came up with one of the better lies I'd ever told.

"Oh no," I replied. "I had the best time of my life. It's the coming home from paradise and landing in the real world again. It's kind of a let-down"

"Well, I'm sorry we let you down."

"I didn't mean it like that!" I kept trying to cover up.

"Hey, neither of us are good-looking Indian guys with black hair down to our butts." Lucy merrily chimed in.

Kate rescued the moment by mentioning how the middle school had a lot more girls in the basketball program now that Rob was coaching.

"You hang on to that one, he's one good catch. And so are you, by the way! It's too bad about that shrieking harpy who keeps following him around."

Rob called twice just to say that he was thinking about me. I felt a shudder of desire at the sound of his voice and the flash of a particularly erotic moment in my mind's eye. It put a band-aid on my sore feelings, but I was really hurting over that fight with Tom. There was something special, really special between us. Shucks, I almost had an affair with the infamous Tom DeVries and there were some real feelings on both sides. We accomplished something together by getting the precious cassettes and reels back to his family. I couldn't believe things went so wrong between us, but they sure had. I was so sorry I'd said that awful thing I was convinced I'd take that comment to my grave.

After work, I didn't want to go home. I was even a little afraid that I'd walk into that cold wind again and be trapped by another angry, possessive guy who was going to have it his way and no other.

But where else was there to go? I let myself in and everything seemed pretty normal. It was still warm in Moab in October and the breeze that swept through the cottonwoods was soft and sweet. I felt no sign of an angry guy spewing hurt and disappointment and making me feel guilty about trying to live my life. But I so wanted to make it up, heal it up, part company on better terms and not remain sitting at the bottom of some giant black hole of regret.

In order to do something normal, I went to the kitchen for a beer, hoping I could pull it together to make myself a good dinner. I so wanted to feel giddy and joyful and sexy about Rob instead of so sorry about my Tom. I cracked open my beer and went out to my back patio where I had first met him, sat down on the stone wall and tried to think of a way to apologize without making some kind of compromise that I didn't want to make.

Then something fell in my lap. It was a long-stemmed white rose in full bloom even though there were no roses left in the garden.

Peace, it said. I surrender. Truce. My Tom was back, every bit as contrite as I was. He wasn't going to leave me hanging. I stated out loud how sorry I was that I had said that awful thing. I felt like I had to remind him of how I really did have a life to live and that I wanted a family of my own but I'd never stop loving him. Tom was sorry too. Sad, sorry that we lived on separate planes of existence but not angry any more. I still didn't fell any better. I cared for Tom and he cared for me but there was no relationship to be had.

My cell phone rang. It was Rob, of course and I really wanted to take the call. I smelled skunk. Tom was still jealous but at least we understood each other.

Actually, since my meeting with Candice and Melissa, I had an important question to ask. Tom wasn't good at verbal communication but there was something I needed to know. So, the next day, I made some time for myself after work and went out to sit on the back patio. Candice's speculation that Tom may have been murdered added a new wrinkle to the thin fabric between our worlds.

"Tom?" I called out loud, not knowing if he'd show or not. I didn't like this new awkwardness between us and I didn't know how to broach it. Made me feel a little peeved that the same old guy problems could span a few lifetimes.

"Tom," I called again. "Did Jim Ed O'Reilly really have you murdered? Candice thinks so. Is that what happened?"

He settled in, like a giant bird landing softly. It wasn't the same as it had been between us, certainly not as sexy or flirtatious but still some kind of connection. I felt a familiar chortle flutter through me. He was amused. He knew Candice a lot better than I did. Maybe she had an imagination better suited to the tabloids than real life. I did get the idea that he hadn't been murdered after all.

The next morning I got in my car and turned on the radio. I didn't get a station. Instead, Tom DeVries came on, singing a song called "Torn" about a guy who had to decide between two women and how come it had to be one way or the other.

"How come "Choose" always rhymes with "Lose?"
Choose is a notion I can't use,
Mama, bless her soul, on her dyin' bed
"Pick one or the other, my son," she said.
Maybe pull up the shades and put a bullet in my head
"Cause I'll always want the other one."

I couldn't tell if he was sympathizing or teasing me.

But then I got one of those messages at the end of the song, the best way for him to talk to me.

"Yeah, Jasmine." I heard. "It was murder all right. That patch of gravel really had it in for me."

I laughed out loud, glad to get that kind of news instead of the other and glad as hell that I still had my Tom.

Chapter 12 - LaToya

"Geez, Jasmine. The only things I don't like about this place are that snake and that skunk. I wish you'd let me call somebody."

Rob and I were lounging in bed one Saturday evening after a lovemaking session where I insisted on keeping the blankets over our entwined bodies, saying I was chilly but it wasn't really true. I wasn't free to feel as passionate with Rob while Tom was still haunting the house.

"Is everything okay, Jasmine?" Rob asked. "You seem nervous or something."

"I am," I admitted. "Something feels creepy...Oh, *Shit!*"

I shrieked at a ghoulish face peering in the window, backlit by the shining moon.

"LaToya! Damn you! What are you doing?!" Rob quickly started to pull on his jeans, hopping on one leg out the door and down the steps. I ran to the front window to see LaToya stumble down the stairs on her ever-present spike heels.

"I'm calling the police!" Rob hollered after her but she made it to her car and peeled out, tires screeching, before he had a chance to confront her. Porch lights blinked on and neighbors peered out doors and windows, all being treated to a moonlit view of a finely honed backside as Rob struggled with his twisted pants leg.

"Jasmine, I'm so sorry," he said once he was back in the

house and zipping up his jeans. "We have to talk about this."

"What do you think?" I asked as I poured us each a glass of wine and sat down on the sofa. "I suppose I could call the police and make a report but it may not stop her."

"She's bound to spy on us every time she sees my truck in the driveway," he sighed. "Maybe we should spend our weekends out of town."

"What about your place?" I asked.

"It's a frat house," he replied. "They're real great guys, same ones that helped with your floors, but I wouldn't take you there for the night. I have an idea, though. Now that soccer season is in full swing, I have to be out of town a lot on weekends. Why don't you come with me and help me cheer on my teams?"

Adolescent soccer games sounded like a real bore but I'd have an exclusive on Rob in the evenings and we'd be out of Tom's presence. Problems solved? Well, sort of.

The Rob and LaToya fiasco was a full tank of gasoline for local gossip and Moab was a small town. People I'd never met knew I was dating Rob Dishta. The two guys at the bike shop couldn't stop teasing.

"Rob Dishta, huh?" The smaller one with the goatee made a face and pretended to be jealous. "What do you see in that guy, anyway? There's a lot more to a man than good looks, brains and a good job. Geeze, you didn't even bother to call *me*."

The taller blond with the dreadlocks got into the act. "She doesn't like us younger guys. Dishta used to coach my soccer team when I was in middle school, you know."

"Well, she can pick out her own bike today. I'm not talking to her."

They gave me a half-dozen energy bars and encouraged me to fill out a ticket for a bike raffle. Rob came in to meet me and the boys made faces again.

"We don't like you anymore." The goatee piped up. "You stole my almost girlfriend!"

"You're welcome to the old one!" Rob laughed back.

"What? No way! A fate worse than death!"

We could make fun of the situation but it wasn't funny. We were out of town almost every weekend, just as Rob had said. I was pleased that he wanted me to come along, involving me with his life and proud to have me there. I was surprised to find myself in the role of the ordinary soccer mom, riding from tournament to game in the front seat of a van, surrounded by the cheerful chaos of the players, although I could have done without the constant, sugary, pop music of Tracy Simon. Rob coached a girl's team and a boy's team so the weekends were packed with activities and I usually didn't get to be alone with him until late evening. I got a little tired of it but at least we were far away from LaToya.

I finally introduced Rob to Tom DeVries's music and he developed a mild interest, saying he needed to turn his dad onto the guy. I didn't mention I knew that guy a lot better than only on the radio. I did tell him about finding the case and tracking down Candice DeVries and about the dirty deal he'd been roped into that caused him to hide the case in my house. Rob was intrigued but there was no way I was going to tell him any ghost stories. No weird voodoo stuff that might freak him out. We had a freaky enough situation on our hands already. As the weather got colder and soccer season came to a close, we realized that we were going to have to deal with LaToya sooner or later but neither of us knew how.

Sure enough, we were at lunch on a workday sitting in a booth at one of the better Mexican restaurants in town, when the dreaded SHE walked in the door, wearing ragged fishnet stockings, ultra-short cutoff jeans and her signature spiked heels. A whole lot of boobage burst out of her open jacket. She was so obviously off the deep end, wearing enough makeup for ten sleazy biker sluts. This woman was thirty years old and dressed like a slutty fifteen-year-old trying to imitate the eighties version of Madonna. To top it off, she looked drugged and dopey. She sat right next to Rob and slid up against him, curling her lip and sneering at me.

"And what are you doing here?" she demanded.

"I belong here," I replied as calmly as I could. "And you don't!"

"Get out LaToya!" Rob almost shouted. "I don't want you here! Get off of me!"

He tried to shove her off but she sat tight. "You've been two-timing me with this piece of white meat?" she shouted indignantly. "You got a lot to make up for, mister! Get rid of that whore and make good on your promises. We're engaged, remember?"

I kept quiet in spite of her venom. A sarcastic retort would have been too easy and prove that I was smarter than she, escalating the whole confrontation right through the roof of the restaurant. Flashback to Greg Ross. I could *so* remember how he used his very short fuse to control every situation.

"God, LaToya! We broke up right out of high school. And we are not engaged!" Rob was doing his best to hold his temper. He growled through his teeth so as not to shout but other restaurant patrons were beginning to take notice.

"Oh that was years ago!" she maintained. "We're all over *that* now. Get this bitch out of here and let's get on with our plans!"

Rob shoved her away and she fell off the seat. One of the waiters came over and helped her up.

"Miss, you are going to have to leave," he stated firmly as he steered her toward the door. She shook off his arm, turned and shouted at the whole restaurant "See what I have to put up with? Did you see that?"

The waiter managed to get her out of the restaurant but he couldn't clean up the atmosphere. He apologized to Rob and me and promised to ban her from coming in ever again. Rob sat with his head in his hands and sighed. "I'm so sorry about that, Jasmine."

"Rob, it's not your fault. Besides, I know a lot about this kind of thing. Greg used to chase me down just like that. I could never get away from him. He was just as crazy and just as stupid and just as dangerous."

"She is, isn't she? Dangerous, I mean."

Rob hadn't thought of her like that before. Annoying, obsessed, obnoxious but not really a serious threat. I thought of her differently. There was nothing left of the high school prom queen. LaToya showed symptoms of something much darker. I'd heard that schizophrenia often emerged in young adulthood. To my way of thinking, her personality had dissolved to the point where any number of evil things might have taken over. Psychology might say bi-polar. As a graduate of the school of Greg Ross, I diagnosed demonic possession.

Shopping for socks and a sweater at a local sportswear venue, I was approached by the shop's assistant manager, a young woman named Tina, a sturdy type of gal who'd probably made use of every item in the store at one time of year or another, who said that she used to be LaToya's friend and wanted to talk to both me and Rob. She said that LaToya had lost her job at the souvenir shop and was sure that neither she nor her mother had any income.

"I'm not really her friend any more but I went to visit just to see how they were doing and it doesn't look good at all. Really weird. Like they're both crazy or on drugs or something. Maybe both. It's probably none of my business but I wanted you guys to know that this thing is getting worse and it might make things worse for you two."

Rob was coming over for dinner anyway, so I invited Tina. I made a black bean chili with tortillas, tomatoes, avocados and cheese on the side and a a nicer-than-usual beer. Tina and Rob greeted each other with a warm hug while I opened beers.

"Tina and I go all the way back to grade school," Rob began. "But we didn't get to be friends until high school when I started dating LaToya." He rolled his eyes at the ceiling. "You were always so much nicer than LaToya."

Tina laughed. "LaToya was like the sun and we were all planets caught in her orbit. She had so much charisma in those days!"

"Yeah, she couldn't sing or dance and she still rocked the hell out of those Janet Jackson songs."

"Nobody had a chance after that." Tina nodded. "We all thought she was the next big thing!"

"So she really did have some talent?" I asked.

"Yeah," Tina said. "But she didn't want to work at it, or anything else really. Rob, have you been to her house recently?"

"Not for years. Not since her dad took off. It's been a long time."

"Well, LaToya got fired after, oh gosh, maybe twelve years of working at Little Thunder's. They got sick of the way she dresses, her crummy attitude and she's been showing up all stoned on something. When they tried to talk to her, she just threw one of her tantrums."

"Tell me about it!" Rob said.

"Her way of controlling things," I surmised.

We sat at the table and started our dinner. No need to make conversation as LaToya's behavior was better than the movies. The woman did know how to get attention.

"She manipulated her girlfriends too," Tina continued. "She was always really popular but, looking back, it's hard to say why. She never came to our study groups or anything. Instead, she'd bully one of us into doing her homework for her, saying say we weren't good friends if we didn't give her the answers on the tests. I could have gotten caught cheating but she was so intimidating! She threatened to tell my mother I'd gone on birth control pills!"

"Sounds just like LaToya." Rob agreed.

Tina continued. "You wouldn't believe what it's like in that house. I mean, I don't think that either of those women knows how to do anything but their hair and their nails. There's stuff everywhere. Overflowing trash cans. Trash on the floor. And it stinks! Really stinks!" Tina clamped her fingers around her nose to illustrate her point.

"LaToya's mother always had someone come in to do the cooking and cleaning," Rob put in. "And it wasn't that big of a house, even. I just don't think she ever expected to do any work."

"I think that's what drove her dad away," Rob said. "Too many demands from two women who thought he was made out of money, I guess."

"When did he leave?" I asked.

"I think LaToya was about twenty. He left five thousand dollars in the bank and just disappeared with the rest."

"I don't blame the guy," he continued. "They weren't nice to him at all. Always making sarcastic remarks that he couldn't make any more money than he did. They did it in front of other people just to humiliate him. Even in high school, I knew better."

I asked Tina about drugs and alcohol.

"I saw a lot of booze bottles. They might be doing pills or something. I don't think it's meth 'cause then LaToya would be running around looking for meth instead of harassing Rob."

"I wonder what they do for money if LaToya doesn't have her job anymore?" Rob wondered. "Social Services?"

Something probably had to be done but none of us had a suggestion. I reminded Tina and Rob of one of my least favorite statements regarding law enforcement, "We really can't do anything until something happens." It was a statement that I hold responsible for the abuse, victimization and deaths of women and children in all parts of the U.S and anywhere else in the world where they use the expression. By the time it's said, something bad has already happened. Either the victims are too scared to say anything or they don't know what to report or they're afraid to tell the authorities about the abuse because they've been smoking pot or doing other drugs in order to endure the situation. LaToya was a time bomb in heels and fake eyelashes. And there wasn't much we could do since she had so far not been a serious physical threat.

Chapter 13 – The Spiritual Side

Rob decided to show me his house, a typical, boring little ranch on the outer edge of town. Beige, of course. The inside was such a man-cave that I felt very out of place. A huge, wide-screen TV dominated the living room. Mountain bikes hung from the ceiling. Shelves by the front door overflowed with about a million types of sports equipment. Hiking boots, ski boots, cross-country ski boots, rock climbing shoes, crampons, Teva sandals and other types of indoor sports shoes were arrayed untidily in the front entrance. On the wall were a couple of hand-made shields with hand-painted hides stretched across a framework of bent branches, painted with symbols that didn't seem traditionally Native American. On the floor underneath them were two drums, hand-made from hollowed out trees with hides stretched over the top. I asked if they belonged to Rob.

"Naw. That's my housemates' stuff. They're kinda weird but they mean it. They made those shields and drums for themselves. They like to go out in the desert with a group of other guys and build fires and sit around naked. They drum and chant and stuff. I don't get it."

I thought you were half-Navajo, I thought to myself. You, the guy with the black braid down to his butt, think these guys are weird. Okaaay.

Rob asked me if I wanted to sit down. Not really, since the leather sofa was all dusty and the recliner was covered with crumbs. I chose the sofa.

The housemates arrived shortly. They dropped hockey sticks and helmets on the floor in the already hopelessly chaotic front entrance. They both smiled brightly as Rob introduced me and went to the kitchen to get beers for all of us.

Dr. Agon, as he called himself, was a nerdy little guy with black hair, black-rimmed glasses and a subversive look in his eye. He spent most of his time in his room at his computer. He said he was working on a project for NASA but wouldn't say any more. Rob told me later that he made a mint but he was saving it for something he wouldn't talk about. Mark was a skinny blond surveyor who worked in the same office as Rob. They had known each other since college in Provo. No, they could never get Rob to come to one of their drum circles. Wuss. They were better Indians than he was.

And they knew all about LaToya.

"Yeah. We just put on the headphones, lock the door and wait for her to go away."

"When I'm not working my real job, I work on formulas that will make obnoxious females disappear." Dr. Agon was in his element. "There'll be a formula for guys too! You can use it on Rob if he turns into an asshole. But all that is still in the developmental stages."

To Rob's annoyance, I asked what had gotten them interested in the drum circles. Dr. Agon was reverent. Mark was enthusiastic.

"I'm from the East Coast. Long Island, New York." Dr. Agon happily told his story. "There's church there, but it was all Christian and it just wasn't me. I'm not saying there's anything wrong with it but I just couldn't get into it."

"Yeah," Mark agreed. "I was the same way. I'm from the Mid-West. It was really important to my folks to belong to a church so I always went with them and I still go when I'm back home. All their friends go there. It's such a social thing. You know, donuts and coffee after the services and stuff."

"So if you're not into the Christian thing and you need something, what do you do?" I asked.

Both Dr. Agon and Mark were happy to expound on their personal spiritual journeys. Rob stood patiently and let them tell their stories but I could sense him wanting to be somewhere else. It made me uncomfortable that he was so closed to even discussing spiritual matters. I also wondered if he didn't like having my attention taken away from him. Red flag? Should I think twice about this guy? But maybe he'd just heard it all too many times.

Dr. Agon, in the meantime, might have been reading his own diary. "So I spent the whole summer working at the Shambala Center in the Colorado Mountains. Really nice place. I meditated my brain off, worked my buns off and chanted all the time trying to be a Buddhist. I was totally Zen for a while. There were a lot of cute girls there too! I finally had to admit to myself that the girls were more important to me than any old religion so I stopped trying to be enlightened and went back to being myself."

I asked him how he'd become involved in the drum circles in the desert.

"It just came to me," Dr. Agon saidd. "I think it was meant to. I was having beers with this guy I'd never met and complaining about the mad scientist, computer geek thing and how isolated I felt. Anyway, this guy, name's Brad, super athletic. He said he'd always been into all the outdoor sports but he never felt so connected until he started drumming with this group of guys he knew. He said his whole attitude toward rock climbing, biking, canoeing and all the other stuff he liked to do took on a whole new meaning. We spent the evening getting drunk, sneaking out to smoke joints and bonding over our spiritual needs. He made me think."

Mark sank into the recliner and cracked open his beer.

"I just didn't care until I moved here. Dr. Agon over there invited me to the drum circles. I was just like Rob and thought he was crazy but I couldn't resist the adventure."

Chuckles. Rob kind of snorted.

"Anyway, I think we both found something," weird little Dr. Agon agreed. "And it's really a guy thing. It just pulls you right into the center of the earth."

"It makes me feel like part of the elements," said Mark "Like I'm growing out of the earth just like plants and animals. Maybe like a hunter or a cave man. It's church. It's my church."

"Yeah, especially since I'm always at the computer, I start to feel like some kind of electronic insect or something. After one of the drum circles I feel human again. Like a real person. Flesh and blood."

I asked if there were Native Americans involved. They said that their team leaders were a Cherokee, an Apache and an Arapahoe. They often brought teenage boys, and Native American guys who had just gotten out of jail and needed to reconnect with their heritage.

Rob stood up.

"We need to go," he said firmly. "We'll be late for the two-step class."

I felt a little weird about us. This may not be true love after all. In the truck, I chose not to ask him about his own spirituality or whether he'd gone to church with this family or any of those things. Someday, I would have to tell him about me, about the second sight and my communication with spirits. I might even have to tell him about my relationship with Tom DeVries. But only if we wanted this thing to be for real.

One morning, I finished up at the ATM and turned around to find this nerdy guy behind me. He had lank blond hair, wore a plaid shirt, jeans and Nikes and his shy smile revealed crooked front teeth. Pale blue eyes peered through wire-rimmed glasses.

"Hey there," he began in a low drawl that didn't fit the rest of him. "Aren't you the one who stole the heart of our very own Rob Dishta?"

I kind of chuckled and replied "I guess."

"Well, you can have his heart but his friends would like you to give his brain back. All he wants to do these days is stare into space and smile a lot."

"Oh, that's so sweet of you. I'm Jasmine."

"Call me, uh, Derek," he replied. And then he went on. "You know, I'd better let you know that we're all a little concerned. And I think you know what I mean."

I may have had other issues in my future with Rob, but I did know that Derek was referring to LaToya.

"Anyway," he continued. "I want you to be real careful for a while. You take this."

He put something in my hand. It was a cylinder of pepper spray. "Yeah, try not to be alone unless you have to be. We'll be watchin' out for the two of ya."

He gave me something like a wink, got his cash out of the ATM and turned to go. There was a curious grace to his stride, kind of floaty, as though he wasn't really touching the ground.

Good to see you, Tom! It didn't look like him at all but I knew he was my Tom. A huge surge of sheer joy exploded in my heart. Tom had altered his role in my life so he could still be with me. My protector. My knight. My dear, dear friend. There was a split second when I would have abandoned my whole life to take off after that skinny dude, but he'd already disappeared. Besides, I'd have to be dead to do that. Didn't matter. I love you Tom or Derek or whatever your name is. I really do.

Theresa Rose

Chapter 14 – Thanksgiving

Rob's family wanted to meet me and asked me over for Thanksgiving. Rob warned me about LaToya but promised if she did show up, he'd do his best to send her on her way.

Meeting the family was a big step and a sign that the relationship might be heading for "something serious", at least in Rob's mind. Part of me adored him. I loved the time we spent together, hiking and two-stepping and cooking dinner and watching TV together. I loved being in bed with him, totally engulfed in that big, strong, sexy guy thing. But part of me had serious misgivings, not the least of which was how I longed for another who also longed for me. But Rob and I had only been dating for a few months, and I knew Rob wasn't at all open to certain modes of perception, like me sometimes knowing things before they happened and talking to ghosts. I dreaded having to reveal this side of myself, certain it would not be well received. Meeting his family would give me another clue.

The tri-level was in a well-established neighborhood, very conservative, with appropriate desert-style landscaping and wagon wheels by the mailboxes. Pieces of antique farm equipment decorated the seasonally brown front lawns. Rob's mother, dad and sister were so glad I wasn't LaToya that I was welcomed with arms wide open. I liked his mother, Sylvie, immediately. Even though she'd been raised in Pennsylvania, she'd hung onto her French heritage and still had an enormously attractive accent that made every simple statement sound elegant and sophisticated. She was very much the French country matron, a tiny bit plump, pretty, hair in a French twist. She and Yvette, Rob's older sister, set the table and poured glasses of Sylvie's carefully chosen wine.

I was happy to see that the Dishta home was decorated with a western flair, including Navajo rugs on the floor and walls and Indian pottery on the selves. I'd gotten the impression that both Rob and Jaime were so disdainful of their Navajo roots that I was afraid that I'd see none of it in their home. But the big slab of a farm table, the heavy dark beams in the ceiling, the carved dark wooden staircases were all warm, inviting and appropriately cowboy and Indian.

Yvette was fashion-model lean with very short hair that showed off her wide dark eyes and magnificent cheekbones. She was apparently quite the clotheshorse. I complimented her on her sweater, which I was sure I had seen in Vogue magazine for five hundred dollars. I guessed her jeans to be in the two hundred dollar range and her heavily embroidered cowboy boots at almost a thousand. I couldn't even imagine the value of her Indian jewelry.

"Rob tells me you own that pretty little adobe on the hill above Big Mesa road?" Yvette appeared impressed. "I always loved that place."

"I do own it but I had a lot of help with it." I told them the story about Kate putting all the money in my bank account and then taking it back.

"But you're keeping it paid for, aren't you?" Jaime was an older, heavier and darker version of his son. "So she's not only pretty but she has a brain in her head. Rob, it looks like you picked a winner this time."

Rob flushed a little. "Well, *I* think so."

It was funny to see Rob looking so awkward around his family. He hadn't mentioned any women in his life other than LaToya to me, so maybe there hadn't been that many. Why not? Moab was a small town and everybody already knew each other. Was that the reason the new girl in town had caught his eye?

Sylvie asked me how I liked living in Moab.

"Oh, I love it." I replied. "I love my job, most of the time, and I love that little house." I mentioned that I'd had to run from Fort Collins to escape from a LaToya situation of my own.

Sylvie's eyes widened and her mouth rounded into an "Oh!"

"That girl is clinically insane." Yvette commented. "It's really very sad and it's not her fault but it's getting worse. I'm afraid that something terrible is bound to happen."

"My ex was crazy too." I had to explain the situation, if only briefly. "He seemed so smart, but he really couldn't take care of himself. He literally couldn't get out of bed in the morning, take a shower and go to work. That's why he was so dependent on me, but he made my life miserable."

"It's not my favorite thing that we have in common," Rob said. "Let's talk about something besides LaToya for once. Usually, she dominates every family holiday. I almost expect her to show up at any moment."

"She was really cute in high school." Jaime recalled. "She was rude and self-centered but you expected her to grow out of that. It is so sad that she's turned into such a monster. She could have gotten some guy to take care of her but she just won't lay off of Rob."

"It's made it really hard to date anyone." Rob sighed. "Hey, I'm serious. Let's talk about something besides LaToya. Please!"

Yvette had all kinds of news. At one point in the previous year, the Navajo nation had almost lost its Internet provider and she'd been involved in a mad scramble to gather all the tribal leaders and find the right lawyers to cut the right deal. She was looking to rent a second home in D.C. since she spent so much time flying back and forth.

Sylvie was going to Sedona with a group of girlfriends for a retreat in January. Yes, it was a spiritual retreat, nondenominational, of course. Yes, she used to go to church but decided it was very old-fashioned and this type of retreat meant much more to her. She liked to take a trip once a year. The last had been to Lourdes, France, where she'd been very important since no one in her group spoke French but her. The year before she'd been to Glastonbury, England. I asked Jaime about how he felt about his wife taking off every year.

"It's her reward for putting up with me." Jaime chuckled. He was an old soul, with many lives behind him and an old-style machismo. Independent women still puzzled him. He'd never quite become accustomed to women who didn't need men to survive. His traditional Navajo self-hung heavily upon his modern American manhood and I wondered if he was aware of the contradiction.

Sylvie had created a thoroughly contemporary French-styled Thanksgiving. The food was superb, seasonal, flavored with herbs she grew in her own kitchen, every course a work of art and nothing out of place. She had seriously mastered the Brussels sprout. Appropriate wines accompanied each course. Yet here at this feast of food from another culture, I felt most intensely the presence of the Navajo ancestors at a gathering of the tribe. Ancient souls and some who were not so ancient surrounded us. Yvette, who had found her calling in life in her tribal identity, was probably tuned in. But there was an odd disconnect within the two men.

"Rob told me your father was a Code Talker." I said to Jaime. "It sounds so heroic. You must be proud."

I thought I'd brought up the perfect topic, so far from LaToya and so close to Jaime. But a silence fell over the table, so heavy I wondered if I hadn't ruined everyone's evening with a dreadful faux pas. After what seemed like a very long interval, Yvette tried to come to my rescue.

"We don't usually talk about that," she said. "You wouldn't know but it's another giant black wound in Navajo history...I won't elaborate. Tell us some more about yourself! Do you have brother and sisters?"

"They all live in Denver," I said. "We aren't real close." Faux pas upon faux pas, the congenial family gathering had stumbled and fallen on its face. I was so relieved when Rob jumped up and turned on the football game.

The evening ended at about eight PM, rescued by football and a chocolate torte. Rob was warm and fuzzy and pleased with me, and also relieved that LaToya hadn't shown up to frustrate and embarrass him again. But as we walked to his truck, we almost tripped over a dead cat on the sidewalk. LaToya had been there after all. From the advanced state of the decomposition, we deduced it was roadkill. At least she hadn't slaughtered it herself. Still, it was creepy and ugly. LaToya wasn't finished.

Rob and I often went two-stepping at the The Arches, since it was too cold for outdoor outings. At the big old dance hall we met with other friendly couples and often switched partners and learned new moves. I wasn't much of a two-stepper yet but everyone indulged me. This particular evening it was really crowded, a favorite way to exercise and have fun when Moab got dreary.

The band was especially good that night and we hardly got a chance to sit down. I got so thirsty that I'd downed four beers before I even knew it. At one point, I got a very nasty feeling and later learned that LaToya had showed up but the bouncer wouldn't let her in, saying that this was a respectable dance hall and hookers weren't allowed. Rob was an accomplished dancer and a popular partner. I didn't mind sharing. Jealousy was a buzz-kill and a deal-breaker, I knew for sure, and I didn't want to spoil anything.

Rob was a good teacher but only up to a point. He soon got tired of the simple steps that I was learning and often had to partner up with other gals so that he could show off his stuff. I felt he didn't lead so much as push me around, obviously impatient with my clunky efforts. I was actually relieved when one of his other partners asked to cut in, and only too happy to oblige.

Then I felt a tap on my shoulder, turned around and found myself face to face with my Derek/Tom friend. He flashed a knowing smile through his wire-rimmed glasses, took one of my hands in his and put my other on his shoulder. Giving me a quick nod, he whirled me onto the center of the dance floor and I felt as though I'd been doing the two-step all my life. Steps that had seemed so complicated with Rob seemed perfectly natural with Derek as he led me from the hip, gently nudging me forward and backward, turning and spinning effortlessly as we circled the dance floor. When the song ended the other couples, including Rob and his partner, returned to their booths. But Derek had other ideas.

The band began to play one of my favorite Hoyt Axton songs, the sweet and passionate "Evangelina". I turned to go, but Derek took my hand and led me in a promenade back to the center of the dance floor where the magic started again, his slim hips guiding me every which way as we floated over the floorboards together. I grinned into his thin face as he smiled back. He wasn't nearly as stunning as my buffed-out Rob, but his lanky frame was as limber as if boneless as we did the daylights out of the dance floor. We sashayed from side to side, pulled apart and came together again, those fluid hips suggestively promising the best lovemaking ever without the slightest hint of lewdness. The song climaxed with the stanza I loved:

"But the fire I feel for the woman I love is driving me insane."

Derek pulled a one-handed maneuver and I spun on one foot, landing in an embrace that was anything but a dance move as the song ended. We stood back and clapped. Derek adjusted his glasses. "Just let Rob know that he needs to get a locking gas cap for his truck."

Then he disappeared into the crowd, just like that.

I returned to my hunky oaf, who was steaming mad as I sat down and casually ordered another beer as if nothing had happened.

"What were you doing dancing with that guy?" he growled. "I've known him since grade school and he's been the same skinny dweeb the whole time. How come you don't dance like that with me?"

"Oh, I don't know," I lied. "He was a really good dancer. I just found him easy to follow."

"Easier than me? You wanna go find him again?"

"Geez, Rob. We've both been dancing with other people and you just left me standing there. What's the big deal with this guy?"

Yep. Jealousy was a buzz-kill and a deal-breaker, just like I said. But how could I blame a guy whose girlfriend had just returned semi-orgasmic from the dance floor, grinning wide enough to split her face and obviously not telling the whole truth?

"Wait a minute!" Rob's frown changed from anger to puzzlement. "I thought he was in the hospital. He's supposed to be in a coma! He was working on some power lines and got electrocuted or something. He shouldn't be here at all!"

Oh boy. How was I supposed to tell Rob that Tom, a ghost, had somehow hijacked this guy's body in order to take me for a spin on the dance floor? Oh well, after five beers I was drunk enough to try anything. I let my guard down. It was now or never.

"All right. I kinda do know that guy, but it's not what you

think."

"Just what DO I think, anyway?"

"Well, I'm not seeing anybody behind your back or anything." I could tell that Rob was getting more and more agitated but the door was already open. "Look," I began. "There's something I have to tell you about myself."

"What?" Rob's handsome face was getting all screwed up. "What have you been hiding from me?"

"All right!" I was getting angry now. Here I was, on trial for being a little different, once again, as though it was some kind of crime. "I'm psychic. I'm clairvoyant, I guess. I communicate with spirits. I read Tarot cards and study astrology. I had to leave all my books and decks behind when I ran away from Greg. The guy you just saw me with isn't really a person. He's more like a guardian angel and I guess he must have possessed Derek or something. He told me to tell you that you need to buy a locking gas cap."

Now Rob looked like a ghost. His mouth fell open and his face blanched.

"I think we'd better talk about this outside," he growled.

I started to pull on my coat. What was there to talk about? I was what I was and Rob couldn't take it. Enough said already.

"Look, it's a big part of who I am and I've been this way all my life. I've been dreading this conversation since we first started seeing each other but it had to happen. Now you know."

Rob was silent until we got outside. As we got to the truck we both noticed a deep, ugly scratch in the immaculate red finish. LaToya had been here. So he blew up at *me*. "Jasmine! This stuff you're telling me is crazy! It's all in your own head! I can't believe that YOU actually believe this crap! You have a good job! You own a nice house...!" He shook his head in shock and disbelief.

By now I was shaking with rage.

"It is NOT crap." I shouted. "It's the heart and soul of my

being and you're saying it's crap. GOD Damn YOU!" Now I'd gone over the top. I knew I was over-reacting but this had been an aching sore spot my whole life. "Why do you think I haven't said anything before this? I knew you'd be this shallow. Damn YOU!!"

He snorted. All scorn and disgust. "Get in the car." His voice was low and threatening and I didn't like him any more. "I'll take you home."

I put up the hood on my jacket. The wind was icy cold and so was I. "I'm not going anywhere with you." I turned and started walking. Rob came up behind me and spun me around.

"I said to get in the car!"

"And I say fuck you!!!!"

I shook him off and turned around again. Rob got into his truck and started the engine but I kept walking. I had a long way to go but I didn't care. I was so on fire with rage that if anyone tried to give me trouble they'd have a fight on their hands.

Rob didn't try to come after me. It took me an hour to walk home. To be perfectly fair, I had just told my boyfriend that I talked to spirits and that he'd seen me dancing with a ghost who had possessed the body of a guy he'd known since he was a kid. Also, I'd felt that mad hate-missile from LaToya as it exploded between us and escalated a sensitive situation into a full-scale war. It wasn't unexpected or entirely his fault that things between us had gone so terribly wrong. But I didn't want to be fair. I wanted to stay angry. I knew if I wasn't angry, I might have to feel the way I really did feel. And I didn't want to feel that. Instead I stayed mad the whole long, lonely march back home.

When I finally returned to my sweet little home, a fire already glowed in the fireplace. My Tom was telling me that he was there, looking out for me, wanting to make it all better. Thanks for the dance, Tom, I thought. You just cost me a boyfriend. I changed into my flannels, sat on the sofa next to the fire and put on the headphones. Boy, that guy could pick a guitar. The lyric used the circus carousel as a metaphor for the ups and downs of love on the ever-spinning wheel of life. It was a new song to me - one I certainly had not put on my I-Pod.

I took off the headphones, put my head in my hands and cried for the next month. Every day.

Chapter 15 - Christmas

Oh, I went through the motions. I got out of bed, went to the gym and went to work as usual. I tried to focus on the task at hand and not think about the fight and especially not think about all that had gone before between Rob and me because even the most insignificant detail would bring forth another flood of tears. The merry chaos of the rodeo mag was a temporary distraction but it brought no real relief. It made it even worse that Kate and Lucy both felt sorry for me. Food had no flavor. Beer made me lazy and dull. TV was stupid. Even my Tom sounded stale. Still sweet, but stale. Yesterday's news.

I had been rejected just for being me, and it was not the first time. As a little girl I scared my conservative, Catholic mother with stories of the nice lady who helped me across the street or the young cowboy who played games with me in the back yard. I wish I never told her about my vision of shadowy Indians with Mohawk haircuts breaking down the door between the kitchen and the garage, probably a past-life memory of a time during the French and Indian War. My mother would scold me for telling stories but as I was not an obedient child, I would argue furiously that these things were real and inevitably end up spending many hours in my bedroom playing with other spirit friends. I was happy there, protected by spirits who were only kind.

Since moving to Moab, I made tentative contact with my family, my parents and a brother and sister. The reception was polite but chilly. Of course, there was no contact at all during the Greg Ross years but it wasn't just Greg who had pulled us apart. When I was a child, both my mother and father insisted I needed to be "cured" of these wild fantasies. We visited counselors and psychologists who gave me medications and I learned how not to swallow. Some suggested I was "gifted" but I never saw them again. My brother and sister would tattle on me if I mentioned there was someone else in the room or if I made some kind of prediction, even if it came true! Like the time I said the thunderstorm outside was really a tornado and we should get in the basement. It only got worse as I got older and went to college. Any mention of the possibility of reincarnation, or astrology may not be a joke, would bring on a furious outburst from my father or a sharp "Jasmine, WHEN are you ever going to get over that?" and another lecture on how none of this was real. According to them I couldn't tell the difference between reality and my silly fantasies. They might as well have been telling me not to have blue eyes.

So the hurt wasn't all Rob's fault. I tried to tell myself this was just a rebound romance, and even the most sublime lovemaking didn't necessarily make a relationship. I hadn't given myself enough time to recover from Greg Ross and hadn't made any attempt to play the field before I got all emotionally tangled up with Rob. But speaking of the field, I wouldn't miss the constant priority held by Rob's coaching. I tried to humor myself. Dead or alive, men are always going to be trouble! But I didn't believe myself. I missed the guy and I missed him BAD. And I wasn't covering it up very well.

I wasn't all that sentimental about the holidays, usually, but it was the Christmas season and everybody was smiling and happily preparing for the holiday. Christmas season in what was supposed to be my new life and it sucked!

For Kate and Lucy, I bought one of those little rosemary trees, re-potted it in a pretty pot and decorated it with miniature ornaments and tiny lights. I brought it into the office and the gals oooh-d and aaah-d but the tiny lights didn't come on. It was just another indication that my flag was flying at half-mast. Kate and Lucy were very business-as-usual and didn't pry or try to get me to talk about my feelings. Instead, they re-arranged the office so my space wasn't so cramped and Kate bought me my own printer. We talked about moving into a better office but we'd have to wait until after January's National Western Stock Show in Denver, one of the biggest rodeo events in the U.S.

One morning, Derek came by the office with a freckled redhead on his arm.

"Hi Kate, Lucy." He said. "How are you gals?" His voice sounded about half an octave higher than when I'd met him at the ATM.

"How are *you*?" Kate looked startled. "I thought you were in the hospital! Are you okay now or what?"

"We need to talk to Jasmine for a minute," the redhead said. "We keep hearing these weird stories about Derek breaking out of the hospital, twice! One time they said he went to the dance hall!"

"Yeah!" Derek said. "I was just back home from the hospital and Dishta came over and yelled at me for breaking you guys up. I didn't know a thing about it. Did we really have a dance that night? I mean, do *you* remember?"

You bet I did! "Oooh yeaah!" I sighed rapturously. "It really was *that good*."

I continued. "Derek, can you *ever* dance! I think I'll remember that for the rest of my life! I can't dance at all and Rob had gone off with somebody else so when you tapped me on the shoulder, I went with it."

"I don't get it. I don't remember at all." A puzzled Derek frowned at the floor while Lucy and Kate stared in disbelief.

"He was supposed to be in rehab for months, even years." The redhead added. "I think he musta sub-consciously known what he was doing 'cause he's always been a good dancer. Rob hates that. Derek's a lot better than he is."

"Yeah, he's always gotta be the best at everything and sometimes he's just not." Derek grinned. "At least I know I'm dancing with somebody and that it's not just about everybody looking at me. Anyway, Heidi here caught on to something and she took me to the Arches just a couple of days after I came home. I guess dancing is the best thing for me 'cause I'm recovering faster than anyone ever expected. I still can't remember how to fry an egg but my motor skills are almost back to normal."

And all this time I'd been thinking it was a mean joke when Tom took over this guy's comatose body just to compete with Rob. Now I was proud of him.

"Well, I hope to see you at The Arches again." I told Derek. "Heidi, I don't mean anything by it but ohhhh boy!" I pointed at Derek.

"Aw, you're not the only one," Heidi replied as she shoved Derek out the door. "I sure hope things work out between you and Rob."

I got another surprise one chilly evening when as I gathered up my stuff to go home. Sylvie showed up. Since she was almost Rob, I was almost glad to see her. She'd come to invite me to dinner.

"Only the two of us." she insisted. "I feel I need to speak to you about my son. There are some times when I am so disappointed with the men in my life!"

I accepted her invitation, backed up with smiles and nods of approval from both Kate and Lucy. Sylvie drove a pristine, older model Mercedes that fit her as well as her smart winter hat and camel hair coat. We went to a tiny, intimate Italian restaurant where Sylvie ordered a bottle of wine and steak tartare to start.

"I can see how sad you are. You should not be punished so because you have the second sight!"

Sylvie's intensity told me this had been an ongoing issue in her family. "These men! They are both very good men but sometimes they are like stones. They do not want to think or to feel. I hear them say that you are crazy and Rob has made another bad choice! I had to go. I do not cook for such men!"

She went on. "I love my son but he only thinks of himself. I hoped maybe you could change him but people do not change!"

I reminded her that I'd dropped this little piece of information about myself rather suddenly and right after LaToya had put a big scratch in his truck. "I could have been more tactful," I admitted.

"Ah, but it would have been the same. These men! Sometimes they are cowards!"

Sylvie described to me how Jaime opposed her pursuing her career after they married and it was a constant source of tension between the two of them. She opted to do her writing from home, but occasionally she would need to visit a particular site to observe a new method of excavation or to see some particularly unusual artifacts. After Yvette was born, Sylvie took the baby with her on some of her trips. Jaime did not want his wife driving around with his baby. Anything could happen!

"So I say I can change a tire and I have my friends on the site to help me. Then he gets jealous! I say I want my children to be proud of their mother and I could not be at home, cleaning the house and watching the TV and growing fat and stupid!"

Obviously, this old-fashioned and insecure man was threatened by his ambitious wife. Jaime came around somewhat but he still felt Sylvie's independence made him look like a poor husband whose wife had to work, and he never quite got over it.

"And he ignores anything about his Indian heritage. All Indians are not just drunk Indians but that is all he sees. Now his son is just the same!"

The waitress brought our entrees, cannelloni for me, cioppino for her. Sylvie remained quiet until the waitress went away and then she went on venting. "My son does not like women who challenge him! But why not? Why not, when Yvette and myself are such smart, successful women? I do not understand!"

I didn't understand it either. I told her about my family and their insistence that something was wrong with me and I lived in a fantasy world. We both agreed it was all about the fear of anything different or outside of their comfort zone. I said I never talked about myself at work, because my Christian employers would probably think I was possessed by the devil. Sylvie was sympathetic.

She dropped me off back at the office so I could get my car. I felt a little better. I was grateful that she'd referred to my "second sight" as something real and natural instead of freakish. I was touched to know that Rob's mother was disappointed in him instead of me. But it didn't feel any better to have Rob's own mother confirm that he could be so closed-minded and self-centered. I felt there was no hope of a second chance.

I did get a phone message from him that almost sounded like he might have wanted to make up.

"Jasmine, you were right about the locking gas cap," it said. "I think LaToya put sugar in my gas tank. My truck is ruined. They don't think they can fix it."

I wanted so badly to call him back and tell him how much I'd missed him and I was sorry and that I couldn't wait to see him again. But I chickened out.

The holiday approached, and I was getting positively bored with all my man troubles and very much in the mood to get my own life back. Kate and Lucy were spending the holidays with out-of-state relatives. Kate tried to apologize for leaving me alone but I really didn't care. To get myself out of my own head and do something for someone else for a change, I volunteered to help serve Christmas dinner at the free kitchen. But for Christmas Eve, I bought a bottle of champagne and a stack of fashion magazines, a pricey cashmere sweater, a skirt to go with it, new shoes and a cowboy hat. Strutting along the street with my shopping bags was Christmas enough for me.

That evening, I got an unexpected present. Stirring up a seafood risotto for dinner, I didn't put on any music, preferring the company of some trash TV to round out my holiday. But someone was playing a guitar somewhere near. As the sound gained volume and richness, I heard my Tom, singing a song I hadn't heard before and the words both shocked and thrilled me.

"Jasmine" he sang. "I can't cross over, and the reason is you.
I know how much you love me.
And I love you too.
My darlin' girl, don't you cry no more, He won't give up on you.
I have seen your future, and maybe I'll be in it too."

He didn't stop all that evening, singing all my favorites, plus some of the new ones, right there in my living room. I'm certain no other air guitar ever sounded so beautiful. I couldn't imagine what he meant although the "he", of course, would have to be Rob. But being this close to Tom, even with all of the impossible complications between us, made me not care about Rob at all.

The next day I put on a hair net and helped serve a fairly good Christmas dinner to the homeless and the poor of the town of Moab. I was pleased to find Bud McClintock standing next to me, also in a hair net, which was funny, because he had a lot less hair on his head than in his mustache.

"Jasmine! What are you doing here? Nobody invited you for Christmas?"

"Oh, who cares," I replied. "Kate and Lucy are out of town. I almost thought I had a boyfriend but now I don't." I told him I'd waltzed around town the day before and spent a whole pile of money on myself.

"Well, if I'd known, I'd have taken you out on the town." Bud grinned.

That would have been fun, I thought.

The folks at the shabby kitchen had gone all out with the generous donations from the city of Moab. We served real mashed potatoes and real gravy. The atmosphere was festive, with decorations of fragrant pine boughs and real mistletoe. All the children got wrapped presents and everyone serving was positively jolly. I saw some sad situations, too. An obviously overburdened mother with four little kids stood next to two old veterans undoubtedly looking forward to their evening drunk. One shy, waifish young woman stood next to a belligerent young man who controlled every move she made. I put my facial expression in neutral for those two, knowing that it wouldn't help her at all if I made my feelings known. The dinner ended at about eight in the evening. McClintock and I stayed late to tackle a giant mountain of dishes and cookware. I felt good. Life was good and Tom had said he loved me. Everything was fine.

I dragged myself up the stairs to find Rob sitting on the front porch. He must have been waiting there for hours. If I'd thought I didn't care about him anymore, now I knew I was wrong. I felt a little shy and ashamed remembering what an awful bitch I'd been that night. He didn't ask me where I'd been but it must have been obvious that I hadn't been out celebrating.

"Merry Christmas," He said, gesturing to a package in front of him.

"Well, you didn't have to wait out in the cold so long." I felt a little embarrassed, actually. "You could have called me on my cell."

"You smell like a soup kitchen."

"That's where I've been." I looked at the carelessly wrapped package, which was actually quite large. I hoped that it wasn't too extravagantly expensive.

"I wasn't sure you'd ever speak to me again." Rob had his arms wrapped around his chest. He looked cold and shy and not at all like the arrogant athlete I'd been dating.

"And I wasn't sure you'd ever want to have anything to do with me! Our first fight and it seemed so final."

"I thought it was over. You were really mad. I never heard you talk like that before."

"*You* were really mad! And then there was that scratch on your truck..." I looked around. "Rob? How did you get here? I got the message that LaToya had ruined your truck."

"Mark dropped me off. I think everybody in the universe took a vote, including my mom. They all decided I should try to get you back."

"Well, I think you're awfully brave to show up here after all the things I said that night." I was finally warming back up to him. "Let's go inside. I've got to see what you brought me."

Rob built a fire and I brought out a bottle of wine and a couple of glasses. We sat on the sofa, still not quite touching, while I tackled the package. I couldn't believe what was inside.

On the top of the stack was an Osho Zen Tarot deck, one I'd heard highly praised but had never seen. There was the classic Wilhelm I-Ching, a little pouch with three Chinese coins and an up-to-date astrology text. But the crown jewel of the whole collection, in a sturdy box, was a crystal ball. It was made of smoky quartz, mysterious and gorgeous. I was stunned.

"Rob! What did you do?"

"You'd said that you had to leave all your books and stuff behind so I went online and found this bookstore in Salt Lake. So I went there and it was all strange and smelled like incense and there were candles and crystals all over the place. I was clueless so I said I needed a Tarot deck for someone who really knew her stuff. They put together this package for me so maybe this could be the start of your new collection."

I still didn't know what to say. "But, I thought...you thought I was crazy! And you might have been right. I mean, I told you I'd been dancing with a ghost!"

"Well, he was a pretty smart ghost and I wish I had paid more attention. But, Jasmine, this has been the worst month of my whole life. I made a bad mistake there. I hope it's not too late."

"I made a mistake too. That was some pretty strange stuff to just spew out all at once."

I decided to tell the real truth.

"Rob, I just couldn't stand lying to you. How was I supposed to explain who I was dancing with? I just couldn't think of a good enough lie and I didn't want to do that anyway. Oh, crap..."

"What, Jasmine?"

"Oh, it's that I've been hating life this whole month. I think I cried every day."

"Not me. Men don't cry, you know. We just sit around and drink and cuss."

We were making up. Something that I thought would never happen. How could someone who was supposed to be a psychic be so wrong? "Look," I said. "I've been working at the free kitchen and I'm not feeling very glamorous. I'd better take a shower."

"Sure." He said. Then he grinned. "Mind if I join you?"

Chapter 16 - Partners

Rob moved in with me shortly after that and the arrangement proved to be both cozy, practical and a pain in the ass for me. We only had one car between us while he waited for his insurance to come through and *that* would take the whole month of January. In the meantime, basketball season was gathering steam and Rob always needed to be somewhere either after work for practices or on the weekends for games. We were on our cell phones frequently, to coordinate who would drive where to and when. I was so glad to have him back and without any big secrets between us, I tried to be patient with the situation. Rob was still skeptical about my psychic tendencies but he was just being smart. Conversations with spirits and predicting the future were still not part of his reality. I didn't care, though. I could finally be myself. I told him how I'd become aware of the presence of Tom DeVries haunting the house, carefully leaving out the parts about how seductive he was, and how he'd led me to finding the case of music.

Rob couldn't understand why I hadn't been scared out of my mind. It wasn't easy to explain how this spirit needed my help with some unfinished business and was anything but scary. Not all ghosts were about floating heads and things that go bump in the night. I told him about contacting Tom's widow and meeting his daughter and handing over the case and, more importantly, how grateful they were that I'd come to them first. Someday I'd be able to tell him how Tom had been such a shining knight regarding Greg Ross, but it was a little early in the relationship for cars blowing up and doors swinging open by themselves and rattlesnakes coming to the rescue. There would be another time for that.

Rob was such a regular guy. He was passionate about his coaching and the kids loved him. He insisted on volunteering for the difficult middle school level, rightly believing they needed sports even more than the grade school or high school level. I wished he wasn't so insistent that I come to every single game to cheer on his teams. While I didn't have anything all that important to do on the weekends, I wasn't crazy about driving long distances in a van full of noisy teens and listening to that candy-coated Tracy Simon.

The potty-mouthed boys could be bad enough but the jealous little girls were far worse. "God! Look at the cowgirl!" I heard as I climbed into the front of the van in a stylish denim dress and fancy cowboy boots.

"I bet she's older than he is," grumbled another.

When they weren't on the basketball court, they hung all over him. I complained to Rob about their inappropriate behavior and rudeness but he only said it was just the age group and not to pay them any attention. Still, I found it hard to ignore when one of his twelve-year-old Lolitas came skipping off the court after a particularly good play and plopped herself in his lap. This time I didn't have to say anything. The girl's mother came marching down off the bleachers, grabbed her daughter by the arm and pulled her off of Rob.

"Get up, young lady!" she scolded her daughter, who sneered back at her mother in a snotty little rage. "Coach Dishta!" the mother continued. "I'm surprised that you allow this kind of behavior!"

"But she made a great play!" Rob protested weakly.

"It's completely wrong! It could get *you* in trouble, letting these girls behave like that! Someone could accuse you of... of *molesting* these girls!" She was so furious that she could barely get the words out. Blushing fluorescent pink under his coppery Navajo skin, Rob relented.

"Okay," he said. "I'll have a have a little talk with the girls when this quarter is over. I just didn't want to hurt anyone's feelings."

The enraged teen glared at her mother and then looked beseechingly at Rob.

"She's right, Cheryl." Rob addressed the pouting nymphet. "You can't be doing that kind of stuff and it isn't only you. I'll make it clear to the other girls too."

Cheryl hung her head and I felt vindicated. But the snotty looks and snide comments continued whenever the opportunity arose. I braced myself for the juvenile hostility, remembering that they were just little girls, but I couldn't help being a little disappointed in Rob that he wouldn't stick up for me.

But then, I never minded sashaying around town with one of the hottest guys in the region, nor did I mind that he was solid and dependable, or that he kept his promises and paid his bills on time. I was charmed by how vain he was, making regular trips to the gym, his pickiness about the cut of his jeans and his addiction to expensive shampoo to maintain that glossy black braid that followed him everywhere. I looked up his astrological set-up thanks to the book he gave me. Sun in Leo, (of course!) Moon in Taurus, Sagittarius Rising. He could be self-centered, stuck in his ways and impulsive. But that's only seeing the dark side.

Since Christmas Eve, my magical Tom seemed to have faded from my life. I did miss my special friend and the occasional whiff of tobacco smoke and the comforting warmth and protection of his presence. Melissa called on New Year's Day to say the reels were being remastered and the new songs were all gems. At least three new CDs would be released in the next few months, the money people had to sort out the details and the possible financial returns could be huge. They didn't know how much they'd be entitled to yet. She promised that I'd be getting a fat little "finder's fee" once they knew more about initial sales and royalties. "Don' worry," she assured me. "We got some good people on the project."

I knew Tom would want to make sure things went his way. His attention was elsewhere. Little wonder he hadn't been around.

Mark and Dr. Agon paid us a visit early that year. Dr. Agon was practically in tears.

"I got a promotion!" he sobbed. "I have to move to Houston. I'll be making a huge amount of money but I have to move away from Moab!" He was really hurting and if the real truth be told, I didn't blame him. A city the size of Houston with all its urban sprawl and traffic congestion, pollution and crime didn't appeal to me either.

"Oh, Frankie," Mark said. "Remember, I'll be going with you. We'll be able to come back to Moab once in a while."

Frankie? Mark was going with him to Houston? What were they trying to say? I ran to the kitchen for beers.

When I got back Mark said that he and Frankie had an announcement to make.

"What's that?" Rob had a knowing look on his face indicating that he'd already guessed.

"Frankie and I are a couple." Mark continued. "We finally figured it out."

"I kind of had a feeling." Rob said through a knowing grin. "I never saw either of you guys dating any girls but you were always going to these drum circles and sitting around naked with a bunch of other guys. Kinda makes you wonder."

"Hey!" the former Dr. Agon spoke with righteous indignation. "Most of those guys aren't gay! But anyway, we didn't even really discover each other until you started seeing

Jasmine and spending all your time over here."

"Yup. We finally realized that neither of us had any chance with you!" Mark was laughing.

"It freed us both up to realize that we liked each other better than anyone else in the world."

"So what happened to Dr. Agon?" I asked.

"Oh, I created this science fiction character for myself so that I could hide from myself. My real name is Frank Sommers. I work for NASA as a radar technician. I've been stashing all my money away so I could buy a ranch in the desert and disappear. I guess Mark brought me out of myself 'cause now being gay seems so normal to me. I guess I'm more bi than gay. I still like girls but I really do love Mark."

"So when do you guys have to move?" Rob wanted to know.

"Really soon. Before February 1st."

"I have to give up my job," Mark said. "Frankie will be supporting me for a while."

"That'll be a good thing." I said. "Won't you be the one who has to find a place to live and buy furniture and all that? I'm sure Frank is going to be really busy."

"Believe me, I can support him." Frank said. " He may never have to work again."

"Would that be okay with you?" Rob asked Mark.

"Actually, it would." Mark answered. "You know, when I was making my shield and the drum, I got ideas for art projects that I never gave myself permission to do. Maybe I'll take some classes. I'm not too old to change careers."

"I'd love to see Mark find himself as an artist. Frank said. "I think he's always had it in him."

"Well congratulations guys!" Rob was happy for them. "You make sure that you keep in touch. Let's not lose track of each other."

"You have both our cells." Frank said.

They descended the stairs hand in hand.

Chapter 17 – Marriage and Babies

Kate and Lucy were getting ready for the National Western in Denver at the end of the month. Growing up in there, I'd always known about it but never been to one. My family had scorned the whole cowboy scene and considered it old-fashioned, uncultured and very much beneath them. Now I was sorry that I'd probably never be able to go. Kate kept me busy with signs, brochures, new business cards and posters for her booth. Everything had to be done at once, of course. I got more accustomed to a manageable pace instead of working myself to death as I tried to keep up with Kate.

I had some good reasons for not wanting to die just yet. As Rob showed some very clear signs of becoming a decent partner, I started to notice a change in myself. An idea had been growing in my head almost since we first began dating and it got a little bolder and brighter. I found myself flirting with the babies in the grocery carts and admiring the little ones in strollers, complimenting the moms and dads. Motherhood was clearly tugging at my heartstrings. Maybe things were going too fast but Rob and I were barreling ahead with our lives together anyway. Rob already spent a lot of time with kids as a volunteer coach. Of course, not everyone who likes teaching or coaching is destined for parenthood. I felt I needed a few more signs from Rob before I brought up the subject, but as it was, I didn't have long to wait for one of those "signs".

I was riding home from work on my new mountain bike raffle winner. Somehow, I don't think anyone else had a chance at it. I stopped to watch Rob playing basketball with the adolescents down the street who he was hoping to recruit for his team. Three boys between the ages of twelve and fourteen were regular players and they were beginning to gather a few more. That day, two toddlers watched, a boy and a girl, probably being baby-sat by one of the older boys. The ball rolled toward the little boy and he caught it in his plump hands. One of the older boys sneered.

"Hey!" he yelled. "You can't play basketball! You're too little!"

"Oh yes he can!" Rob swept up the little guy who still had the ball in his hands and held him up to the edge of the hoop. "Drop it in, little dude!"

The little boy dropped the ball through the hoop with a delighted squeal. Rob put him down, made him catch the ball again and held him up to the hoop once more. The ball fell through and one of the older boys caught it.

"Hey, there's a WNBA! Don't you know?" Rob scooped up the little girl in pink tennis shoes and pigtails.

"Come on. Let her have the ball." Rob held her up to the hoop and let her drop the ball through. She grinned and kicked her little legs. They did it one more time.

I was pretty sure I knew how to fill that empty space in my life, and watching Rob with those kids was just what I wanted to see. It was time to talk about it.

So after another of one of those sublime, magical, sexy as hell lovemaking things we always did, we were lying in each other's arms staring at the ceiling, and I tried to work up the nerve to ask the big question.

"You know," I began, avoiding the issue entirely. "Your mother is very sorry you and your dad have no interest in your

Navajo heritage. She wishes you cared more about your traditions."

"My mother is an anthropologist and thinks we're something to study." He rolled over on his side and propped his head on his arm. "Crap, Jasmine, I don't want to be the fuckin' Indian cliché that everybody expects. I just want to be myself and my dad is the same way. I like football and coaching sports with kids and hanging around watching TV with a beer in my hand. I want out of this one. I really do."

"Hey dude. What about the braid? That's soooo Indian. No wonder everyone expects you to be one."

"Vanity. I grow great black hair and I love to show it off. You're a great looking gal who likes to strut her stuff. You must get it."

Okay, I'd been hedging for long enough. "Rob," I took a deep breath. "I've been thinking…"

"Uh oh, Jasmine's been thinking. What about, my lady love?"

"Well, it's just that, I'm thirty four…"

"And you're thinking about kids?" He totally nailed it.

"I'm thinking about kids."

"Well, let's do it then. But don't you want to get married first? Is this a proposal?"

"I didn't say that!" Well, not exactly. I really wanted a baby but hadn't thought about a wedding. "I suppose that's part of the plan," I said. "I'm not really a gal who dreams of her wedding as the biggest day of her life."

"Let's get back to my original question. Are you proposing to me or not?"

"I must be. I just said it backwards. What do you say?"

"Let me think about it. But we can work on that baby right now!"

"Rob!" I pretended to be annoyed but I knew he was just teasing. He rolled over on top of me and I got squished, at the same time thinking that someone had just said, "Let's get married" and someone else had said "Yes, let's".

That night I threw away my pills with a ceremonial flourish.

But the next day, I got a surprise that put our plans on hold. The mailman brought an envelope containing a letter signed by both Melissa and Candice, a check for $15,000, and an invitation to a gala at the Grand Ole Opry for the official launching of the new collection of Tom DeVries songs. The letter was quite formal but stated that me and a "plus one" would be honored guests. I would need to RSVP as soon as possible so they could reserve a room at the hotel and spaces at the banquet. A note at the bottom, written in Candice's broad, loopy hand, warned me not to skimp on something special to wear, as most of the gals at the gala would be as dressed up as they could possibly get. She invited me to call if I needed her help.

Boy, did I need her help!

I was practically reeling as I climbed the stairs. It was Monday, and Rob was already home from work.

"Guess what, Rob? I just won the lottery!"

"You what?"

I dangled the check in front of his face and his jaw dropped open. "Oh it gets better!" I continued. "We're invited to the gala at the Grand Ole Opry! Candice says we have to get all dressed up."

"Wow! We could fly to Dallas or L.A. just to go shopping!" My vain darling was getting all lit up about the idea of an expensive new suit. "We have to do it this weekend, though. It's the only weekend of the season that I don't have any games to coach. You'd better tell Kate first thing."

I ran into the bathroom and fished my pills back out of the wastebasket. The gala was two months away and I wasn't about to show up without my waistline. I felt a little annoyed that our lives always had to revolve around soccer or basketball, but then I remembered Greg Ross. If I was going to be annoyed with a guy, I'd rather be annoyed with a guy like Rob than terrified by a guy like Greg.

I talked with Candice that evening.

"Well, Jasmine. How ya doin, honey? This had better be my RSVP." I was pretty sure the ice I heard clinking wasn't in a glass of ice tea.

"I wouldn't miss it for all the world! How are you? This is so exciting!" I was almost more anxious than excited. I didn't know anything about this kind of event and I was capable of committing any number of total faux pas. "But Candice, I really do need your help. Where do I get a dress? What fork do I use? Where can Rob get himself a really great suit?"

"You got a Rob, huh?"

"I sure do. The best accessory that a girl could have, and he's all excited about dressing up and going to a gala. But Candice, help! How do I start?"

I could sense Candice feeling wise and smug over the phone as she geared up for some serious girl talk. I gestured for Rob to bring me another beer.

"Well, now that you have that big ol' check, you can go to Austin" Candice was saying. "All my favorite places are there."

"Rob! We're going to Austin, Texas!"

"We are? Coool!"

"Yeah, Austin is THE place as far as I'm concerned." Candice was stepping up to the plate. "I'll e-mail you the directions and the names of my favorite sales folks. There's a great place for men that my Tom used to go to." Big sad sigh. "Oh, I do so miss my Tom so much sometimes. But anyway, Roche's is still doin' good business. They'll dress up your Rob real nice. I'll call 'em and let 'em know your comin'"

"That sounds perfect!" I couldn't wait. "For me and Rob to go and buy a suit in the same place that Tom DeVries used to get his suits? It would be like making a pilgrimage. The Tom DeVries tour!"

"You're gonna have so much fun!" Candice enthused. "Oh, and another thing...I'll send some pictures of dresses that we like and them that we don't. You can spend a whole lot of money and then have everbody laughin' behind your back. I won't let that happen to you."

"I intend to take every bit of advice you have to offer. I really don't know what I'm doing."

"Oh hey, girl. You're pretty enough that you don't have a whole lot to worry about. Anyway, I need another gin and tonic. Watch out for that e-mail."

Chapter 18 – Austin

"You what!!!" Kate was stunned speechless, and that almost never happened to Kate. "You wanna go where? Just to go shopping?"

"Well, Kate, if we're going to Nashville to a big event at the Grand Ole Opry, we'd better do some dressing up. Candice DeVries gave us the name of a place where Tom used to get his suits so that we can get Rob something real special."

"So let me get this straight. You need a four-day weekend so you can get ready for another four-day weekend, huh?"

"Well, I know but it's only March and the gala isn't until the end of May. I mean, it's not like we're in the middle of cowboy Christmas or anything…" Much as I loved Kate, it was starting to feel like she might not let me go. Was I going to have to beg or lie and call in sick?

"Well it doesn't mean we don't need you. Go on and take your weekends, but damn! I have to think about hiring somebody else and that means a bigger office. When am I going to find the time to do that?"

"That's gonna have to happen anyway. Besides, Rob and I are talking about kids and I'm not getting any younger…"

"Oh, why would you want kids?"

"Kate!" But I knew it was another one of those Kate comments.

"Oh no, I didn't mean that." She backed down, as always. "Of course you want kids. You'd be a terrific mom. Anyway, this will get my butt in gear to look for that new office. Which job would you rather do, graphic design or office manager?"

I thought I heard a choir of angels singing heavenly joy. This was going to cut my workload in half!

"I'll take the graphic design job. I don't think I'm much of an office manager, anyway."

I took the check to the bank on my lunch break but sat outside in the cool breeze and thought about it for a while. Rob felt perfectly entitled to the money I had nearly risked my life to get. How was I supposed to do this? If I kept all the money in my account, then Rob would have to ask me if he needed some. If I set up an account in both our names and he got carried away…? Would he run off and buy that new 4x4? He was living with me and we were talking marriage and kids but I still had to keep some control of the finances. I marched into the bank and deposited $10,000 into my account and took out $5000 in cash to spend in Austin.

Rob had managed to wrestle permission from his boss to take the two extra days off. He frowned when I told him how I'd deposited the money.

"But I thought you'd be opening a new account for the both of us! It makes me think you don't trust me."

"It's not that." I assured him. "This is called budgeting. I don't want to spend it all in Austin."

"Yeah, I suppose, but Jasmine, we're supposed to be partners. You should have talked to me about it first." He still looked disappointed.

""Look, I took out $5000 in cash to take to Austin. We should be able to have a pretty good time with that."

"But why do you have to be so controlling about it? This is supposed to be fun, remember? Now your turning it into some kind of business deal and *you're* calling all the shots."

Me calling all the shots? Grrrr!

"Rob, yes I should have talked about it with you first, but just because we've had a windfall doesn't mean we can go crazy with it. We'll be doing this all our lives if we're married."

Rob softened up a bit after the comment about marriage.

"Ok, Yeah, you're right. My Jasmine's just being smart." He ruffled my hair. "Let's sit down and work on this together."

So we did. We sat at the computer together and worked it all out, hotel, plane tickets to both Austin and Nashville, entertainment, and food. Our new clothes would come out of our own accounts.

Later that evening, Rob called Mark and Frank to see if we could meet up with them in Austin and got a good, solid "maybe".

We caught a small jet from Grand Junction to Austin.

We agreed on a few extravagances. We rented a room, no, a *suite* at the Driskill Hotel in downtown Austin. The Driskill was old, built in 1886, really fancy and probably haunted. We arrived at about five in the afternoon on Wednesday and immediately asked for a bottle of chilled champagne, which we drank while relaxing in the spa and testing out the various water jets. The windows were floor to ceiling and we made love without closing the curtains so we could watch the sunset over the Austin skyline. Damn the binoculars! Let 'em have an eyeful, we joked! Although I doubt anyone saw us.

Later that evening, we held hands and walked around downtown Austin looking for a drink and some dinner. I had always heard that Texans dressed to the nines when they went out and it surprised me that Austin seemed so casual. I saw Danskos and Birkenstocks and skirts from India, lots of jeans and cowboy boots. There was music everywhere! Indoors and out, music halls and outdoor venues, every bar had its own live performers and bands and there were street musicians on every corner. Then I gasped!

"Rob! Look!"

"What is it, Jasmine? Oh, wow!"

In an elegant display window shimmered the only dress for me. Navy blue, sleeveless, V-necked and cocktail length with a generous flounce. I took a picture with my cell phone so I'd remember where it was. We then located Roche's where we had an appointment, secured for us by Candice, for 11 a.m. the next day.

I insisted that we show up at Lillian's Boutique, where I saw my dress, as soon as it opened. I didn't want to take any chances on someone else getting it first.

"I have to try on that dress in the window!" I said to the saleslady, who was staring at Rob as if he'd put some kind of a spell on her.

"Oh the navy silk charmeuse?" The gal came back to earth long enough to grasp that there was a female in the store who wanted to try on a very expensive garment. "Oh yes, I love that piece! And it should be very nice on you. I'll get it right away."

Another woman came out of the back room. "Lillian, do you need my help?" So there really was a Lillian! Lillian responded from the window where she was carefully undoing a series of tiny buttons on the back of the dress. "Yes, Jeanine. Could you offer our guests a cup of coffee?"

Jeanine was either a lesbian or somehow accustomed to very good-looking guys. She politely sat us both down in a couple of plush chairs and brought us coffee in china cups. She then introduced herself and asked me for what occasions I would need the dress.

"It's for a big gala in Nashville at the Grand Ole Opry." I said. "We're going to Roche's after this so Rob can get something to wear."

"Well, besides that, I'm going to need something to wear to the wedding." Rob said.

"Wedding?" For someone who was supposed to be so

psychic I could be as dense as a brick sometimes.

"Ours, of course!"

"Oh, yeah."

Jeanine was amused. By then, Lillian had the dress on a hanger, waving it slightly so I could see the shimmering weave. "I'll have to help you with this." She insisted. "Those little buttons are very difficult to do by yourself."

My red espadrilles hardly went with the luxurious silk but the fit was almost miraculous. The dress caressed my modest curves as though it had been made just for me. I loved the line of tiny buttons dotting my spinal column. Lillian suggested I purchase a bra with a bit of a lift to fill out the top a little better and recommended a lingerie shop. $1800 dollars later, Rob and I walked out of Lillian's with a shopping bag, complete with a padded hanger and a silk sachet.

Roche's was something else entirely. An elegant, gray-haired woman in a black suit sat us down at a table and began a detailed discussion of the upcoming event, how often Rob expected to wear his suit and what he had in mind. A gentleman with a tape measure wanted to know how we'd become acquainted with Candice DeVries. I began to tell the story about how I'd found the case in the closet and tracked down Candice while he had Rob stand up and began to take measurements.

"Tom DeVries," he said nostalgically. "They just don't make them like that anymore. In fact, they didn't make very many like him in those days either."

"So you knew him!" This guy had made suits for Tom! The adoring fan within me wanted to know more and more about my guitar hero with great taste in suits.

"Inseam, shoulder width, waist size..." the tailor smiled smugly. "Tom always knew what he wanted. He made my job so easy. I never had to worry or make any guesses. And such a fine figure of a man, too!"

I would have pressed the tailor with more questions but the

gray-haired woman steered the conversation back to styles and fabric swatches.

"Here's a classic design that should really show off a fine, athletic build like yours." She spoke admiringly as Rob soaked it up, loving the attention. Sometimes he could be so full of himself! The woman continued.

"Your hair is a bluish black so I would not suggest a brown or even a gray. But plain black is so boring, so funereal." She picked up a swatch with a sheen to it. "This is a subtle pinstripe. I love this fabric! The weave is tight but soft, and durable also. But look! The stripes aren't gray, they're silver! So therefore, we line the jacket with this." She picked up a silver silk. "And we also line the vest, and the whole back of the vest will be silver. And then we line the pocket flaps and the pockets themselves so that every time you pull something out of your pocket, you flash a little silver!" Rob was enchanted. He couldn't think of a thing to say.

"Our Alice is such a genius!" The tailor continued his careful analysis of Rob's assets, taking detailed notes. "She can design the perfect suit for any man alive in less than half an hour."

"Oh, this man is so easy to design for." She looked up. "So well-proportioned and handsome. I am not often so fortunate."

I was fascinated to observe a level of tailoring that I'd never imagined, middle school sewing class being my only experience with tape measure and sewing shears. Rob was so excited that he reminded me of a little boy getting his first two-wheeled bike. He could barely bring himself to ask about the cost and the time it would take.

As it was, the suit would be ready on Saturday morning. It would cost $2800, a whole thousand dollars more than my dress! Wow! I could tell that Rob was balking at spending all that money but too embarrassed to say so. He also wanted the suit. I offered to cover $1000 for him. After all, it had been a windfall.

We were looking for a place to have lunch when he spotted a jewelry store.

"We have to go in here."

"I do need something to go with my dress." Jewelry was totally foreign territory to me, my little gold hoop earrings being the entire extent of my jewelry wardrobe. I spotted a two-strand necklace of deep red coral beads that would be perfect with the navy dress. "Oh, how lovely!" I exclaimed, but Rob had other ideas.

"Jasmine, come over here and tell me what you think."

I joined him at the counter. "Rob! These are engagement rings!"

"Yeah, and we can get the engagement ring to go with our wedding set so you can wear both rings for the rest of your life! Look Jasmine, we might as well do it now. They have some nice things in Moab but not like this."

A handsome young salesman approached us and introduced himself as Ahmed. "We do have an extensive selection of unique designs, but it can be very overwhelming and it's lunchtime. I'll order lunch and we can sit at the table over there. Wedding rings are very special and not to be rushed."

"Lunch sounds wonderful." I agreed. "But before we start to look at wedding sets, I would like to see those coral beads over there. I need something to go with this dress." I held up my Lillian's shopping bag.

We spent three hours in the jewelry store over sandwiches, ice tea and all kinds of gold, silver, diamonds and other dazzling items that I'd never thought about before. Rob apparently had. He had definite opinions about what he liked and what he didn't. I ran the smooth coral beads through my fingers as I decided against the diamonds, loved the rubies and sapphires and decided that the opals were my favorite. But the salesman cautioned me about the opals, as they were delicate stones and not for everyday wear.

"Opals actually have water in them. They shatter if they're frozen." He informed me. "A wedding or engagement ring is meant to be worn every day, all day long. Opals are for rare occasions."

In the end, my engagement ring would be a slender lightning bolt design in white gold set with three tiny sapphires. The wedding rings were the same lightning bolt design in yellow gold. Both of my rings would be made to lock together perfectly.

Then we got to the checkout counter where Ahmed meticulously totaled the cost of the engagement and wedding rings, my coral beads and matching earrings. Rob waited, clearly expecting me to cover the cost.

"Shouldn't you pay for the coral and the engagement ring, since all of those are yours? Then we split the cost of the wedding rings," he suggested.

I felt irritated but I wasn't quite sure why. This was in keeping with our agreement, wasn't it, or was it? The jewelry store had been his idea in the first place. Couldn't he have been more, oh, gallant?

"I didn't think I'd be buying my own engagement ring," I said. "That sounds more like LaToya, buying her own ring to try and trap you."

Ahmed also seemed to disapprove. "Traditionally," he began as politely as he could manage. "The groom purchases the engagement ring as a gift to his future wife. It's a symbol of his commitment to her."

"Maybe we should talk about this outside." I said.

"What?" Rob flushed even as he frowned, embarrassed again. "Of course. Sorry, I don't know anything about weddings and rings and stuff. I'll pay for the engagement ring and we'll split the cost of the wedding rings. Does that work for you?"

Rob's ring cost about a third more than mine did but I agreed just to keep the peace. I didn't want to have a fight in an elegant jewelry store. I paid for half of the wedding rings and my coral beads.

Didn't all couples have to work through these things? Wasn't compromise a part of the deal?

We went shopping for more stuff, and paid for it all out of the rapidly dwindling $5000 I had budgeted for the trip. I picked up a pair of red heels (an inspiration from Melissa DeVries) and Rob bought a fancy pair of cowboy boots at Allen's Boots. By then it was almost dinner time and we were both too tired for night life so we went back to the Driskill to sit in the spa for a while, order room service and spend the rest of the evening watching Texas TV. The Austin skyline glittered through the windows as Rob joked with me about the rumors that the hotel was haunted.

"But you probably knew that already," he teased.

"Yeah, the fourth floor. Two brides killed themselves in separate incidents. I have to wonder what's up with that but I don't think I'd want to meet either of those gals. They also say that the original owner still hangs around. I wouldn't mind running onto him."

"You sure like those Texas guys!"

"I only know the one and he's a ghost too."

"Oh. Then you like Texas ghosts, but only if they're guys."

"Oh Rob. You stop that! I'm going to try on my dress and shoes while we're waiting for dinner."

Rob was struggling with the tiny buttons on the back of the dress when our dinner arrived, being pushed on a cart by a crisply dressed waitress.

"What a pretty dress!" she exclaimed. "And it fits you so well!"

"I still think she needs that push-up bra to really do it justice."

"Rob!"

The waitress laughed as she opened our wine. Rob asked her

about the best way to find out what music was playing so we could choose a concert to attend. She picked up the remote and tuned into the Austin Entertainment channel, where everything that happened anywhere in Austin was listed. Our evening was complete. I reluctantly took off my dress, not wanting to ruin it with steak sauce.

We ate our steaks and drank wine and scrolled through the vast array of possibilities, most of them unfamiliar to us. Frank called, saying they could catch a small plane and meet us the following evening. Mark picked up his phone and we argued pleasantly over jazz, blues, rock or country/western, became overwhelmed and almost couldn't decide on anything. The four of us finally decided to do it my way and go to a small lounge where Lyle Lovett and John Hiatt were doing a show devoted to Townes Van Zandt. Rob ordered the expensive tickets with the excuse that this might be the closest thing to a honeymoon we'd ever have. It was quite the fairy tale, really. Just a couple of short years ago, I would never have imagined that I'd be doing anything like this with anybody like Rob, but here we were doing it up as much as we possibly could.

We spent Friday morning strolling around the city. That afternoon, we rented a canoe and rowed around Ladybird Lake. We met Mark and Frank in the Driskill for an extravagant dinner for which Frank insisted on paying. Rob and I bragged about our rings and the proposal that hadn't been but was a commitment after all. Mark and Frank were trying to decide how to commit themselves to each other in a more public manner, still a problem for gay couples all over the world.

Both of them had changed. Frank had traded in the heavy black-framed glasses for a lighter version that no longer hid his eyes. I had never noticed that they were so blue or how long his lashes were. He was no longer sneaky and secretive looking but more open and vulnerable. His clothes were stylish and fit him well. He also smiled frequently and easily, which he'd never done before.

Mark looked taller than he had; more confident, and glowing with something like inspiration. He planned to attend art school in the fall and he'd already completed a couple of new pieces that were a variation on the shield he'd made.

"These are a lot more developed and I'm using better materials. I really think those drum circles got me going. I'm using some traditional stuff but then I'm inserting contemporary found objects, like bottle caps and plastic six-pack holders, into the designs."

"He brings home a lot of weird shit," Frank said. "Sometimes the whole place smells like a dumpster but I think he's doing great. This move to Houston hasn't been so bad. I really like my job and I like the people I'm working with. I guess the inner nerd never goes away."

Our concert that evening had been well chosen, at a small, intimate venue with two musicians whom I already loved performing all these songs I may have heard at one time or another but never knew they were all by the same guy. I thought about Tom and how wonderful it would have been to see him performing in this same place. His life had been so short. I was stricken by the magnitude of the loss. He would have continued to write and perform with the same brilliance well into his old age. Privately, I grieved for my Tom and all he could have been, even as Lyle and John paid tribute to another superbly gifted songwriter and musician who had also departed too soon. I wondered how often and how many artists had performed Tom's songs and not given him the credit. How many jukeboxes had listed the song and the performer and not credited the songwriter? These two musical giants thought so much of Townes Van Zandt that they devoted an entire evening to him and no other, possibly in an attempt to right a wrong. I wondered if I'd helped do the same thing for Tom. It was an enlightening performance and one of those that stay with you long after the lights come back on. The four of us walked back to the hotel without speaking so as not to break the spell.

"Wow," Rob finally spoke. "I always thought that Willie Nelson wrote "Pancho and Lefty". It's time I got some Townes on my iPod." I agreed.

Rob went in for a fitting on Saturday morning. While the designer and tailor exclaimed enthusiastically about how handsome he looked in his suit, I agreed the suit was great but had to admit that Rob looked fabulous in a paint-stained t-shirt and old jeans. The tailor put a few pins in the shoulders, pinned up the pants cuffs and cinched in the darts in the waistline just a touch more. They told Rob to come back at three that afternoon when the suit would be ready. Rob decided that he needed a new cowboy hat and a red silk shirt and began discussing menswear shops with the gray-haired designer lady. I was too burned out to do any more shopping and begged off so I could go back to the hotel and watch trash TV. Rob understood completely, and walked me back to the hotel before he took off on another spree.

I really didn't want to watch TV. The concert of the previous night and being in the same shop Tom used to frequent put me in a thoughtful, melancholy mood. Tom had just about finished what he'd set out to accomplish when he'd haunted the little house for fifteen years waiting for the person to come along who could actually communicate with him. The dreaded moment when I'd really have to say goodbye hung a dark cloud over the crazy good time that Rob and I were having, throwing money around, planning our future and buying our wedding rings. So I sat on the balcony, sipped a glass of cold white wine, watched Austin bustle around and allowed my own thoughts to roll.

I've heard people say, when they've been exposed to an unfamiliar degree of luxury, "I could get used to this!" I was not one of those people. Impracticality and conspicuous consumption were making me uncomfortable. My tastes tended to be simple and my needs were not that many. I wondered if I'd ever have any place to wear my beautiful dress after the Nashville gala. At least Rob's suit was a good investment. Three days in Austin, spending more money that I'd ever spent in my life, had been great fun but I was more than ready to go home. Rob, on the other hand, seemed to thrive on this lifestyle. Would it lead to conflict in our future? We were talking about starting a family and had just ordered our rings. Had we given ourselves enough time to really know each other?

Rob came in, put down a big shopping bag, and fell on his back on the king-sized bed.

"Jasmine!" he called. "Bring me a beer! I can't get it myself. Spending all this money has wiped me out. I guess I'd make a lousy millionaire."

All my cloudy, gloomy thoughts, sorrows and fears fell with a thud and rolled off the edge of the balcony. I went to the mini bar and picked out a beer for my Rob and poured myself another glass of wine. I sat on the bed next to him and leaned back against the cushy down pillows.

"You know, that's just what I was thinking. I don't think I could have bought another thing."

He took my hand and squeezed it and we sat in contented silence. We really were soul mates in so many ways.

Chapter 19 - Nashville

Back home and back to work. Rob had a new truck by now, a white Toyota, much more modest than his magnificent Ford 4x4. We both hoped LaToya wouldn't find out which one was his, but Rob bought a locking gas cap just in case. Surprisingly, there hadn't been any encounters or any sign of LaToya for a couple of months, but just after our return from Austin, I got a call from Tina.

"I just thought I'd let you know," she began. "LaToya and her mom got evicted. I don't know if they're at the homeless shelter or living out of her car or what."

"Boy, am I glad I'm not the social worker on that case!" I exclaimed. "If they could get a diagnosis of mental illness, they'd be eligible for some benefits, but it's really hard for someone to admit that they're crazy."

I remembered Greg Ross, refusing any kind of evaluation of his mental health and thereby disqualifying himself from any assistance he might have received. The problem was always society, other people or, nine times out of ten, me.

LaToya and her mother had been living the illusion that they were beautiful princesses and entitled to be taken care of. But no rich, handsome prince had come to their rescue and now they were out on the street. At least LaToya had been too involved in her new and unfamiliar lifestyle to harass us.

Our Nashville adventure was less than a month away and I was a little nervous about it. I anticipated going to a giant party of glamorous stars who all knew each other but didn't know Rob or me or pay any attention to us. None of them would suspect I had the best connection there in Tom DeVries himself but I expected Candice and Melissa to be far too busy to give us any real attention. I imagined another big, unfamiliar city. Rob and I wandering around, doing tourist stuff, and trying to kill time until the gala finally happened. I decided to book plane tickets for one day to fly in, one day for the gala and the next day to fly out.

One afternoon, I was staring into my crystal ball, seeing a crystal ball and nothing else, when a welcome drawl rolled through my head.

"Jasmine! Come talk to me!"

Well, this was certainly new. Tom had only talked to me so directly twice before, when he'd manifested on the physical plane and gotten me in trouble with Rob at The Arches. I was so glad that Rob was coaching and I had the space to give Tom my full attention. I went out on the back patio and sat on the wall. "What is it, Tom? Must be important."

There it was again, not only a voice in my head but that clean-shirted scent that I loved so much, along with the ever-present tobacco smoke.

"Tom, tell me!" I felt a sigh, and then another.

"Jasmine, somebody's got to talk to Melissa. I don't like some of the songs she's doin."

"But Tom, isn't that her choice? It's her career now and she needs to learn to make her own decisions."

"Well not this one. Did you listen to the cassette me, Emmaline and Dirk made when we were so drunk?"

"Is that the one with all those raunchy songs on it? Oh dear! You can't tell me she actually wants to sing those songs."

"Yep, she and the band got carried away and decided to do a burlesque section. They've been rehearsing 'Boom Boom Girl', 'What a Drunk Man Wants', 'The Backside of Nights Like These', even 'The Devil Between the Knees'."

"Oh no, Tom. Not that one! I wonder what Candice thinks?"

"Candice doesn't know. They're working so hard on it I don't think they've told anybody. They even hired a horn section for a New Orleans jazz sound. Melissa's got herself a French whore outfit that she just loves but she's too skinny to fill it out. She looks awful."

"I don't know what I could do about it."

"Can't you just tell her? You met her, right? You must have told her something about yourself."

"A little, but not that," I said. "How can I just casually tell Melissa that I'm a psychic and her dad doesn't want her to do those songs?"

"Jasmine, I don't want anyone to know I helped write those songs. It was a joke between the three of us. We were never going to release any of it."

"Oh crap, it's Rob." I'd heard the front door open.

"So he doesn't let you talk to your friends?"

"He's not real comfortable with my spirit friends."

Another sigh. "Then I guess I'll go."

"Jasmine! Who's that you're talking to?" Rob came out to the back patio just as Tom evaporated into space.

"Oh, Tom." I really hated lying to Rob so I didn't. "He's all upset about the way Melissa is doing some of his songs, but I don't think that's really the whole problem."

"I'd be mad if I couldn't be part of my own gala." Then Rob surprised me. "Hi Tom!" he said brightly. "I can't wait to hear all that new material."

I barely heard an "Ah ha!" as it rolled through my brain, but it seemed like Tom and Rob had actually communicated and it wasn't so bad. I let Rob know that I'd ordered plane tickets to fly in, go to the gala, and fly home the next day.

"That sounds fine to me," Rob agreed. "We're going to be real outsiders looking in at this thing. I bet the country music scene in Nashville is a pretty close group."

"And I'm probably the closest person in the world to the guest of honor! Right now, anyway." The irony of the situation had not gone unnoticed.

"Oh yeah," Rob's voice lost some of its lightness. "I saw LaToya and her mom sitting on a bench in the park today. I don't think they saw me..."

"Oh, I hope not! What were they doing?"

"Well, I didn't look too closely but her mom had a mirror in front of her face and I think she was doing her make-up."

"They're probably expecting to be rescued. Oh God, what a mess! What's her mom's name, anyway?"

"Dolores."

"The sorrows. How appropriate." I really knew so little about these gals. "What's their last name?"

"Mendes."

"We'll have to leave it up to social services. They're both so obviously wacky. I don't think there's a thing we could do."

Rob looked apprehensive. "You know, It's giving me the creeps. Crazy people do crazy things. I wonder if they still have the car and how they pay for gas and insurance and stuff."

Two crazy women with nothing to do and a grudge against Rob and me. The thought made me feel queasy too.

But we had too much going on to worry about the Mendes gals. We had a couple of tentative conversations about our wedding, where it was going to be and whom we were going to invite. I wanted to get married in my own home, even though it would limit the guest list a lot. But our Nashville trip was coming ever closer. Wedding plans would have to wait.

I lived on lettuce the week before we were to leave, and tried to keep the beer to a minimum.

Candice DeVries called and asked about our itinerary so she could send someone to pick us up at the airport. "You're not staying any longer than that?" She was incredulous. "There's so much to do in Nashville! I thought you'd stay at least a week."

"Oh, I'm sorry." I said. "We both have jobs and we already took time off to go to Austin. It was really fun, though. We stayed at the Driskill."

"The Driskill! Tom and I used to stay there sometimes. When he did good at the poker table, that is."

"It was great. We ordered room service and everything."

"Didja go to Roches for your Rob?"

"We did!" I was doing my best not to get all jealous of Tom's widow but the idea of her and Tom together at the Driskill was, if not a knife in my heart, at least a fork. I went on as pleasantly as I could. "Candice, the same people are still there!"

"Oh yeah, I know." She left the past behind and returned to the present. "We'll send a limo for the two of you. I'll have 'em holding a sign that says 'Jasmine and Rob'."

"A limo?" I wasn't used to being treated like royalty.

"Well, yeah! None of this would be happenin' if it wasn't for you."

"I suppose not. Thanks, Candice. I can't wait!"

"And Nashville can't wait for you. Bye bye, hon. Gotta go."

Candice hung up. She was such a nice lady, at least to the people she liked. I was still a little jealous, though.

We had to get up at four in the morning and drive all the way to Salt Lake to catch our plane to Nashville. The weather didn't cooperate; it was rainy and windy all the way there. The plane was crowded and the stewardess paid way too much attention to Rob and practically none to me. Still, the flight wasn't all that long and we flew into Nashville that afternoon. "Wow!" I said. "There's a river cutting right through the city!" I really could have done a little more research before we took off.

"Look at the stadium! I don't even know what river that is."

Rob confessed. "Geography wasn't my strongest subject."

A pleasant looking black woman with a wide-eyed baby chewing on her shoulder helped us out.

"That's the Cumberland river y'all are lookin' at. There's a lotta history in Nashville."

I made faces at her baby, who had two teeth on the bottom gum that were just coming in. "What's the weather like?" I asked.

"Oh, humid!" she answered. "The air is real thick. Ya kinda have ta chew it and swallow it. I like the culture in Tennessee but I know I like the air in Utah a lot better."

We landed, got out of the plane and even in the air-conditioned airport, I knew what she was warning us about. Not only was it humid, the air was thick with the smell of flowers, dense foliage and slow-moving river. Just as Candice had promised, an elegantly dressed black man held a sign that said: Jasmine and Rob. He introduced himself as Chad, took our garment bags and carry-ons, and neatly stashed everything in the trunk of a long, black limo. In spite of his formal appearance, Chad was open and friendly.

"So where y'all from? This your first time in Nashville?"

"We're from Moab, Utah." I answered. "And Nashville already feels like a whole other country."

"I think that's 'cause the South *is* a whole other country. But Utah is too, from what I hear."

"Oh, we're not Mormons." Rob commented.

"But you must be some kind of Indian then. They got a lot of Indians in Utah?"

"I'm half Navajo but it's not that important to me. There *are* a lot of Indians in Utah. All different kinds. Not many black people, though. I think there's two in Moab and I know both of them."

"What's Moab, anyway?"

Rob went on to explain that Moab had been a mining town

Theresa Rose

and now it was a tourist town. He mentioned Arches and Canyonlands and the Colorado River. "It's a great place to live but it's hard for a lot of people to make a living wage. I make pretty good money and so does Jasmine but she has to work her butt off."

"I think a lot of folks in Nashville feel that way too. Oh hey, we're almost there." Chad gestured at a giant complex.

"That's a hotel?" I didn't believe it. "It looks like Disneyland!"

"Yup, it's a theme park." Chad looked around at me. "How come you didn't know?"

"Somebody else made all the arrangements." I put up my hands and shrugged.

"So, you goin' to that big gala tomorrow? Word has it that some little gal found a whole pile of this guy's music that nobody knew about and tomorrow's the release party. I'm gonna be workin' it, I can tell you that."

"This is that same little gal." Rob bragged.

"Hey, I'm not that little!"

"Well, whatever you did, it's a real big deal. Here we are, folks."

Chad pulled up to one of the lobbies, held open the car door for us and carried our bags into the hotel.

Suddenly, we were surrounded by cameras flashing and microphones in our faces. I'm sure the pictures were horrible. I had no choice but to answer their questions.

"Jasmine! What's your full name?"

"Jasmine Anders. That's A N D E R S." I figured I might as well get my name spelled right in the papers.

"Who are you with?"

"My fiancé. F I A N C E. Did everybody get that?"

"Rob Dishta, D I S H T A." Rob was not to be left out or have his name spelled wrong either.

"Where did you find the case?"

"I found it in a weird little closet in my house. I'd just bought the house"

"Were you a Tom DeVries fan before that?"

"I was. I love him."

"What kind of compensation did you get for all the music?"

"That's too nosy!"

"Come on! What did you get?"

The questions just kept coming and some of them were getting personal.

"How long have you and Rob been together?"

Chad ran back to us, grabbed each of us by the arm and steered us away.

"Now all you folks can just lay off. They just got here!"

A nice lady clerk greeted Chad by name and confirmed our reservations. Chad carried our bags up to our room, which was a good thing because we never would have found our way by ourselves. As he hurried us past a giant, plant-filled atrium, Rob asked him if there was a machete on the list of hotel amenities.

"Oh, you won't need that." Chad answered. "You gotta be careful, though. I think some of these plants really do eat people! This publicity thing is gonna be trouble for y'all. I hope you don't get trapped in your room."

Rob tipped Chad a twenty and hoped he'd done the right thing. Our room was much more modest than the one we'd stayed in at the Driskill and there was no spa or mini bar. A gift basket offered gourmet snacks, a bottle each of red and white wine, and a bottle of champagne. I felt a little dizzy, having been up since four in the morning so I flopped down for a nap. Rob lay down beside me, planted a warm kiss on my neck and started to unbutton my sweater, so we didn't get to sleep for another half hour. By the time we woke up it was dinnertime and we were both famished but if we left the room, would we ever find it again?

The phone rang and it was Candice, checking up on us.

"Hey y'all. Waddya think of the Grand Ole Opry Hotel? Is the room okay?"

"Yeah," I said. "But we're afraid to leave it. We're going to get lost for sure."

"Oh, don't you worry. There's a map somewhere in the room."

"You know what else? Reporters in front of the hotel lobby swarmed us. I don't know what I'm supposed to do about that."

"What!!! Oh no, I wonder who let the cat out of the bag? I sure hope it wasn't me! I'm sorry if it was!"

"The chauffer rescued us. But what are we supposed to do if it happens again!"

"Oh, just blow 'em off. This is one of the biggest to-dos to happen in Nashville for a long time though. Some of this kind of thing is bound to happen."

"I guess it's going to keep happening to us."

"Some of it will. We got some media folks linked up for you tomorrow. It's gonna be a busy day. Say, I was wantin' to ask you two to dinner tonight, but I'm just too tired after all the work to put this shindig together. All I want is a gin and tonic or two and to hit the hay early."

"You do just that, then. You get some rest and we'll take care of ourselves."

"Well, after all you did for us, I feel like a bad hostess. I want you to know that anyway."

"You're not a bad hostess." Maybe a southern belle like Candice just had an inborn need to over-apologize. "Just tell us where to eat and we're good."

"Oh, probably the first place you come to. Just make sure you take that map with you." Candice did sound tired.

So it was up to me and Rob to navigate the vast Southern fantasy that was the Grand Ole Opry Hotel. Surprisingly, no one else followed us and I suspected the hotel was particular about reporters and their credentials. We held hands as we circled down the spiral staircase to the Delta Atrium, to begin daunting process of finding somewhere to eat. We strolled through the luxurious atrium with its elegant pavilion and its abundant botanical garden.

"You know," I commented. "I think this place got flooded a few years ago."

"How could they tell?" Rob studied the vast water feature that encircled the atrium.

"Oh, it was for real. They had to do a lot of remodeling...Hey look! There's a steakhouse."

"That's fine with me. But it looks like a mansion! Do you think they'll let us in wearing jeans and cowboy boots?" We chickened out and found a pizza place.

The dazzling décor was fun but the people watching was spectacular. There were families of every imaginable nationality; groups of Japanese with cameras, veiled Muslim women, a group of Mennonites or Amish or something like that, one of the girls showing off knee-length hair. We saw a group of dreadlocked Jamaicans with spouses and children. We even saw a decrepit-looking Kris Kristofferson, complete with entourage, and probably there for the gala. Rob and I, in our jeans and cowboy boots, were very much the southwestern representatives.

We explored the grounds as the sun went down, stopping outside of the Jack Daniels Restaurant where the band was covering a Tom DeVries tune.

Rob said, "Let's go back to our room, drink one of those bottles of wine and go back to bed." He gave my behind a playful squeeze.

"Good heavens, Rob. You're amorous today!" He always had a healthy appetite for lovemaking. Our first couple of months had been wild and crazy, of course, but then we'd settled into once a day lovemaking.

"Of course I am! I'm having another wild adventure with

Jasmine! I'm doing all these things I never thought I'd ever do!" His grin showed off his fine white teeth. "My life was so ordinary until I met you, and now it's all glamour and craziness and places I've never been. I love it. And I love you!" He grabbed me and gave me a big long kiss right in front of everyone. People stopped to watch. What's more, they gave us a round of applause.

He put his arm around my shoulders and I put mine around his waist and we went back to our room. I thought about all the women who were jealous of me. Of me! But remembering where I came from, I tried not to feel too full of myself. As the soon-to-be Mrs. Rob, I had much to be thankful for.

He opened the wine and brought me a glass. He gazed at me with such love and pride I thought I would melt right into the mattress. Gently, he pushed the hair away from my face. "Jasmine, I don't know how to tell you how I'm feeling right now. You've opened up my life so much that I feel like a different guy."

He laid his head in my lap while I finished my wine. I stroked that rippling mane of black satiny hair from the crown of his head all the way to the end and then wound it around my fingers. This was a different Rob. He's always been romantic, playful, athletic and adventurous in our bed, but this was something deeper. I put down my empty glass and started to undo his belt. He in turn pulled up my shirt and kissed my belly, working his way down, undoing my jeans and sliding them off my hips. At last he arrived at my most intimate parts, where he pushed my thighs apart and slid his tongue into the cleft. I couldn't help but moan with sheer erotic ecstasy of it. And that was only the beginning; we must have made love for a couple of hours.

Chapter 20 – The Gala

The day of the gala promised to be a tornado's worth of activity. Candice called at 8 a.m. and ordered us to get our butts over to the Grand Ole Opry itself by 10 a.m. for a back stage tour and to meet some people. We walked into a frenzied scene of lights, cords, and equipment being hauled around and familiar billboard faces everywhere. I wished I had done a little more research into contemporary country stars because there were a lot of faces I should have been able to put names to. But Candice got between us, took both of our arms, escorted us everywhere she wanted us to go, and introduced us to everyone she wanted us to know. She sat us down with a newspaper reporter, an older woman with coifed blue hair.

"When you found that case, did you realize what you had?"

"Yes I did. It was a little scary." I admitted. "I was already a Tom DeVries fan. I bought an old cassette player at a pawn shop to listen to the tapes, and that's when I knew what I had."

"How did you know to contact Candice DeVries?"

"It was a lucky guess." I lied. "I did some research and found out she was his widow, instead of an ex, so she seemed like the right gal to contact. I went on Peoplesearch.com, got her number and gave her a call."

"How did you convince Candice that you were for real?"

"I sent her one of the cassettes."

She asked us about our lives in Moab, how we met and when we were getting married.

"Moab's a small town and the dating pool is pretty shallow." Rob said. "She was the new girl in town so I didn't waste any time."

We posed for photo after photo and spoke to more reporters. I let it slip that I'd never heard of Tom DeVries before the drive from Colorado to Moab, and called it an amazing coincidence. White lie upon white lie. But how was I supposed to tell the real story? Rob was careful to go along with what I said and not blow my cover.

We were getting cheers and applause wherever we went. Rob, looking dashing in his braid and new cowboy hat, was sparkling with all the attention. I was feeling claustrophobic.

Apparently, being a celebrity means being a good sport. Maybe being psychically sensitive means being easily crushed by too much attention. I could sense everyone's moods, their reactions to Rob and me and could tell whether they were glad to see us or whether they found us a distraction from some very important task. I could sense who had their eyes on me and who might be interested in Rob and it felt strange and predatory. (Some people just don't believe in monogamy.) Finally, I asked Candice if there was a place I could go to catch my breath and have a cup of coffee. She was her usual gracious self, finding me a quiet break room with an espresso machine delivering a full-bodied brew and a red leather recliner to relax in. Then she ungraciously took off with Rob, who looked back mouthing, "I'll be right back." I believed him.

I sipped my espresso and took a few deep breaths, feeling drained and overwhelmed and glad for a moment of solitude. The recliner was cool and squishy. I put my feet up on the footrest. Tom's voice and guitar were playing over the loudspeakers and I recognized the song as one of the new ones, the way Tom had meant it to sound, pure, heavenly Texas Tom.

The Tom I had fallen in love with. The Tom I adored. The oppression I'd felt began to ease. I leaned my head back and let the song and Tom's voice serenade me; rich, cool, smooth as old whiskey. The scent of freshly showered male in a clean shirt surrounded me along with that familiar warmth. I felt protected and cared for. Of course Tom would be here, but that he'd bother with me, at an event of such magnitude, dedicated to him...Oh, my Tom. You really are everything that I'd hoped and dreamed that you were. My dear dark angel. He stayed with me for as long as I sat there, not attempting to communicate anything but simply being with me, for as long as I needed him.

Rob finally came back escorted by Melissa.

"I told my mama that she was gonna have to give him back someday. Feelin' a little better, Jasmine?"

I felt a squeeze on my shoulder and a tap on my cheek as Tom made his exit, knowing I was all right.

Rob had a glow on. "You'll never believe who I just met!"

"Who?" I asked, already knowing the answer.

"I met Tracy Simon! Melissa introduced us! She's even prettier in real life than she is in her videos! Wow! And she's so sweet! Like a real old-fashioned southern girl."

"I'm glad you were introduced. Did you get an autograph?" I was trying to be nice but I felt annoyed. Come on, Rob, what do I have to do to remind you that we were talking about kids? He seemed to forget we had ordered our wedding rings. I had to bring him back to earth.

"What next?" I asked. "Are there any more plans involving us?"

Melissa drawled out the next item on the agenda.

"Well, me and my mama would like to take you two out to lunch with a couple o' other folks. One of 'ems the guy who remastered all my daddy's new music and we think he really did it right."

Lunch with the perpetually shining star that was Melissa

DeVries was a treat not to be missed. This time, I was truly happy for the invitation, but I was still going to need a long break before the banquet at six and the performances at eight thirty.

"Will Candice let us go back to our room after that?" I asked. "I don't know if I could take another round of introductions. And please! No more reporters! I don't even remember the names of anybody that I met this morning."

"Oh, don' you worry. She'll have a couple of glasses of wine with lunch and she'll have to take a nap too. You'll get your downtime. They'll be pictures and people wantin' to talk to you at the banquet, though. You'll be in the papers tomorrow."

Rob and I actually slept that afternoon, due to a combination of wine at lunch and a genuine need to sleep. But the intimacy of the previous night seemed to have evaporated. We showered separately, and took our time getting ready for the gala. We weren't at all used to dressing up.

"Melissa will probably show up in her jeans and red high heels." I said. "I bet her mother will be dressed to the nines with the biggest hair in the room."

"Melissa doesn't need to dress up. She shines enough already. So what do you think?"

Rob buttoned his jacket and strutted around for me. He'd left his hair loose, slithering down his back, every inch the Navajo warrior prince.

"I think you're prettier than me and it's making me jealous."

He was stunning. I could see why Tom had insisted on having his suits made at Roches. Even with the silver pinstripes, the cut was so elegant and so subtle that Rob looked perfectly at home in the unfamiliar garments. He'd opted out of the tie and left his shirt collar open, looking just like my Rob, long, strong, a little exotic, native southwestern and comfortable. I felt so proud. But in love?

"Let's get you into that dress. Then you'll be the pretty one again. Did you ever get that push-up bra?"

"Rob, geez. Okay, I did."

"Let's see if it works!" Sigh.

The Magnolia ballroom was cathedral-sized, with a lofty ceiling and a champagne fountain in the middle of the room that shot up almost as high. Arriving at the entrance, we were nearly blinded by what felt like a million flashbulbs. We finally composed ourselves to actually pose for a few of these and I hoped the publications would use the good ones. Our photos would be on all the major news stations that evening. Rob was basking in the limelight, posing like a pro, but I wanted to hide behind him.

Our very efficient hostess led us to one of the linen-clad round tables. A number of people were already seated. There were eight of them, including an older guy in a wheelchair who was accompanied by a nurse in a sharply tailored gray ensemble. The hostess put her hand on my back and shoved me forward, also taking Rob by the arm.

"I'd like to introduce Jasmine Anders. She's the lady who found the lost music of Tom DeVries! If it hadn't been for her, none of you would be here today! And with her is her fiancé, Rob Dishta."

Everybody except the guy in the wheelchair stood up and clapped and cheered. There were more flashbulbs. The hostess introduced everyone else at the table, deftly averting some potentially awkward moments, especially for Rob and me. One of the couples was a producer and her husband. The other couple shared a publicity and promotion business. The guy in the wheelchair turned out to be Daniel Clark, whose name had appeared with Tom's in innumerable venues. I was glad to be close to someone who had been close to Tom who wouldn't make me jealous. He grinned at me and nodded.

"Well done, my girl, well done!"

The older British gentleman with the shining silver hair and the obviously too young girlfriend looked familiar but I couldn't place him. Then to my absolute amazement, he was introduced as Jason Poole. My teenage crush! I wondered how long it would be before I melted into a fourteen-year-old groupie. But I went ahead and allowed myself an expression of delight at finally meeting my old flame.

"Mr. Poole!" I began. "Oh, I would have been such a Poole groupie if I'd only been born in time! But my folks would never have let me out of the house anyway."

There was a round of polite laughter. Then the champagne arrived.

I was happy to be seated next to Daniel Clark. I asked him to tell me a favorite Tom DeVries story and he was happy to oblige.

"Oh yeah, I loved Tom! I just loved him. We were always raisin' hell together. Made some great music, too! It was a damn shame Jim Ed was always tryin' to clip his wings." He paused to take a big swallow of champagne in spite of the disapproving eye of the nurse.

"But anyway, let me tell you my story," he continued. "Tom got wise to Jim Ed and started bookin' his own gigs. He also started packin' a pistol, knowin' what Jim Ed could be like. Well, sure enough, Jim Ed had hired a couple of creeps to jump him in the parkin' lot after one of those gigs, thinkin' they'd teach him a lesson. But Tom was ready for 'em. He musta smelled what was goin' on 'cause he shot 'em both in the foot before either one had a chance to lay a hand on him!"

Everyone at the table either gasped, or laughed or both. Daniel Clark went on.

"The first night I heard DeVries sing, we were both shitfaced drunk. I'd never heard of him before and I thought *I* was *the guy*. We were outside of Amarillo in somebody's trailer. It was sunset and Tom picked up the nearest guitar. I'm pretty sure it was mine. Anyway, he twanged and tuned like all us guitar players do…"

Daniel looked up at the ceiling; rapture on his face, smiling broadly. "And then he sang. And then I knew."

"Like dark chocolate!" I offered.

"Or Irish whiskey," Daniel called back.

The conversation turned to Jim Ed O'Reilly and how the person who'd shot him had never been caught.

"That's because she did ever'body in Nashville a favor, that's why not." Daniel had already succumbed to a combination of champagne and prescription painkillers. The word "she" rose like a phantom in the middle of the table and no one dared to discuss it further, but still, my eyes went straight to Candice.

"Has it ever been proven if Tom was actually murdered or not?" one of the gentlemen asked. Here I was, the only one at the table who knew the truth and I couldn't say a word. But Daniel Clark didn't have any illusions about his old friend.

"Oh, I don't think they ever proved that anybody had messed with his brakes or anything. Plus, he'd made himself so scarce that nobody knew where he was!" He took another swallow of champagne.

"Nope. Tom was just bein' Tom, racin' around in the desert, probably celebratin' with a bottle of whiskey in his hand." He took another swig of champagne to demonstrate.

"He was just like that. Reckless, wild. He never outgrew the cowboy in 'im. But, ya know, I don't think he was ever mean to anybody unless they really deserved it." Daniel paused, knowing he'd get a laugh. "He had a real kindness to him, real kindness."

"I think *I* would have slept with that guy." Jason Poole said. There was another round of laughter. Jason Poole was notoriously heterosexual.

"Hey! Why don't you tell the one about the legendary jam session in that basement bar in Houston." Daniel called out. "I never quite heard the whole story."

"Yeah!" I said. "I only heard a little bit of it from Melissa."

All eyes turned to Jason Poole, anticipating another fond anecdote, but Jason's expression had changed. He glanced quickly around the room.

"I was looking for Melissa since she may not want to hear this," he said. "That jam session never happened."

"But..." Daniel Clark looked puzzled. "I've been hearing that story for years. Tom told it all the time! What do you mean it never happened?"

"Oh, we met at the bar all right," Jason began. "I was excited. By that time, Tom was one of the great legends of American music and I felt utterly privileged that he would pay me any attention at all, much less invite me out after the show. So he went down to his lounge gig and I went off to the stadium where I was so distracted, I didn't play well. Not that I cared very much."

He swirled his champagne in his glass. That Tom had been telling a tall tale was certain. Maybe it was just a case of not letting the truth get in the way of a good story.

"Once the show was over, I dashed off the stage as soon as I could, fought off an army of screaming girls and barely got into a cab with my guitar and amp. When I got to the lounge, Tom was sitting at the bar having his supper. He motioned me over when he saw me and I felt like a teenager on a first date.

"He was such a class act in his black suit and string tie. I was getting so sick of the raging orgy that was every Radio Lightning tour, sick of being drugged up all the time and sick of being sick. Tom ordered a shot of Wild Turkey, a Coors and a steak for me, joking that even rock stars couldn't survive on booze and dope alone. He paid for it all, too! Such a gentleman.

"So we talked about music mostly. I gushed about "Cowboy Angels" and "River of Gold" and he told me that he'd played "Fire and Ice" so many times, he wore out the grooves on the record. I didn't think I'd ever met a cooler guy. But this is the thing…

"He had just asked to see my guitar and I was all psyched for a jam session. But then this white-haired guy in a suit came up and tapped him on the shoulder, saying something like:

'Hey Tom, we got a game going on. You gonna wrap this thing up?'

"So Tom hands my guitar back to me and says he's got to go."

Everyone at the table, except Daniel Clark, looked disappointed.

"Oh, that was Tom's dark side," Daniel said. "He never could resist a poker game. It was like a bad drug to him. A couple of times he was late to a gig 'cause he couldn't get away from the poker table."

"I was quite crushed," Jason admitted. "This was the Seventies. Oh, I suppose I had it coming, considering the way I was treating the girls at the time, but I was rock and roll royalty! And here I had been dismissed as if I were a nobody."

I noticed that Rob hadn't said a word or even been listening. He was staring across the room at the strapless and sequined Tracy Simon, who was staring right back. I happened to spot her just in time to see her smile and raise her glass to Rob. Shit. Here I'd been soaking up all of the Tom I could get and hoping Rob didn't feel out of place or jealous. I knew how he loved to be the center of attention.

"Hey y'all!" Melissa DeVries strode up to our table, grinning with those huge teeth and casting a ray of starshine over the whole table. "Dinner's just comin' out so it'll be here real soon. Ever'body got enough champagne?"

"Melissa!" Jason Poole was all smiles again. "Thanks so much for the invitation! I feel so honored."

"Aw, it weren't nothin'. I just picked up the phone, talked to your secretary and sent out an invite. I'm so glad you're here. I'm always tryin' to copy your guitar playin' but you don't wanna hear it. Believe me."

"This is supposed to be about your dad, anyway. He was all about acoustic."

"Yeah. He might not like the way I do some of his songs, though. He always said that pluggin' in a guitar was a way a' coverin' up lousy technique."

"Some of them would be really good that way." Daniel Clark said. "That new one, 'Eyes Blazing Blues'? That would be really great on electric guitar."

"I'm opening with that one. It's plugged in all right."

"You're going to be great, Melissa."

"I hope so," she said. "But just see if I don't break a heel or trip over a cord or somethin'."

"That kind of thing always happens." Daniel Clark broke in. "Doesn't it Jason? It's good luck!"

Jason winked. "Don't worry, Melissa. You're going to knock 'em all dead."

"But then I'd be playin' for a bunch a zombies!" She waved. "I gotta go." Melissa strode away, swinging a long ponytail.

The banquet was served and many more bottles of champagne were consumed. The show was eventually announced after coffee and the tables were emptied in an orderly fashion. Rob and I found our seats, second row center, right behind Candice and Brandon DeVries. Rob was silent and distracted, glancing around in all directions. I was high on champagne and wired on coffee, not in a good condition to confront Rob with anything, but what would I say? The idea that I would have to remind him that I was wearing his engagement ring was just too humiliating. Besides, I was jittery with anticipation, preoccupied with the possibility that Tom may have to do something to stop the performance. Being so damn old-school, he just might. To make it worse, Melissa was late. Everyone was waiting, making puzzled conversation. Then the lights went down.

The rest of the band slowly took their places. Ten minutes went by. The band members looked at each other and began a warm-up tune that seemed to go on for a very long time. They kept looking off stage and the crowd began to murmur.

"I wonder if it's a prima donna moment or stage fright?" I speculated as I leaned over to Rob.

"What?" he said, unaware of the delay as he scanned the darkened theater. Brandon DeVries turned around.

"Melissa never has stage fright. She usually can't wait to start. There's somethin' up. For sure."

"Must be," Candice agreed. "I hope it's nothin' real serious.

Finally, after another five minutes, Melissa strutted up to the microphone, electric guitar in hand, grinning her giant grin.

"Hey everybody! I'm sorry I'm late but I had a technical difficulty. My bra strap broke!"

She waited for the laughter to subside. Then she managed to look every member in the audience right in the eye at the same moment or at least I thought so. What an ability to have for a rising star, to make everyone feel as if she's there just for them! And she did!

"Let's get goin'!"

She started with a slide playing one of Tom's southern guitar riffs. Sure enough, it was "Eyes Blazing Blues". A sparkling red spike heel on the end of the skinniest of all skinny jeans began stomping a hole in the stage floor. Her long dark ponytail swung from side to side as the nineteen-year-old Melissa DeVries did her daddy proud. She effortlessly belted out some of Tom's more raucous tunes just to get everybody all fired up, all of them 'lectrified and all of them fabulous. She then switched out her electric guitar for an acoustic (one of her daddy's favorites, she declared) and began a set of his ballads and love songs. I waited nervously for the burlesque section, wondering what Tom would do if she actually showed up on stage in a bustier, but she couldn't have known how he felt about it. The band seemed to be mostly college age. They probably thought they were having a frat party with no clue about being inappropriate.

Other musicians joined her on stage including the long-suffering Emmaline Hughes and Dirk Castellano, their years of effort finally paying off. Emmaline was still slim and pretty, although the waist-length red hair had turned completely white. Her dimples deepened as she smiled at the crowd. Dirk Castellano had gray streaks in his hair and mustache. He was small and slim except for a bit of a belly, almost disguised by a fringed leather vest. They played a song called "Dreamtime", a spooky, surrealistic imagining of a desert under a full moon. Dirk added an eerie mariachi wail that gave me the shivers. Then Tracy Simon appeared on stage and I heard Rob gasp. She glittered all over, her long, white gown gracing her willowy body, angelic blond curls framing her cherubic face. Even her acoustic guitar was white.

I wondered how the sugary pop princess could possibly do justice to Tom's music, and steeled myself against the inevitable spoilage. The song was one of Tom's sweet, sad ballads about a beautiful girl from a coal-mining town whose hopes and dreams are crushed by the grueling lifestyle. I had to admit, no one could have done it better. Her young voice expressed the plight of the dreamy mountain girl, reaching deep inside to bring out the emotion written within the song, the longing, the disappointment and the helplessness. She brought tears to my eyes. I didn't know that she could sing like that. I began to view her in a more sympathetic light, certain that she had been pigeon-holed into the saccharine pop tunes just for the money when she was capable of so much more.

A beaming Melissa came back on stage and the astonished audience drew in a collective breath. She was wearing a black and red lace outfit with a camisole that drooped over her small breasts. The short skirt with a series of tulle petticoats sat atop her skinny legs. Her sparkling heels, so fancy and fun on the end of her jeans, made her feet appear disproportionately large. The other band members all came out wearing black suits and black bowler hats. Following them were the four horn players, blowing a dirge that sounded just like a New Orleans funeral.

"And now," Melissa announced. "Welcome to the Tom DeVries Memorial Burlesque Extravanganza!"

The band played a single note and the whole theater went black

"Tom!" I shouted inside my own head. What else could he have done? There were startled murmurs all over the theater as the stage manager began to shout.

"Everyone please remain in your seats! You will all be escorted out beginning with the very last rows. We apologize for the inconvenience."

Ushers with flashlights began the tedious process of emptying the dark theater. Rob spoke to me for what seemed like the first time all evening. "Jasmine, what happened?" he whispered, not wanting Brandon or Candice to hear and complicate things even more. Fortunately, the two of them were chatting it up about what could have gone wrong with the power. "Do you know?" Rob asked.

"I do," I whispered back. "And it was Tom."

"Why would he do a thing like that? That was his daughter up there. Why would he want to play such a mean practical joke? I got the impression at dinner that he was this real good guy."

"These kids found a cassette that was supposed to have been a joke between Tom, Emmaline and Dirk." I whispered. "It had all these awful, raunchy songs on it and they never meant to release them but Melissa and her band thought it would be great fun to do this show."

"Oh. I see." Rob nodded. "Did anyone else know about it?" he said quietly.

"If anyone had, this wouldn't have happened."

"It's a good thing it didn't go any further," Rob said. "Inappropriate doesn't even describe it."

There would be no performance of River of Gold.

The flashlights finally came to our row and everyone squeezed into the aisle. As the crowd crushed together, I dropped back behind Rob, got stuck for a few moments and then was left even further behind. Rob disappeared into the darkness ahead as I waited for the crush to disperse enough to allow the crowd to resume shuffling forward.

When I finally got to the entrance there was still a mass of people to weave my way through. I didn't see anyone I knew. Not Candice, not Brandon and most of all, not Rob. I felt a wave of panic as my intuition revealed the awful truth. Rob wasn't looking for me. He wasn't waiting for me. He wasn't concerned for me at all.

I found myself walking toward a willow where the crowd seemed less dense and in the shadow of the sweeping tree, I finally saw Rob. He wasn't alone. He was with Tracy Simon, holding hands, gazing into each other's eyes, oblivious to the rest of the world. I had a couple of choices. I could barge in and collar Rob, claiming him for my own and making it very clear that he was mine. But that wasn't my way of doing things. As I steeled myself up to get my feelings crushed, I felt the warm presence that I loved so much circle behind me. Whisky and cigarettes and the embrace of a fresh, clean shirt distracted me from Rob and Tracy and suddenly, I didn't care what they did.

"Follow me, Jasmine."

Tom escorted me away from the tawdry scene. Weaving through the milling mass of humanity, I followed something that only I could see, a shadow figure, yes, but not a dark shadow. It was luminous, a guiding light weaving gracefully between the other concert attendees, finding the least conspicuous spaces. No one noticed me.

By then, the lights had come back on in the theater and I found myself back in the break room with the recliner and the espresso machine, alone with my Tom.

"Jasmine, I'm sorry about Rob but I guess you already knew."

"Oh, Tom," I said softly. "I just don't care that much and I don't want to marry Rob. I love you and that's that. I'm pretty disappointed in Melissa but I don't think she realized that her burlesque show was such a bad idea."

"She's a kid, and so are her band mates. Superbly talented but kids after all. Come on. Let's go back to your room."

We returned to the hotel and Tom stayed with me. I undressed, changed into my nightgown, laid down on the bed and Tom lay down beside me, warm and strong, sweeter than Rob ever was. Even without a body, Tom was all heart. I imagined having a weekend to myself, not driving all over Utah to watch some boring Middle School kids play basketball. I looked forward to making my own decisions, spending my free time cooking, watching trash TV and biking around Moab. Maybe I'd cultivate a few female friends. Rob's presence in my life had been so large that he'd been the only person I'd gotten to know outside of work. Having my own life back was beginning to have a lot of appeal except for one thing. Where was I going to get my baby? The degree of sorrow I felt as the prospect of motherhood slipped away surprised me. I'd known I wanted kids but I didn't know I wanted them as bad as that.

Rob didn't come in until sunrise. No explanations, no excuses. He crawled into bed beside me just as if things were the same as always. But he didn't smell the same as always. Maybe he actually thought that he could fool me.

Chapter 21 – An Agreement

Back in Moab, Rob and I resumed our life together, not changing our wedding plans but not moving forward with them either. Our rings arrived via FedEx. I put them in a drawer and said nothing to Rob about them. I didn't even open the box. We played house and made love and I obediently attended all of his games until the season was over. By June, Cowboy Christmas was getting into full swing and The *Rodeo Review* once again took over my life, a welcome distraction from the deception and dishonesty at home. I pretended not to notice when Rob took his calls outside, or from inside his truck, claiming they were about work. While I was sure some of them were, I was also sure that some of them weren't. To myself, I made grim jokes about needing my stud service for a little while longer. It surprised me that Rob wouldn't realize that I knew all about him and Tracy but it was probably the most convenient thing for him to think. He was deceiving himself more than me.

We were celebrities. Tom DeVries was all over the airwaves. Sales of the new CDs were soaring. There were TV specials to be produced and my phone never stopped buzzing with reporters and camera people all wanting to get my story. The local publications descended first and then the calls came from New York, L.A. and Salt Lake. When CBS sent their team over, Rob and I stupidly allowed them to photograph the two of us, my house, and the cabinet where I had found the case. Rob and I and my sweet little home were on the national news! I had no clue as to the consequences of trying to please every newsperson and fan that showed up at our door.

Kate was frustrated with all the attention I was getting at the office but it wasn't my fault. I just couldn't put everybody off even if I was sick of telling the same story over and over! Would it ever stop? Finally, Bud McClintock found himself a job, hanging around the office and screening my calls and my visitors. He made a terrific bodyguard, polite but firm, both kind grandfather and tough old-school cowboy at the same time. Thanks to him, I was able to concentrate on my real job. But then Rob came by one afternoon, bringing one of those terrific hamburgers from that place near my old apartment and asking how late I expected to be. I introduced him to Bud McClintock, who was polite as usual but also stared at me with a look of confusion and rage on his face. Rob gave me a quick kiss and ran off to another coaching job at the high school, leaving me alone with a very disappointed old man.

"You have a boyfriend? When did that happen? Last Christmas, you were single, weren't you?"

What? I'd thought Bud was just being friendly. There had to have been forty years between us. But if only he knew the real truth!

"Last Christmas, I thought I was." I said. "We'd had a falling out. But he met me on my front porch that evening and we made up." Then I added something else. "I didn't think I was coming on to you. If I led you on, I'm sorry!"

"I'm sorry too! I didn't expect you to be the type to take advantage of an old man."

"I was not taking advantage! I let you buy me lunch a couple of times. I just thought we were friends."

"Well not any more we're not!"

And then Bud, who I thought was my "buddy", walked out on me! Oh...Men! I really hate it when people make all kinds of plans revolving around you and don't tell *you* anything about them.

Late in June, Kate called from Las Vegas. It was almost 11 p.m. and she knew to call me at the office. Was she ever going to hire anyone else? She told me that she'd seen Rob, my house and me on the evening news.

"Everybody's talking about Tom DeVries, and his CDs are for sale all over the fairgrounds. You might want to hire some security or something 'cause people are gonna start comin' to your house to see one of the last places that he ever was."

"Oh no!" The magnitude of having appeared on the national news in front of a growing Tom DeVries cult was just beginning to hit me. "Oh no!"

"Yeah, Jasmine. Here it comes. There's a whole new generation of fans headed your way. And you know what? I'm one of 'em. I bought all three CDs and then I bought all his old stuff. He's really good!" Kate too. Now everybody wanted a piece of my Tom.

I was putting off any attempt to contact him, knowing that the inevitable goodbye was imminent and not wanting to say it. So when I felt that warmth and smelled that scent as he called me out to the patio, I almost felt dread instead of joy. It was Sunday, so Kate was at church in some other state and not at work for once. We had each other all to ourselves.

Tom sounded tired, sad and discouraged and not like himself. He was a normal human spirit and did have his moments, just like everybody else, but I wished he didn't feel so sad.

"...and you're the only person I can talk to," he was saying. "My own wife and my own son and daughter don't even know I'm there. That's it, I guess. There's nothin' left for me to do here."

"Well, Tom," I replied. "You did it. You did what you've been hanging around for. Your family's all taken care of and the music has been released to the public. Brandon is going to music school and Melissa's career is taking off." I didn't want to say the next thing but I had to. I took a deep breath.

"You're done with this lifetime, Tom. I wish you weren't but I can't hold you here. It's time to head toward that light that everybody talks about. But oh boy..."

"What is it, Jasmine?"

"I'll just miss you so damn much!" My throat got tight and my eyes welled up. It was for real this time. I was going to have to let him go if I really cared for him as much as I thought.

"Jasmine, you're the only thing that's holding me here. I don't want to give you up either."

"Real love is so fucking complicated!"

We sat in silence. There really wasn't any more to say. Both of us knew that we couldn't live in each other's worlds and both of us hurt for it. Some things just couldn't be. We were saying goodbye.

But then I thought again. I'd just had the weirdest thought. I had to put it to Tom.

"Tom, I have an idea."

"Tell me, my darlin'."

"Well, you know, you're going to have to cross over so you can end this lifetime. But..."

This was going to be a hard thing to say.

"What are you thinkin'? I'm listening."

"You have a standing invitation if you want to come back in."

"What?" He sounded intrigued.

"Tom, you must know how much I want a baby..."

"Yeah, I do but I know things aren't goin' that well with you and Rob."

"Oh probably not but I still want to try. Anyway, this is what

I want to say. Would you want to, uh, be my baby?"

There, I'd said it. I'd spit it out and it was met with dead silence. I decided to try and sell this one for all it was worth.

"Please, think about it. You and I already know we love each other and Rob seems to carry a pretty good set of genes. Just imagine being a little kid again on family vacations. Imagine being a teenager again and falling in love for the first time. Think about having your whole future ahead of you. And think about having me for a mom!"

There was another long silence. I started to feel embarrassed. Maybe this wasn't quite the right proposal for a guy like Tom DeVries. But I was wrong again. Sometimes it was great to be wrong.

I felt that deep-throated laugh that I'd loved so much roll through me.

"I probably won't remember you, you know." Tom was beginning to sound like his usual self.

"But I'll know who *you* are!" This was crazy and I loved it! I'd take my Tom any way I could get him and this just might be the way.

"So I'll finally get a taste of those pretty little tits of yours? I thought that was never gonna happen! I'm starting to like this idea a lot!"

Boobs and guys again! Works every time.

"Watch out, though." He continued. "I drove my mom crazy."

"You've already been driving me crazy. So come on back and do it some more!" I was beginning to feel hopeful. He really seemed to like the idea!

"Yeah, I think I'd want to come back to earth for another go as soon as I could. Sittin' on a cloud playing a harp just ain't my style."

"I bet you'll be playing guitar before you can walk!"

"There's one thing you gotta consider, Jasmine darlin'.

Nothin's gonna happen if you and Rob can't be honest with each other. Now you think about that."

This was probably the strangest conversation that either of us had ever had, alive or dead. And what he said about Rob and me was true. I wanted Tom to exit this life with no regrets about having to give up someone he loved, and I didn't want to hold him back. We were making a deal, our secret. Somehow, I was going to have to talk with Rob.

Rob got a call a few days later. It was Tracy Simon, asking if he would like to come back to Nashville to be in a music video. He'd be the brave, handsome Indian who rescues her from the outlaws and a tidy sum of money was on the table. The guy who, just a couple of months ago, didn't want to be the "fucking Indian cliché" jumped for joy. He immediately began making plans to take time off from work, and never once asked my opinion. I should have been furious with him but I wasn't.

"Sounds like some real good money," I commented. "But can you really take that much time off work?"

"Aah, I'll just find a new job if they have to replace me. I have a good reputation in this town."

"What about coaching? Don't you do a summer basketball program?"

"They can do without me for one season," he answered. "I'll make it up to them in the fall."

Oh, Rob. What was happening to you?

Chapter 22 – An Attack!

Rodeo season meant that Kate and Lucy were gone for almost the whole month of July. I didn't mind all the work this time. Kate and I had come up with a plan so I wouldn't be so overloaded, meaning ten-hour days instead of twelve. The downside was, I'd be alone in the office again, without even Bud McClintock to keep me company. I missed Bud and his protective, grandfatherly presence. He never came to visit any more now that he knew he'd gotten the wrong idea. Tom seemed to be around a lot. I could feel him tailing me, checking on me at the office, following me home. Something worried him. I kept my mouth shut, my eyes and ears open and my cell phone handy.

The weeks passed without incident but I still had a creepy feeling. I was being watched. Pretty sure I knew who it was, I still had no idea what to do about it. Smudging the office with a sage wand every morning, I could count on my Tom to watch over me, but I still didn't feel safe. Not at all.

It was about eight o'clock on a Thursday evening and I was wrapping up the day's work. Cheyenne Frontier Days were almost over and Rob had been gone for a whole lot longer than it would have taken to make a music video. But the girls would be coming back on Monday and I could have some of my life back. As I was closing up, I felt nervous. The hairs were standing up on the back of my neck and my palms were sweating. Something wasn't right, but that was all I knew. I considered leaving through the back door but there was no light out back and my car was in front of the building. I shut off all the machines and locked the back door.

I had my cell in my hand as I turned off the last of the lights. The front door lock was old and rusty and was always a struggle to open and close. I had nearly succeeded when I heard a familiar male voice shout, "Don't open that door!" and I shut it again.

A giant ball of flame exploded on the front porch as all the windows, the cracks in the walls and around the door lit up like the Fourth of July. I could hear a horrid shriek as I hurried to let myself out the back door. The single shriek exploded into a continuous series of screams. I called 911 and gave them the address, then ran around to the front of the office to see what had happened.

It was LaToya. She had fallen backwards off her spike-heeled pumps with her hair on fire. I ran over, peeled off my own shirt and wrapped it around her head to smother the flames. I don't think even she knew who I was. The screaming subsided to panting and whimpering and her movements were weak and feeble. Behind me, the flames on the porch leaped higher. The old wicker chair had ignited and the fire threatened to consume the whole office.

Oh LaToya! Whatever she had intended to do to me had backfired in the worst way. Her pretty little doll-painted face was all blackened with burns and bleeding wounds. She may have even blinded herself. All the gels and sprays that she used to achieve that big-hair look had ignited and she would probably have bald patches where the hair would never grow back. I was horrified, sad, scared to death for the office, and helpless in both situations. There was nothing I could do beyond what I'd already done.

I wasn't much of a nurse and was easily grossed out. LaToya's burns horrified me. Her long, lacquered claws were all charred and hanging off of the ends of her fingers. I felt traumatized, nauseated, and grateful that she hadn't carried out her plan, but sorry for her anyway. I had been warned. My Tom. Thanks, Tom. You were there for me again.

The ambulance and the fire crew arrived within a few minutes of my call and within seconds they had LaToya in the ambulance with a morphine IV in her arm. The fire crew put out the flames on the porch as soon as they arrived, so the front door and walls were black but still standing and everything in the office was safe. I was standing there in my bra and shorts and one of the officers gave me his jacket to wear. When they asked me what had happened, I told them everything I knew but I doubted that they would believe everything I said. I insisted there were other witnesses to LaToya's crazy behavior. I didn't know what had caused the explosion.

"Hey, take a look at this!" One of the policemen said. A can of AquaNet and a lighter lay on the ground in front of the porch steps. LaToya's firebomb! Only LaToya would think of such a weapon. They would have her fingerprints on them, which would exonerate me, but I doubted that they could get any prints off of those burned fingers to compare them to. She'd probably been arrested before. They wouldn't match mine, anyway.

The police station wasn't as scary as I had expected. They sat me in the front office and a friendly female officer brought me coffee.

"I just don't understand how a nice lady like you could get into so much trouble."

Officer Gravdall stood in front of me with his arms crossed over his chest. He shook his head from side to side and clicked his tongue in mock disapproval. Another officer asked me if I wanted to press charges, attempted murder being one of the possible counts, but I didn't see any point to it and there was nothing in it for me. Proud, mad, bitchy little LaToya, once the pampered darling, prom queen on the arm of the handsomest high school hunk, was now reduced to an impoverished freak, possibly living on the streets if she got out of the hospital alive. She'd be punished enough.

Later I heard from Tina that LaToya's mother had moved in with relatives in Tucson but LaToya hadn't gone with her. Tina didn't know why she hadn't gone but she suspected she still had her sights on Rob and wanted me out of the way permanently. Another sad thought; was LaToya not welcome in Tucson? Did her mother abandon her? Or did LaToya refuse to go? It was anyone's guess but the real story was a long way off. We'd probably never know.

Chapter 23 – More Tragedies

I called Rob to tell him what had happened.

"Oh no, Jasmine," he exclaimed. "Are you okay? That's terrible!" He did sound concerned.

"I'm fine," I replied. "Tom warned me just in time. But LaToya is in terrible shape. She may not even live through this and it might be better if she didn't."

"I gotta come home, then." Rob surprised me. "I'll get the first plane out of Nashville. I'm so sorry I wasn't there for you!"

"See you soon," I replied, a little bit puzzled. He didn't need to come back for my sake. "It's been quite a while," I said, probing for an explanation.

"Yeah, I know," he said. Then he lied. "It's taking a lot longer than I thought to make this video. I'll get there as soon as I can."

Hmmm.

The gruesome story about LaToya's attempt on my life showed up on TV, and in the newspapers, and was talked about by everyone we knew in Moab. To make it even worse, reverential fans of Tom DeVries kept coming to my house, just like Kate said they would. There were candlelight vigils held at the bottom of my staircase. Sometimes I'd get home from work and have to wade through a sea of people I'd never met who all wanted to express their love for Tom. Some begged me to show them the cabinet where I had found the case. As much as I understood, they were crowding me out of my own life. Most of the fans tried to be polite and to move out of my way but some could be really obnoxious, imagining that their love for Tom and his music gave them special rights.

One woman from Oklahoma claimed to have followed Tom from his earliest days. Her effrontery was unbelievable. She parked her camper at the foot of the stairs and refused to budge.

"I was there, in Austin, when he first sang "River of Gold," she reminisced. "I kept every ticket stub to every performance I ever went to. I got him to sign a photo that I'd bought. Then I asked him to take a picture with me and him and he did! I'll never forget standing next to him. Oh, he was so handsome..."

I was actually horrified. I don't know what she had been like in the seventies but the woman who stood so firmly in front of my house was sloppy, vulgar and defending herself with brazen snobbery. She identified with her fan-aticism so much that she imagined herself to be at one with Tom DeVries. Her toenails were long, thick and painted bright pink. Her feet in their worn flip-flops were cracked and dirty. She wore an old t-shirt with a nice photo of Tom on it but it was threadbare, with holes in it, hugging every roll on her body. Intimidated, I politely asked her not to park her camper in front of my house but she turned on me with an attitude of full-blown righteousness that actually scared me.

"I'm the biggest fan that ever followed Tom DeVries!' She shouted at me. "You have no right to keep me from him. He knows me. He knows why I'm here! He won't let you chase me away!" Her cigarette breath in my face was disgusting.

This monster was adamant. She shoved me aside and began a determined march up my steps with every intention of letting herself in. I had to let her go. Glancing around at the other fans and seeing their bewildered faces, I almost appealed to them for some kind of help but they all seemed as vexed and helpless as I felt. As her broad, fluorescent blue clad butt ascended my staircase, I considered calling the police when she suddenly shrieked, jumped and ran back down the stairs in response to a familiar rattle. Fred to my rescue, again!

"You have a rattlesnake under your stairs!" she screamed into my face. "I hate snakes! I'm calling the police on you! What kind of a woman are you, anyway? That has to be illegal, keeping a poisonous snake on your property."

She climbed into the cab of her camper, muttering to herself indignantly.

"You haven't heard the last of me, you know!" she shouted out the window as she drove away, black exhaust spewing out of the back of her camper. Oh yes, I had.

I got enough complaints from the neighbors and visits from the police that eventually I hired a security team to stave off the adoring crowds. I couldn't wait for winter when the cold would keep them from coming.

Rob showed up the day after I called him, just like he said he would. He could be reliable after all, as long as it suited him. He met me in the office and took me in his arms, insisting that I take the rest of the day off. Knowing it would get me in trouble, I called Kate and left her a message that I had to be out of the office. Rob and I had business of our own. It would have been torture to try to work the rest of the day.

"Oh Jasmine. It must have been terrible. I'm so glad you weren't hurt."

"It was close," I said. "You saw the front of the office. Tom warned me not to open the front door."

"Tom, huh?" Rob grinned.

"Yeah, Tom." I said. But we had other concerns. "Rob? Could we get some beers and go sit by the river? I think we need to talk."

"Yeah. We do," he sighed. "Let's go."

We sat under a stand of trees by the river while the cottonwood seeds snowed down on us, just like on our first date. The cloudless turquoise sky burned above the red canyon walls, majestic, all-powerful, heavy and sweltering. Canoes and rafts drifted by, loaded with vacationers who kept jumping into the muddy river to cool themselves off. The awkwardness between us, as oppressive as the summer heat, forced me to break the silence.

"Rob," I said. "I have to tell you. I've known about you and Tracy ever since the gala. I saw the two of you under the willow tree beside the entrance. I've been deceiving you, too"

"What?" Rob was shocked. His mouth fell open. He looked around, trying to make sense of what I had told him. "What? You knew? And you didn't let on? Jasmine, what were you thinking? Don't you hate me?"

I took a big swallow of beer.

"Look, Rob. We were going too fast. I was almost relieved that it was over. But..." Shit! This was going to be hard to say. "I want a baby, Rob! What else was I going to do?"

"What? Jasmine!" His expression turned from shock to disgust as the whole sordid situation between us came into the light of the scorching sun. "So you've been pretending all this time just because you needed a stud?"

"That's not a very nice way to say it, Rob. I wanted you to father my child."

"But you're not pregnant yet, are you?

I shook my head no. A wave of disappointment rolled over me, tragic as an oil spill. My relationship was over and my baby was so far out of reach I thought I might never be a mother. All my sweet fantasies, from buying baby clothes to holding the little hand of the new person that had once been Tom DeVries faded from my view as the tears began to flow. Rob took my hand and stroked my cheek.

"You really want that baby, don't you?"

I nodded, trying to find something to mop up the tears with. Rob handed me a crumpled tissue.

"Look, Jasmine. I have some things to wrap up here before I go back to Nashville. Now, I don't want to have to pay any child support or take any responsibility for your kid. This is your thing and I want to be clear about that, but if you'll let me stay with you, we can try again. That is, if you can stand to have me around."

"We'll have breakup sex," I said, not feeling the humor I'd intended. "It would be a good time to try. I'm right in the middle of my cycle. But how are you going to get away with this? Are you going to have to lie to Tracy?"

"I don't have to say anything at all. I'm giving up my job, you and Moab to be with her in Nashville. I've taken a job as a roadie in her entourage. Doesn't that say enough?"

Oh God, Rob. *A roadie?* I had an awful feeling about this.

But we went back home to my little house, carelessly dropping clothes on the floor as we made our way to the shower stall with the smooth floor tiles and the old-fashioned copper fixtures. The cool shower streamed over our bodies, running from head to shoulders, down his chest and over my breasts and then down our legs. We kissed as we always had, slowly, open mouthed and trusting. With no secrets between us, there was no need to pretend. We focused on genuine lovemaking. Rob kissed my neck and caressed my small breasts (I'd always been pleased with my pert little set), running his hand down my belly and finally between my legs, gently probing, expertly stroking. I sighed with pleasure. He finally reached under my thighs and lifted me onto his hips. I wrapped my legs around his waist and we came together in smooth, rhythmic waves, so easy. We both climaxed at once.

Toweling each other off, we started kissing again. I felt like I needed to be back at work but Rob took my nipple into his mouth and it started all over. Freshly showered, we could do all kinds of things, crawling all over each other like new lovers. I got between his legs and he got between mine. I pushed his black mane to the side so I could kiss the back of his neck. We napped in each other's arms as my responsibility toward my job became irrelevant.

"Jasmine, you can't be thinking about going back to the office. It's already 4 in the afternoon!" Grinning and stretched out naked on the bed, he made a good argument.

"I have to, Rob! I left some things undone that can't wait."

"What about dinner?" he asked. "Do I need to bring you something or are you coming back in time?"

"In time for what?" I asked.

"I was hoping you could help me pack. I don't always do it that well, you know."

I was so glad I wasn't marrying Rob, after all. We agreed to order a pizza

I went back to the office. There was just too much I had to do and I wasn't interested in any of it. Naturally, I got an irate call from Kate.

"What makes you think you could take the afternoon off during Rodeo season?" she shouted. "I need you there every minute."

"I was breaking up with Rob," I said. "He's moving to Nashville to be with Tracy Simon."

"What? Rob and Tracy Simon? Oh Jasmine, you poor thing!" She stopped for a minute. I could hear the beer bubbles effervescing over the phone. "I"m so sorry!" she gushed. "What happened? I thought you two were engaged!"

"Oh, it's not that bad, really." I said. "He's a great guy but there were too many things that didn't work between us." I didn't mention I'd been in love with someone else the whole time.

I got back at about 9 PM and Rob had cardboard boxes half-packed all over the house. He'd cleared all of his athletic equipment out of the sunroom. On his cell to Tracy, he explained that he'd rented a U-Haul and was packing up, but he had a few more loose ends to tie up before he could leave Moab for good. Yes, he was staying at his old girlfriend's place. No they were not having sex! He rolled his eyes and then winked at me. *Our* secret. We made sweet love again that night. Cowgirl style, which was his favorite way.

"But what about your teams, Rob?" I asked, after I'd rolled off. "Is there anyone willing to take over? You mean so much to them."

"I think I have a few hopefuls waiting in the wings," he said. "It's something I'll work on while I'm here."

He certainly was doing a tidy job of closing up his life in Moab.

Later, I woke up, certain I could hear Tom singing, but I couldn't make out the words. It was a full moon at the end of July but the breeze blowing through the windows was sweet and cool, carrying with it the faintest hint of whiskey and cigarettes. Rob slept like a rock, which was good.

I donned sweatshirt and clogs and went out to the back patio. The way the wind was spiraling around wasn't the way wind usually behaved. It spun and it swirled, sparkling like phosphorescence. Images that must have been desert spirits whirled around with the wind, looking sometimes like Kachinas, sometimes like petroglyphs, and evolving into mysterious angels with wings like light rays. I was surrounded. I wanted to go with them. My physical body felt heavy and clumsy, weighing me down as the spiraling spirits soared higher. The singing continued, broke up into facets and sounded like many Toms singing together. The voices rose upward on the wind, growing fainter, until at last, they were gone. My Tom had crossed over.

I sat down hard on the stone wall. Crickets chirped, the stars sparkled in the indigo sky and the moon shone silver inside a halo of blue. I felt a glow inside me. It wasn't exactly a heat of temperature but an emotional warmth, a feeling of love, of being loved and of being elevated beyond myself into another realm, strange and fairy-like but still firmly planted on earth. The cottonwoods bent over me, strong and protective. The rose bushes smiled approvingly and even the rocks and yucca cactus sent their blessings. I sat on the wall until sunrise before I went to bed.

Coming home from work that day, I saw Rob's U-Haul in front of my house with boxes stacked inside and Rob bringing another box down the stairs.

"This house isn't really move-friendly," I mentioned as we climbed back up the stairs together, stomping on the step as usual. But there was no answering rattle this time. I didn't smell the skunk anymore, either. Tom had gone and taken his animal spirits with him. I couldn't help feeling a little pang of grief.

Rob saw the pregnancy test in my hand.

"This looks promising," he said. "You'll at least let me know, won't you?"

"I might be able to tell you right away," I said.

When we got into the house, almost all of Rob's stuff was gone except for two large gym bags that held his clothes. A big bouquet of sunflowers sat on my coffee table.

"Oh, Rob!" I exclaimed. "Thank you! How pretty!"

"I had to do something to thank you for being so good about this," he said. "I saw my mom today and she's so disappointed that she could hardly talk to me. I sure hope she gets that grandkid out of you as long as her son is being such a jerk."

"I don't think you're a jerk," I said. "I think you just got carried away and now you have to deal with the consequences." Then I remembered something. "What should we do with the rings? They're just sitting in that drawer."

"Let's say that whoever gets married first gets the rings." Rob said.

"I'd like to wear the engagement ring as a memento." I said. "We did have some great adventures together." I smiled. "I think we can part as friends."

"Of course we can," he replied as he taped up one more box. Then he looked straight at me. "You don't think this is going to work out, do you?"

"That's not for me to say. I don't have a good feeling about this but I'm not in charge of your life. I may be a psychic but I don't know the future." I held up the box containing the pregnancy test. "I'm more interested in the present, anyway."

"Well, go pee on your stick, then. Let me know what happens."

The stick turned blue.

Rob took off that evening, trying to put in as many miles as he could as soon as he could, wanting to get back to his Tracy. I wasn't angry. I didn't want to hurt him, knowing that he was doing that to himself. Instead, I carefully lifted my old poster of Tom out of the closet. It was a little scratched from the broken glass and some shards poked out of the sides from under the frame. Back to the frame shop, I promised myself. This was my show now and I was the star. I couldn't wait to spread the news.

Chapter 24 – Welcome Changes

I waltzed into work with my blue stick and waved it around.

"What's that?" Kate asked.

"Jasmine passed the pregnancy test!" Lucy sang. Kate looked puzzled.

"How are you gonna get any work done?" she scolded. 'Specially when you're puking your guts up all day long?" Then she added, "We'll have to get you a nice comfy chair so you can bring the baby to work. You're gonna want to nurse it, you know. Helps you lose the weight."

We chatted about the complications. Kate had been a single mother herself so she was full of advice, some welcome and some not, but I was happy we could relate to each other on such an important issue. We were all sad about Rob. It didn't take a psychic to know he was headed for some kind of disaster.

The other best thing to happen that fall was that Kate finally found a new office. Hallelujah!

The new space was on Moab's main drag upstairs over two quaint little shops in a renovated 1870s building. Two big windows with thick leaded glass, arched on top, offered a wide view of the street below. I was overjoyed when I learned that it was air-conditioned. I was also elated that she hired a gal to manage the office. Grace was in her fifties with years and years of office experience behind her. She began to make changes right away.

"To begin with..." she issued her orders to Kate. "We'll have no beers during working hours. It's unprofessional and causes unnecessary errors."

Kate didn't argue but she sure screwed her face into a prune about it. I was shocked that anyone would be able to boss Kate around, but Kate actually took Grace's suggestions and put them to work.

The way Grace organized the move was so orderly and efficient that we knew we were in good hands. She called the recycle truck to haul off the stacks and stacks of outdated magazines threatening to either swallow us all up or burn the place down for real. She found room in the budget to take the best and most valuable of the old rodeo posters and photos to the frame shop. "Kate, I have to tell you." She gushed. "This year's profit margin is so far through the roof that I think all three of you can have a raise."

"Really?" Kate was surprised. She had sold ad space like crazy, secured a number of sponsors, and collected at least 10,000 subscribers. But she hardly ever looked at the numbers unless she was paying the bills.

"Yes, really." continued Grace. "And as top sales person, even if you are the only one, you also deserve a bonus. There's plenty of room in the budget."

The two became much better friends after that.

The new office meant I could walk to work. I was strolling down the sidewalk one morning when I spotted a familiar figure heading toward me. Tall, thin and blond, it was Mark! I hadn't expected to see him again, at least not without some kind of notice. He recognized me and waved.

"Mark!" I called. "How are you? And what are you doing back in Moab?"

"I got my old job back," He said. "Frank and I aren't

together any more. He met a girl."

"What?" I didn't feel particularly surprised. "But the two of you had such plans. You seemed to be good for each other. What happened?" As if I could be surprised at someone's partnership breaking up.

"Mostly, it was all the money Frank was making." Mark shrugged. "His life changed and so did his lifestyle. I couldn't fit into his new social circle and he was starting to resent having to support me. Those people don't think anything of flying off to Europe or somewhere like that for a long weekend so I was home alone a lot. The whole thing just fell apart." He sighed, seeming relieved. "I'm so glad to be back home. Oh yeah, and I'm sorry about you and Rob."

"I'm not," I replied. "I let Rob take over my life and just did whatever he wanted. And LaToya! Did you know what she tried to do?"

"Yeah! I saw it in the papers. You're OK, though, aren't you?"

"Yes! I'm better than OK." I smiled proudly. "Rob did one good thing before he moved to Nashville. I'm pregnant!"

"Jasmine! That's terrific. You're not worried about being a single mom?"

"Not one bit," I said. "Hey I'd better get to work. Do you still have my number?"

"I do." Mark pulled a business card out of his shirt. "Give me a call. We'll have dinner sometime."

I called my folks about the baby and got my mother first.

"But Jasmine, you're not even married! How can you be sure you can raise this child by yourself?"

"Oh, mom," I sighed. "There are all kinds of resources for single mothers. I really want this baby and I'd rather do it by myself. The father was a real cool guy but not very reliable. I'm sure his family will help me, though."

"Jasmine, I do want to be happy for you but I just don't

know, especially after that last guy you got all involved with. How can I possibly trust your judgment? This is my first grandchild, Jasmine. I just wish that things could go right for you for once."

My mother knew only the straight and narrow and I was always stepping out of the box. Nothing was going to change her.

The call to my brother, Peter, was better. He seemed glad to hear from me. "Sounds like Jasmine to me. You always did have an individualistic approach to life. I bet you already know if it's a boy or a girl."

"Maybe" I replied. "But you'll have to come to Moab. We'll be sure to make time for some sightseeing."

"Oh, I'd love to check out Moab. Arches, Canyonlands! I can't wait for spring!"

Then Peter surprised me. I almost fell backwards in my office chair. "I'm glad you're doing so well in your life out there. Jasmine, I just have to say that I'm so sorry that we always made you feel like there was something wrong with you or that you were weird or crazy."

"Pete!" Staring at my cell phone, I wondered whether I had the right number or not "All right, who are you and what have you done with Pete?"

"I mean it, Jasmine. We've been talking about it. All of us. God, what a bunch of idiots we were! We didn't even get it when you predicted that tornado and saved all our butts." He paused for a moment. "Then we just abandoned you when you got caught up with that creep in Fort Collins."

"I understood that, actually." I admitted.

"It was a crummy thing to do." Pete was emphatic. "This baby is going to bring us all together. I'm sure of it."

I turned off the phone. This just didn't seem real.

Even if I'd never been close to my family, it was a great relief to have some of those old wounds finally heal up. It really isn't natural to be estranged from your family, whether you get along with them or not. I knew that they'd be taking a few vacations in Moab in the future.

The magical little adobe where my adventure with Tom DeVries first began became even sweeter as I imagined how I'd feather my nest. Dreams of once again filling the shelves in the basement with jars of my homemade, fruits, jams and pickles danced in my head. Visions of planting flowers and vegetables in the little garden beckoned me. I'd always wanted to put plants in the room with the glass bricks and now that Rob's athletic equipment was gone, I actually could.

I called Sylvie. She'd been reluctant to call me, ashamed of her self-absorbed son.

"Sylvie, Rob did one thing right. You're going to be a grandma!"

"I'm what?"

"That's right, Sylvie. I'm pregnant and Rob is the father."

"Oh Jasmine! No! I'm so sorry! Will Rob pay child support or are you on your own?"

"I'm *not* sorry!" I insisted. "This is *my* thing! I can take care of a baby on my own but you'll want to be involved, won't you? This is your first grandchild."

Sylvie was sniffing back tears.

"It may be the only one I'll ever get!" she wailed. "I'm so disappointed in my son! Oh, Jasmine. I'm so sorry for you!"

"*I'm* not sorry for me," I said again. "I wanted a baby but I didn't want to marry Rob. We were going too fast, things between us weren't working at all but I wanted this baby anyway. I don't have a good feeling about what Rob is doing but he is a grown man and he's been in Moab almost his whole life. Maybe he'll grow from this. Maybe it'll even work out between him and what's-her-face."

Sylvie was unconvinced, needing to hang up and cry some more, but not before she invited me to dinner that night.

I got a puzzled call from Candice shortly after Rob had left with the U-Haul.

"Jasmine," she began, getting right to the point. "Did that Tracy Simon steal away your Rob?"

"Rob was a big fan." I said. "Things weren't going that well between us anyway. I liked him a lot but I just wasn't in love with him. I mean, he was so good-looking and nice and everything. We had pretty good sexual chemistry but there were just some things…"

"Yeah, I get it." Candice agreed. "Still, I don't like it that Tracy could just move in on somebody's boyfriend like that. She's real spoiled. Thinks she can have anything she wants whenever she wants it."

"I'm worried that this won't work out for Rob." I admitted.

"Oh no, it won't. She'll get tired of him and move on like she always does. Just so long as *you're* okay with it."

"Actually, I'm fine. Better than fine really."

"Why's that?"

"Rob got me pregnant before he left. I'm gonna have a baby!" I made my proud announcement.

"What! No husband? Jasmine, you're gonna be a single mother!" Candice had been a single mother also and it must not have been easy for her.

"It's fine. It's just fine," I insisted. "I have a good job and I own my house. I really wanted a baby so I'm happy."

"Oh, if you say so. Just don't forget to send me some baby pictures."

I promised I wouldn't.

A few days later, a big bouquet of magnolias arrived at the office. The women were thrilled. When I got home, there was a package on the doorstep from Candice and Melissa. Inside were some pricey skincare products, a stylish red maternity dress and a selection of adorable newborn baby clothes. I still had some friends in Nashville.

Chapter 25 ⟡ Families

The weather got colder and the DeVries fans stopped clustering around the house as the novelty wore off.

That Thanksgiving, Rob was conspicuously absent and the Dishta family seemed strangely lopsided. Yvette wore a black leather pencil skirt that showed off her slim hips to perfection. Her eyes were unusually bright and she seemed anxious about something, frequently refreshing her wine glass. Finally, Sylvie spoke.

"Yvette, we haven't seen you in months and you usually have so many things to talk about. Is something wrong?"

Besides the obvious, I thought.

"Well, no. But yes, I have to tell you all something..." Yvette's eyes got even brighter and she seemed to gasp for air.

"I'm, I'm...I've decided that I'm going to run for state representative of New Mexico!" she finally spit out. She poured another splash of wine into her glass and sat down hard on her chair.

"That's my girl!" Jaime grinned. "Sure doesn't surprise me. You're gonna win, hands down!"

"When did you decide that you were going to do this?" Sylvie didn't share her husband's enthusiasm. "Yvette, you have no personal life as it is. No husband, no children. You are married to your career! Is this really what you want?"

Yvette smiled at her mother. "I know, I know. But this *is* my life! Running for congress wasn't my idea but so many of my constituents mentioned it that it got me thinking. The next two years are going to be pretty crazy but this *is* what I do."

"It sure doesn't hurt that you're so good looking." I put in. "Geez, TV, campaign posters and billboards. You might get elected just for those cheekbones."

Everybody laughed at first but it didn't last long.

"I just wish that Rob was here to share this!" Yvette cried. "Why do I feel that I've lost my brother for good?"

"Maybe he'll grow through this." I offered, weakly. "I think he made a mistake but we're supposed to learn from our mistakes. We'll just have to see."

There was silence for a while. I suggested that we watch the video that Rob had made with Tracy. We looked it up on Jaime's wide-screen PC.

It was as bad as I expected. Tracy was all decked out like a dance hall girl from the 1880s or something, singing a song that seemed to have little to do with the scene being played. She was sitting on a wagon, held tight around the waist by a nasty looking bad guy with a bandana over his face. Two other bad guys in cowboy hats sat in the back of the wagon with guns held ready as they thundered across a landscape that was far too green and far too tame to be the Wild West. When Rob appeared he was shirtless with his hair loose. He'd had his chest waxed. At least he was wearing fringed buckskin leggings instead of a loincloth. I had to admit that he played his part with a dashing athleticism, hauling himself onto the back of the moving wagon and convincingly disarming both gunmen. Maybe he had a career ahead of him as an actor? But the family was obviously uncomfortable and we switched off the video before it ended.

The rest of the evening we quizzed Yvette about what to expect and how her life was going to change as she entered the roller-coaster world of a political candidate. We asked her about fund-raising, her political platform, if she had any wealthy supporters and what she hoped to accomplish. The excitement grew, and distracted everyone from Rob's situation. No one mentioned LaToya.

Come spring, it was time to invite my family out to visit. I wanted to see them before the baby arrived so that I wouldn't be preoccupied and could devote my energy to getting reacquainted with them. We settled on a date early in April when my parents, sister and brother could come out together. I was more nervous about seeing my family than even the impending birth, which was only weeks away. They had booked three rooms at the Big Horn Lodge, with its southwestern styling and log furniture, located right in the center of town. The four of them drove together from Denver and arrived at the lodge in the late afternoon.

Sylvie and I had planned a gourmet picnic for my family including herself and Jaime. We prepared roast chicken, French bread with an assortment of cheeses and jams, a vegetable tray, potato salad and a seven-layer torte for dessert. Sylvie chose the wines and I brought mineral water. I carefully packed a tablecloth with matching cloth napkins, real silverware, china plates and cups and wine glasses, wanting so much to impress. All of my old fears were surfacing again. I would have to disguise who I was, and not mention certain things on a very long list of things not spoken of. It would be foolish to assume that anything had changed.

I got the call from my mother that they'd arrived and I met them in the lobby. My sister, Amelia wore a t-shirt, jeans and clogs, happy to be on a short vacation. She and my brother both hugged me, genuinely glad that we were all together. My dad was somewhat stiff, cuffs buttoned and tie knotted tight, but he'd always been like that. My mom was cordial but stuffy, as usual. She always seemed to be in a state of disapproval and looking down at my pregnant belly, she sighed.

"Honestly, Jasmine. I just don't know."

"Mom!" Both Pete and Amelia spoke in chorus.

"I really don't blame you, Mom." I replied. "But I know I can do this. Things have changed a lot in the last few years. You haven't even seen my little house yet. You'll see."

"Well, you do look good." my Dad admitted.

We went to one of the more civilized picnic spots on the banks of the Colorado. Even my mother admired the craggy, shady rock face on the other side of the river. I set the picnic table with a vase of fresh daffodils and tulips in the middle, a last minute purchase made in a firm commitment to make everything perfect. We chatted casually as Sylvie and I laid out the food.

"All Pete and I ever do is work." Amelia complained. "I always thought that a realtor did a lot of sitting around and fretting about the next sale, but I'm always doing something, whether it's showing the next house or finishing off the paperwork on the last one. Did I hear that you really own your house?"

I nodded. "And wait until you see it! It's sweet!"

"You own your own house?" my Dad exclaimed. "That's wonderful, Jasmine. How did you do that?"

I went on to explain that I'd had a lot of help from my boss and maybe some from the cosmos.

"That's our Jasmine." Pete smiled broadly.

"At least you and the baby will have your own home. Where did you say you work?" My mother had no tact. Sometimes I wondered what my father had ever seen in her.

"How's the food?" I asked as I handed her a copy of *The Rodeo Review*.

"Oh, very good." My mom had to admit. "I didn't know you could set such a nice table. Where did you get your dinnerware? It looks antique."

I couldn't remember having had such a pleasant time with my family. Pete and Amelia talked mostly about their jobs. My mother spoke cattily about her neighbors, the ladies in her bridge club, and the fundraiser she was working on. Sylvie talked about her latest spiritual retreat in New Mexico, and Jaime agreed with my dad that retirement was boring. I didn't feel like I had to hide anything any more, nor did I feel a need to say anything that might be too challenging. I gave them a brief account of my finding the case of music, tracking down Candice DeVries and meeting her and Melissa in Grand Junction, leaving out the parts about Tom's ghost and the car chase.

"I don't like country music," my mother said. "I thought we'd raised you in a more cultured environment than that."

"Oh but Tom DeVries isn't mainstream country!" Amelia shot back. "I love his music! I have all of his CDs now. Jasmine, I'm just so proud of you for finding that case and everything you did to bring all those wonderful songs to the rest of us!"

"Still," my mother insisted on expressing her irrelevant opinion. "There is simply no comparison between Tom DeVries and Mozart or Bach."

"Of course not!" Pete practically shouted. "You might as well compare a Lexus to a pick-up truck."

"I happen to prefer the Lexus." She spoke in that sour tone of voice that indicated that hers was the superior opinion and not open to discussion. Jaime came to the rescue.

"So what shall we do tomorrow?" he asked. "Have any of you ever been to Moab before?"

"I've always wanted to see Arches National Park!" My father did love the outdoors, in his own old-fashioned way.

At the end of the evening, the sun was just setting and Pete stood up to propose a toast.

"I want to say how pleased we all are that you, Jasmine, have done so well for yourself. As your family, we all feel that we let you down and we'd like to say how sorry we are. You have a gift. You're different from other people and we just couldn't accept it. Now we do!"

My mom and dad and Amelia were all looking at Peter as he spoke and all were in agreement. They must have discussed this beforehand.

"We'd like to start over." he continued. "Maybe now we can be a real family."

I didn't know what to say. I'd gotten so used to my family I thought they could never change. Here they'd done it right in front of my eyes and in front of the Dishtas.

"Let's be fair," I said. "Some of that stuff can be pretty scary. It's who I am, though."

I shared my stories of my adventures in Austin and Nashville and tried to explain how I really hadn't been disappointed in Rob. Sylvie and Jaime soon changed the subject to the story of how they had met, how she'd expected him to be angry with her for having complicated his project and instead, he'd asked her out.

"He stepped up on his chair and right over the desk. I thought he was trying to intimidate me but instead he asked me out to dinner."

"I'm no idiot." Jaime said. "She was so pretty and that accent put me over the edge. No way was I letting this one get away."

That story was always good for a chuckle and successfully diverted the attention from the errant Rob who was obviously considered a hole in the fabric of the Dishta family. They spoke enthusiastically of Yvette and her political ambitions with Sylvie fretting as usual about her driven daughter's lack of a personal life.

"Also," Sylvie continued. "Even without Rob, Jasmine will always have a family in Jaime and myself. We fully intend to support Jasmine in whatever way we are able as grandparents to her child."

Jaime nodded. Pete raised his glass in another toast. I

shouted, then laughed as the baby drummed on my bladder.

We spent the next two days touristing around Arches and Canyonlands. I was actually enjoying my family but I also found myself missing Rob for the first time since the split. He was often in my face at the grocery store and newsstands, in the tabloids and on the cover of People magazine, posing with Tracy Simon as they announced their engagement. Another whirlwind romance for Rob, I thought as the symbolism of the lightning bolt wedding rings dawned on me. I truly didn't want to see him hurt and I prayed one afternoon, asking the universe to bring true happiness to Rob and Tracy.

Chapter 26 – The Baby

The *Rodeo Review* continued to grow but the pace was no longer crazy and my hours were actually reasonable even with a summer of Cowboy Christmas looming large. Grace was terrifically good at her job and Kate, once she came around to Grace's methods, noticed that she herself was more efficient and that her own job actually got easier. Lucy had started dating a champion bull rider and expressed her affection on her cell phone by worrying frantically about him every time he went to a rodeo.

"You'll be super careful, won't you?" She'd whine over the phone. "I swear that if something happened to you, I'd die. I really would!"

"Lucy!" Kate would shout. "Don't say those things. It won't help him at all!"

"But I love him!" Lucy would shout back. "He might get hurt real bad!"

"You're dating a bull rider!" Kate would yell. "Get used to it! If you love him that much, you might try praying for his success instead of making him all worried about you worrying about him when he really needs to focus on his bull riding. Turn it over to someone who can really help him out."

"But I don't know that!" Lucy would fret.

They went around and around like that for hours on end.

Some things never change.

Pregnancy brought a few bonuses. As I attended my pre-natal classes and went for my doctor visits I began to meet other mothers and find the female friends I'd been missing. Now I collected phone numbers and made dates with the women I found particularly interesting. A pretty blond named Dierdre was a practicing Wiccan and had a magical quality about her. I loved visiting her home, which was festooned with herbal wreaths, charms and crystals. She and her husband, Fergus, had wed in an ancient Celtic ritual called a hand-fasting. Their two children were named Morgana and Bran. While the two of us happily hung out together on weekends, shopping, baking cookies and watching kid TV, her husband would sometimes take the kids to the pool or ice skating in order to give us some time to ourselves. Then Dierdre would light her candles and incense and we would chant and meditate together. One day I brought over my crystal ball to ask why it wasn't working and if she could fix it. Dierdre gazed at it and then gasped in horror.

"This crystal hasn't been cleansed!" she gasped. "Its energy is completely opaque! Oh Jasmine!" she rolled her eyes teasingly as she pulled a book off of a densely loaded shelf. "You *must* read this!"

I had a flashback to one of the more pleasant aspects of my relationship to Greg Ross but this time I wasn't stoned, drunk or drugged and the lessons and rituals presented in the text had real meaning. My spiritual life began to grow in some new ways.

Sylvie and I became better friends as my due date drew nearer. She had lost a daughter to her career and her son to God knows what, so that the prospect of a grandchild was even more important to her than if Rob and I had stayed together. I was a frequent guest for lunch and dinner.

My time came one morning in late April with a big splash in the kitchen, drenching my sandals. I was getting ready for work and realized immediately that I would have to change my plans. I called Sylvie, who promised to drive me to the hospital and then I called Kate.

"Jasmine!" she hollered angrily. "We don't have the time for this! Can't it wait?"

"Kate, my water just broke." I answered, slightly amused. "I am *not* coming to work today."

"No, I guess not," she snorted. "Okay, go do your thing. We'll come to see you at the hospital as soon as we can."

Sylvie and I went to the hospital, found out that I wasn't far enough along and came back home. We tried to watch TV but neither of us could pay much attention while my contractions got stronger and stronger. We finally met Jamie, Kate and Lucy at the hospital at about 7:00 PM and I was whisked off to the labor deck.

My attendants were two young nurse midwives in training, smiling, bouncing around and excited to have such a healthy mother to work with. Though curtained off, I could hear the groans and cries all the other mothers on the labor deck, almost in some kind of rhythmic chorus against the amplified heartbeat of my baby as he made his slow, steady progress through the birth canal. The nurses rubbed my back, fed me ice chips and cheered me on while Sylvie stood by, her hands clasped almost in prayer in front of her face. If it hadn't hurt like hell it would have been fun but it took a long time. My labor lasted all night. Finally, after a few giant heaves my little boy slid out and my exhausted young nurses cheered and high-fived each other, Sylvie and me. I felt exhilarated as they placed my baby in my arms, exhausted but also excited, thrilled even. As much as I'd been looking forward to motherhood, I didn't know it would be *this* good.

I was sure his first cry had a drawl in it but I may have been just hoping. I needed to get to know my baby for who he was and not just what I hoped him to be, so I named him Zachary

Jaime Anders. I loved the idea of a son named Zach. His June birthday made him a Gemini, with his moon in Taurus and Cancer rising. In every Gemini two personalities try to merge into one. His Taurus Moon would give him a stubborn streak but the Cancer would contribute an emotional sensitivity and a loving nature.

Tom had been a Scorpio/Sagittarius, having been born on the cusp of the two signs. I never knew his time of birth so the rest of his chart was a mystery. I thought he may have had Gemini rising. The rising sign is always the sign that the personality will strive for in a lifetime. Still, imagining that my tiny baby boy was the dashing Tom DeVries was quite a stretch, and I was madly in love with my son no matter who he was.

I got a week's worth of parental leave before I had to go back to work. It was a good thing there usually were no men in the office since I was struggling with nursing and often exposing a whole lot of boob in the process. I also burst into tears at inconvenient moments. Sylvie stopped by frequently, dropping off food for me, making sure I had a bottle of water at all times and taking some of the baby chores off my hands. Thanks to Grace, my workload was cut in half and all I had to do that summer was to build my ads and make Kate's wild scribbles and photos into articles. But still, between the magazine and my hungry little Zach, it was a very trying season.

Deirdre had her baby about a week after I did but I didn't get to see her until the end of August. By then, we were both determined to lose the last of the baby fat we'd accumulated, so we began taking long walks in the evenings, sometimes along the river and sometimes through town, often accompanied by Sylvie and Fergus. We were strolling along Moab's main street on one of those magical late summer evenings, cool and breezy and so pleasant we couldn't stop walking.

"You know," observed Fergus. "New babies don't really seem human. I'm watching these big brown eyes looking around and he seems like something else. Maybe a baby elf or something."

"Maybe somebody took the real baby and substituted an elf, like in the old fairy tales," I joked. But I knew what he meant. Zach was wide-awake and looking at the street lights, taking in everything that a baby could see. I could only imagine what the world looked like to him.

We passed a little bar that featured a folk trio. Zach seemed fascinated at the blinking Christmas lights that lined the front window.

"Oh, listen!" Sylvie exclaimed. "They're doing that song that's so popular now!"

"That's my beloved Tom DeVries; 'River of Gold.'" I said. We stood quiet so we could listen. The trio, two guys and a gal, were doing a nice rendition with some interesting harmonies that made an old song sound fresh.

Zach started to make a noise, but he wasn't distressed or crying. Instead, he let out a soft "Aaaaah" and then another and another. He was trying to sing along!

"Listen!" Dierdre whispered. "I think he's singing!"

"He's a Tom DeVries fan already." I said. "Coming out of me, what else could he be?"

We waited until the song ended and the trio began a version of Lyle Lovett's "North Dakota". Zach stopped singing and snuggled against me.

"Hey, little dude. That's a pretty song too," said Dierdre. But Zach was through singing. I had a fleeting thought that he couldn't sing a song he didn't already know.

Chapter 27 – A Surprise Visit

Three years later, Rob's divorce was all over the grocery store tabloids, same as his wedding. It hurt to see Tracy wearing the ring that was supposed to be mine, but the curse of the lightning bolt had come around again.

I was dating a rancher who had lost his wife to breast cancer two years before and was interested in bringing a little boy into his life as well as recruiting a mother for his two little girls. He also played guitar in a local band! The little girls were not one bit pleased at having to share their father with another woman, so I planned to win them over by taking them on a $200 shopping spree in Salt Lake. I was packing for a weekend in the big city, aware that bribery wasn't the best idea in the world but I did want to make friends in a hurry. I'd also made reservations at a nice hotel for the four of us and paid for it all. Zach would stay with his adoring grandparents.

Zach was singing to himself like he always did when I put him down for a nap. I was laying out my clothes and Zach's, when there was an urgent pounding on my front door. Puzzled, since I hadn't been expecting anyone, I swung the door open.

It was Rob but not the one I remembered. He was thin, unshaven and haggard, nowhere near the buffed out athlete I'd almost married. I looked past him to the bottom of the stairs where a beat-up old Mustang waited with a couple of sleazy looking guys inside. As I looked at his face, he must have sensed the wave of horror, pity and disappointment that washed over me. He dropped his eyes and looked sideways.

"Rob? Is that really you?" I couldn't think of anything else to say.

"Yeah, Jasmine. I know, I know!" He sounded impatient more than anything else. "I'm gonna get right to the point. These guys and I are on our way to LA where we've got some jobs lined up. Right now we're short on gas money. You got anything to spare?"

Gas money. Right. Rob was shaky and sweating. "Meth, cocaine or heroine?" I wondered, feeling achingly sad. Rob had never taken anything stronger than wine or beer when we'd been dating, not even marijuana, even though Frank and Mark had lived in a cloud of it.

"I'll give you all the cash I have on hand," I said. My years with Greg had taught me how to get rid of a guy with a habit and that was to buy him off. I'd have to ATM another bundle of money in the morning for the trip to Salt Lake with my rancher and his girls. As I turned around, three-year-old Zach padded out of the bedroom and stared at the visitor with a displeased look on his face.

"Mommy! Who dat?" My little boy was suspicious.

Rob's fierce expression softened a bit, almost into a smile. "Is that...is that our baby?" He asked.

"No, he's *my* baby, remember? You didn't want anything to do with him."

"I never even knew if it was a boy or a girl!" Rob wailed. "Jasmine, he's beautiful! Please! Can I just have a look at him?"

He dropped down on one knee and motioned to Zach to come over. Zach looked at me.

"It's all right, darlin'." I told him. "He's an old friend of mine and he won't be here that long. He just wants to meet you."

Zach toddled over reluctantly. Rob took him by the shoulders.

He stared at Zach, and the reality of having a son. Zach had straight black hair, deep brown eyes and a café con leche complexion. His looks truly favored his father. Rob looked at me, then back at the Mustang and then at Zach, the truth of his own situation rising up and blazing in his face. All the shame, regret, and sorrow that he'd suppressed were growing inside him and his expression hurt me to look at. Rob was still Rob but with a raging drug habit. I had to fight the urge to rescue him, invite him back into my life and try to make it all better. But I already knew it would never work. To my surprise, Zach put both arms around Rob's neck in a warm hug. He knew his father!

Oh no! I started to panic. I didn't want Zach to bond with Rob, father and son or not! What if Rob decided he wanted a relationship with his son? The courts would insist on it, whatever Rob's condition or ability to offer financial support. Rob could use his son as a bargaining chip to shake me down for money or to demand I take him back. No! I thought. No! Not another Greg Ross!

But Rob's shoulders began to shake and tears ran down his face.

"I'm sorry, Jasmine. I'm sorry about everything." He couldn't look at my face.

"Well, *I'm* not," I said. "Come here, Zach."

I swung Zach up onto my hip, no easy feat with a healthy three-year-old, went back into my bedroom and got the $200 out of my jewelry box. Rob made no attempt to come in the house. I was grateful for that. He obviously had other things on his mind. Even $200 didn't exactly please him.

"Is that all you've got?" he asked.

"You're lucky I had *that*!" I snapped. "I don't usually keep that much cash around unless I have something specific that I wanted to do with it. Which I did!"

"I'm going," Rob assured me. "You'll never see me again. Please don't tell my folks you saw me."

"Don't worry," I said, having no intention of making any promises. I couldn't keep such a thing from Jaime and Sylvie when I had grown so close to them. They had a right to know.

Rob descended the steps with his head down and his hands jammed into his pockets. I could have cried too but I didn't want to upset Zach.

One mistake made in the passion of the moment could send someone hurtling down an icy slope with jagged boulders and chasms so deep a person could disappear forever. I felt terrible about Rob but I could understand how it happened, having lost a big chunk of my own life to the wrong guy. Rob had sacrificed his whole self to Tracy and now he couldn't get it back. Time for a prayer session with Deirdre, I decided. It was the only other thing I could do for him.

Chapter 28 – River of Gold

In the fall I was in my kitchen, putting up some jams and pickles, as I'd been doing for the last couple of years. I was proud of the pickles. Each jar contained the usual cucumbers gracefully framed by an entire dill sprig, grown in my own garden, as well as two creamy white garlic cloves and one long, dried, red pepper. Zach was remarkably cooperative for a three-year old, staying far away from the spitting pressure cooker. He remained in the living room, playing with his Legos and singing to himself as always. The tune sounded familiar. Of course Zach had heard Tom DeVries ever since his first day on earth but certainly not exclusively and not every day. As much as I loved my Tom, I didn't want to burn out on him so I limited my listening time.

"What are you singing, Zach?" I called out.

"Sumpin I made up."

"What's it about?"

"A river."

I never told anyone about the deal I'd made with Tom because that would have been too weird even for me. But if I had needed a final clue, I'd gotten one.

Hello Tom. My Tom. My friend, my protector, my love, my son.

Purchase other Black Rose Writing titles at www.blackrosewriting.com/books and use promo code PRINT to receive a 20% discount.

BLACK ROSE writing™

CPSIA information can be obtained
at www.ICGtesting.com
Printed in the USA
FSOW03n0641060915
10669FS